# Praise for
# Shades of the Deep Blue Sea

*Dead or Alive? London's approach to this question thrusts the reader into their own vision of immortality and an immensely entertaining story of the life/death struggle of a character that dramatically makes you want to see his destiny.*
> — **Dan Witt,** author of *Marsh Musings* for the
> Great Bend Tribune in Great Bend Kansas

*… an intriguing nautical adventure as well as a ripping good historical fiction complete with typhoons, spirits, and cannibals.*
> — **Mark Bowlin,** author of The Texas Gun Club novels

*The plot twists blew me out of the water. Narrowly avoiding burial at sea, born again Bart's heart is in the right place but the avalanche of his military misdeeds can only be held back so long. A depth of great writing with a creative approach to character development.*
> — **Robert Goswitz,** author of *The Dragon Soldier's Good Fortune*

*Bart is a cheat, black marketer, forger and is clearly less than honorable. As the central figure in the book, he will take the reader on a roller coaster ride of epic proportions, putting the book down will have to wait until the last word on the last page. I found myself rooting for Bart and believe every reader will as well.*
> — **Jim Greenwald,** multi-award winning poet

*Fascinating and almost impossible to put down.*
> — Jane Frederick, Reviewer

# SHADES OF THE DEEP BLUE SEA

Jack Woodville London

Vire Press, LLC, Austin, Texas

Editor-in-Chief: Mindy Reed
Book Design by: Danielle H. Acee, authorsassistant.com

ISBN: 978-0-9821207-0-5
Cataloguing-in Publication Data
London, Jack W. 1947-
French Letters: Virginia's War
p. cm.

Fic LonPS642 L86 2019  20080821

**Shade:** a noun.

> 1. A time or place of little light.
> 2. A distinction of light between colors or tones.
> 3. The soul of a dead person as it appears to the living.
>
> From the Merriam Webster Dictionary

# Part I

The (very brief) War Diary of Bart Sullivan,
Seaman Second Class

# Chapter 1

*Diary, September 20, 1944: I've got my orders.*

The peaks that rose above the jungle were clearly visible from the rope ladders that hung over the side of the troop ship *Renegade*. Less visible but more apparent were the palm trees five hundred yards away. Long fronds swayed in the brilliant sunlight, shaking in the breeze, then shattered when artillery shells blew their tops off. Thirty soldiers climbed down the *Renegade*'s rope ladders and dropped, fell, or were pulled into the landing craft, a Higgins boat that bounced on the water alongside the troopship.

"DROP! DROP! DROP!" the chief petty officer yelled. He stood by the coxswain, rising and falling with the boat, yelling at the top of his lungs. "MOVE! MOVE! MOVE! INCOMING!" A blast hit the water and rocked the boat. "AWAY! AWAY BOW LINE!"

The soldiers fell all over the deck, hanging on to their rifles and ammunition boxes. Some of them held on to a howitzer that had been loaded onto the tiny boat. The others held on to each other, or the Higgins boat, or simply crowded themselves into the scuppers and tried not to pee in their pants. The bow line was thrown clear.

"AWAY, COXSWAIN!" The engine strained. The landing boat swung away from the *Renegade*'s hull, its bow lifting in the swell, surged forward, and stopped dead in the water. "I SAID AWAY, GOT DUMNIT," Chief Petty Officer Olafson screamed. "WHAT THE HELL'S GOING ON?" The bowman had cast off his line. The engineer was at his deck station. The coxswain had shoved the engine to full throttle. And the sternman...

The stern rope was still tied fast to the ship.

3

"STERNMAN, YOU SON OF A BITCH! I'LL KILL YOU!" Olafson shouted. The chief climbed over the engine cover, into the machine gun well, and grabbed Bart Sullivan by the ankles as Sullivan tried to climb out of the Higgins boat and back up the rope ladder to the *Renegade*. "LET GO OF THAT GOT DUMNED LADDER." Olafson almost fell into the ocean as he tackled Bart's legs and began to pry Bart's hands away from the thick ropes. "TURN LOOSE!"

The boom of artillery drowned out the noise of the other landing craft racing toward the beach. The Higgins boat swung around its stern line until the coxswain realized what was going on behind him and pulled the power back to idle. The bow settled onto the water and the hull drifted back against the *Renegade*.

"LET GO MY LEGS! I'm not supposed to go, Chief," Bart screamed as he tried, vainly, to climb back up the ropes to the safety of the deck. "I've got orders...." He reached his right hand over his left and strained to grab the next rung of the rope ladder, but Olafson got a grip on his wrist.

With one jerk the two sailors tumbled back into the Higgins boat. Olafson grabbed Bart by the neck and yanked him down into the machine gun well, then took Bart's hands and forced them to pry the stern line loose from its cleat. The Higgins boat floated free of the *Renegade*. In the distance, the beach began to swarm with soldiers as the other landing craft dumped their men on shore. The assault was on.

The little boat strained as it bounced off the low rolling breakers and surged toward the beach. Shells screamed overhead and the men shook when the boat bounced hard on the rough water. Ahead of them, palm trees arced gently over the sand, their leaves shaking while the battle raged.

"DOWN! DOWN! DOWN!" Olafson yelled. A shell hit the water and rocked the boat. "READY! READY! FIFTY YARDS TO RAMP! FORTY! THIRTY!" A gush of saltwater almost swamped the overloaded boat as it rose over a wave, then nosed down into the boiling sea. "TWENTY YARDS! READY AT THE RAMP!"

A dozen other landing craft bounced around in the surf while guns boomed from behind the palm trees. The strains of the engine surging for the run-up to the beach caused the little boat to shake so violently that every man on board had trouble gripping his weapon. Four soldiers stood over the howitzer that threatened to roll forward and crush the bow before the boat ever made it to the beach.

With one final surge the Higgins boat lifted its bow, Olafson yelled, "RAMP DOWN," and the boat hit sand. The soldiers surged forward to get out of the landing craft and into combat. "GO GO GO!" he screamed as another geyser of sand and sea water erupted alongside the ramp. Some men pushed the howitzer onto the beach while the other soldiers raced onward, digging into the soft sand, tripping, dragging each other, pushing, falling.

"GET OFF THE BEACH! INCOMING! INCOMING!"

A machine gun rattled at them from the jungle. For a quarter-mile on either side of them the men of their battalion tried to run across the beach and into the tree line. Behind them, the lagoon boiled as yet more Higgins boats raced toward the island. Empty landing boats shuttled back to the troop ships where even more soldiers clambered down rope ladders into more Higgins boats that would bring them into the war. For most of them, it was their first action under fire.

"REVERSE! REVERSE! REVERSE!" Olafson screamed at the coxswain. "RAMP UP! AWAY! AWAY!" The bowman and the engineer heaved on the winches and the ramp began to jerk its way back into place. The coxswain shifted the engine into reverse. The engine sputtered and died.

"COXSWAIN!" No one moved. "COXSWAIN, GOT DUMNIT!" The crew looked at each other, glancing from winch to winch to wheel to machine gun and then back at Olafson, each of them shaking his head. "RE-START THE GOT DUMNED ENGINE AND GET THIS BOAT OFF THE BEACH!" Sand and water erupted alongside, spraying Olafson and the crew. No one moved. They began to drift aimlessly in the surf, the half-lowered ramp taking on water, the stern swiveling from side to side, the crew and Olafson staring at each other, waiting for someone to snap to and rescue them. No one did.

The coxswain pushed the starter button; nothing happened.

"No power, Chief." The coxswain, Smith, was a pimply nineteen-year-old from Olathe, Kansas. He crawled out of the steering position and began to heave at the plywood engine cover, whose latches kept it locked in place. "Gretel, gimme a hand!"

Gretel, the engineer, whose real name was Hantsel, dropped his winch handle to turn and help Smith, causing his ramp cable to go slack and thus overpowering Barker, the bowman. The loose ramp slapped down into the shallow surf, causing the bow to go under water.

Smith and Hantsel peered at the dead engine, hoping that something would declare itself as the cause of death. Nothing did.

"STERNMAN!"

"Huh?" Bart croaked.

"What the hell are you doing, Stern?" Olafson demanded. "Your boat's dead in the water, ramp's down, the whole dumned crew is stupid, and you've got Japs shooting at you from fifty yards away! Do something, you idiot!" To prove his point, a line of machine gun bullets zipped the water ten yards to starboard. Bart, terrified, huddled as far down in the machine gun well as he could get and put his hands over his helmet.

"Got dumnit, Stern, you're the only thing keeping this got dumned landing boat from being blown off the beach while they start the got dumned engine. Get on your weapon or I swear to Got I'll shoot you myself." Olafson took his rifle off his shoulder and drew the bolt.

A blast swamped the tiny vessel and cloaked them in smoke.

"OFF THE BOAT! OFF THE BOAT! GET OFF! RUN!"

Smith and Hantsel dropped the engine cover and scrambled forward, knocking Barker into the surf. Bart climbed out of the machine gun well and stepped onto the engine hatch, cracking the plywood cover. Olafson slapped him on the helmet.

"Where's your weapon, Sullivan? Get your got dumned weapon!"

"It was blown up, Chief," Bart yelled back at him. The machine gun had not been blown up; it was still attached to the gun mount.

"I'll blow your ass up, Sullivan. Get the got dumned machine gun and get off this boat or I swear to Got I'll shoot you right here." Olafson lifted his rifle and aimed it at Bart's helmet.

It took Bart almost two minutes to knock the swivel pin out of the machine gun mount and lift the weapon onto his shoulder. He stepped onto the narrow starboard deck and was tip-toeing his way forward when Olafson kicked him in the hip, knocking him off the boat and into the shallow surf. He landed on his face.

"Get that machine gun out of the water and get your ass across the beach, Sullivan! RUN! RUN! RUN!"

It took the crew five minutes to hike across the sand. A beachmaster near the palm trees yelled at them to run for the trees, but when they tried they tripped, or dug in, or fell on their faces. Hantsel twisted an ankle. Barker dropped his helmet, then ran back for it. All of them floundered in their life jackets. Olafson came along behind, slapping at their helmets. Bart was the last off the beach. The crew huddled at the base of a palm tree, facing the ocean.

"What the hell are you gonna do now, sailors?" Olafson screamed.

"Do?" Gretel asked.

"Wait for the next Higgins boat, Chief? Then go back to the *Renegade?*"

"No! Hell no!" Olafson glared at them. "You lost your got dumned boat! You're on land. You're under fire. So, you numbskulls just became soldiers. Now get your asses in gear! Find some more soldiers and go to war!"

The crew looked around. Fifteen or twenty yards ahead of them the troops that they had just brought to the beach were crawling toward cover under the palm trees. Some were digging foxholes. Others inched ahead on their stomachs, trying to stay out of plain site. The howitzer crew had unfolded its gun and was setting it up. Farther inland, two tanks crashed through the jungle, soldiers huddled alongside with rifles at the ready. The boom and smoke of artillery crashed overhead. Machine guns chattered at them from beyond a low ridge.

Bart Sullivan stood up, leaned against a palm tree, and lit a Lucky Strike.

"No way José," he declared. Bart took a deep drag from the Lucky, inhaled, and blew the smoke out toward the sea. He slowly backed up to the palm tree, slid down on his haunches, dropped his machine gun onto the sand, and crossed his arms. "I'm not a soldier."

Chief Olafson turned, pointed his rifle at Bart's chest, and said "On your feet, Sullivan. Or on your back. I don't care which."

Smith, Hantsel, and Barker waited for Olafson to shoot him. Bart, however, tilted his helmet forward on his forehead, bent his knees to make sitting more comfortable, and reached into his shirt pocket. Olafson jabbed his rifle into Bart's chest. Bart took out a mimeographed sheet of paper and held it up to the muzzle of Olafson's rifle.

A hundred yards inland the tanks clanked along behind a flamethrower that shot a blast into a thatched hut, setting fire to it. The pop of rifles and a first *whump* from the howitzer broke the silence that loomed between Bart and his chief petty officer.

"No, Chief. No combat for me. I've got my orders. Read for yourself."

He handed his orders to Olafson and inhaled deeply, then blew smoke into his chief's face.

CincPacPersCom
Honolulu, Hawaii
Serial 090216 of 20 September 1947

To: CincPacTrngCom
CincPacAmphibCom
CincPacFlt

SECRET
Subj: Seaman Second Class (Signalman) Bart Sullivan s/n 548333 TX

Action:
1. Subject enlisted personal to be withheld from all combat training pending re-posting as essential war personal per request of United States Congressman Wirtle of Texas.
2. Subject enlisted personal not to be deployed at sea.

Signed,
Everett Landrum, Lt. Cmdr, for cincPacPersCom

In the brief eternity between the moment when he tried to hand his orders to Chief Olafson and the moment when Bart's brain stopped, Bart Sullivan's short, miserable life flashed before him.

In his mind he saw Emma, his mother, heaping biscuits onto a breakfast plate and Poppy, his father, steadying him on a new bicycle. There was the moment he swam across the quarry by himself, the time he put a ladder up to the window of the girls' dressing room at the high school gymnasium, the night he figured out the proper combination of yeast, sugar, and peaches to make brandy. He saw himself dancing with Shirley Fleming at the prom, receiving his driver's license, taking the 1937 Ford to the State Line bar in Clovis. There was the secret mastery of Poppy's printing press, Carmen, the bar dance girl, and Doc's fake letter to the draft board saying that Bart had high blood pressure. Bart saw the highlights, the few happy highlights of his past.

Best of all, as it flashed before him, he saw none of the disasters that had dominated Bart Sullivan's brief, miserable time on earth. He would have been happy except for seeing Chief Olafson turn the page upside down, then right side up, then sideways, and the horror Bart felt when he remembered that Chief Olafson couldn't read.

But by that time Olafson had picked up Bart's machine gun, turned it around, grabbed it by the barrel, and swung it.

Then Bart's head exploded.

# Chapter 2

*Diary, September 20, 1944: A white light, and a look through a window.*

Purgatory, or limbo, or the white light, whatever it was, was very sooth-ing, tranquil, unhurried. Bart floated up, off the sand, away from his machine gun and away from Chief Olafson's boots. He rose above the palm trees and over the jungle that stretched away in the distance for as far as the white light shone. As he ascended he saw Chief Olafson turn toward his crew mates, say something to them, and then saw them slowly face the jungle and begin to ease themselves into it. He saw clusters of troops in twos and threes, crawling along, aiming their rifles, ducking their heads, jogging in very slow motion toward tanks clanking along a ridge.

There were no sounds. One of the lovely things about limbo was its quietude. At the very most Bart might have heard a gentle, soothing clarinet that might be playing *Moonlight Serenade*, and if he did, he might have seen the fading outline of the girl he had danced with at the Black Cat Dance Club, once, in Pearl Harbor, a week ago, and would have danced with more if, instead of selling most of the dance cards he had counterfeited, he had kept more for himself.

But *Moonlight Serenade* might only have been limbo playing a trick on Bart's imagination, a nice trick because, as the battle in the jungle below him began to recede from view and the white light became brighter, others began to emerge through the light and appear to Bart, people he had known but hadn't seen in a long time. There was Bart's grandfather Sullivan, a kindly old man who had held Bart on his lap and had let Bart pull his nose and who had bought him a tricycle. His grandmother, who had made peach cobblers for him and had taken Bart to pick tomatoes out of her garden. Mr. Calvin, the preacher, who died from pneumonia. Eddie Toliver, who fell off the water tower, sort of. Old Mrs. Wooten, who looked like an Egyptian mummy and died from cancer. There was more.

---

Johnny Bradley appeared, smiling, not at all angry, forgiving even, with open arms, inviting Bart to join him. It was a very kind thing for Johnny to do since Bart had ratted on Johnny and Hoyt Carter to Sheriff Hoskins, who charged them with drinking moonshine that Bart had sold them, and who then had forced Johnny and Hoyt to join the Army, which sent them to Bataan, where the Japanese had killed Johnny.

All of them appeared to him, looking just the way they had looked when Bart had known them best, not at all wrinkled or pallid or with gaping dead eyes, as he had last seen them.

As Bart floated higher into the white light he felt calm and tranquil, not at all upset about what Chief Olafson had done to him. He wondered if there was a way he could tell Olafson that it was all right. He also wondered if Smith and Gretel would be all right, or if Barker would get them all killed.

It did occur to him that the light *behind* him was not bright. He turned to study it and a window began to take shape, a very large double-hung window. He looked through the window and saw things he wished he had not seen. There was the mimeograph machine in the clerk's office on Pearl Harbor, and the Black Cat Dance Club, again, and Chief Olafson telling Bart he needed some help with something. Bart wanted to look away but couldn't.

Deeper in the dim light on the other side of the window there were more things that he had never seen before. A sea snake. His Higgins boat going into battle. A periscope and an explosion. The *Renegade*, disappearing in the distance across the deep blue sea. A typhoon. More islands. Japanese. These all seemed to be future things, bits and pieces that might be true or might not be true, but things he was better off not seeing. Bart forced his eyes to turn away from the window.

Bart then looked downward, at the beach. There was a beachmaster walking leisurely across the sand. The beachmaster headed straight to Bart's palm tree.

There was Bart's body, crumpled on the sand, eyes open, hands twisted. The beachmaster rolled Bart onto his back and looked for wounds but, apart from trickles of blood coming out of Bart's left ear and the corner of his mouth, and the bashed-in lobe of Bart's steel helmet, there didn't appear to be any fatal wounds.

"CORPSMAN!" Bart heard the beachmaster yell. "CORPSMAN!" He watched the man jog back to the beach and blow his whistle. The Navy had set up an evacuation station fifty or seventy-five yards away, under the shade of some palm trees that arched out over the sand toward the lagoon. "OVER HERE!" the beachmaster waved until he got their attention. Two medics flipped their cigarettes into the surf, picked up a stretcher, and stumbled along in the sand, following the beachmaster to Bart's body.

"Christ, what happened to him?" Bart heard them ask.

"Don't know. Found him here, looks bad." The beachmaster looked at Bart's helmet. "Still wearing his Mae West; must be off one of the Higgins boat crews." The man stepped back while the medics rolled Bart onto the stretcher. One of them checked Bart for a pulse while the other looked into Bart's lifeless pupils and closed his eyelids.

Bart's white light dimmed a little.

He watched them, far below, carry him to the evacuation station. The walk along the sand was pleasant, a stroll, even when they stumbled. When they reached the aid station a third corpsman wrote on a clipboard while a fourth groped for Bart's dog tags and read them off to the clerk.

"'Michael Barton Sullivan. 548333. A positive. 7-15-44. C.' Hell, he's just been in the Navy since July. Must have pissed somebody off to get shipped out here that fast." Bart watched the others nod in agreement.

They rolled him over again; Bart watched them remove his life vest.

"What the hell happened to him? Killed by a coconut?"

"Don't know. He was alone on the beach, crew gone, no petty officer on site. There's a Higgins boat with the ramp down floating in the surf right where they went into the jungle. I figure whatever happened, they left him there and went inland and joined the Army." Bart could see that the beachmaster was anguished; Bart probably was his first casualty. "So, get him out to the ship."

"Aye aye, Chief." The medics put a tarp over him.

It was becoming harder for Bart to see, but even then, covered up as his body was, he was certain from the gentle motion of the water that they were taking his body out to the flagship. He wanted to laugh because all he had wanted in life was to get off the *Renegade*. Now, here they were, taking him to another ship. Life was funny like that.

The medical crew hoisted him up to the main deck of the flagship. Bart expected that once his body was brought into the sick bay he wouldn't see anything at all, not through his closed eyes and the tarp and all the steel decks, but in fact he had no difficulty at all in making out what was happening.

He saw a dozen or so injured soldiers in the sick bay recoil when his covered body was brought in on a stretcher and laid out on one of the steel tables. He felt special in a way that he had never felt in life, with men his own age, armed men, staring at him and asking what heroic deeds he must have done to get killed in battle, even though the battle was just a training exercise on the big island of Hawaii. The medical corpsmen who had brought him in and the pharmacist's mate who took custody of him spoke about what to do.

"Report it to the XO up on the bridge. Then get graves registration in here. We can't have this corpse scarin' the shit out of these guys," the pharmacist's mate said, jerking his head in the direction of the other patients. "Who is he, anyway? What happened?"

"Don't know, some poor bastard named Sullivan. Beachmaster found him under a palm tree. Anyway, I can't turn him over to graves registration until the XO signs off on it. Soon's he signs off, graves can have him."

Bart liked the sound of that. 'Graves registration' sounded like men who would bury his body in a real grave, not wrap him up and dump him over the side at sea. Bart had never seen an ocean before boot camp and had been terrified of it when he was shipped over to Pearl Harbor. The notion of being buried at sea had terrified him again that morning when he had climbed down the *Renegade*'s rope ladder. Even now his spirit recoiled at the memory of what he had seen through the window in the sky and at the thought of being dumped overboard, his burial tarp rotting away in the depths, schools of scaly fishes pecking away until his body was exposed, then all of them, fish, dolphins, whales, snacking on him like a bag of Fritos. But if they buried him on land Poppy could come out to Hawaii some day and visit his grave. Maybe that was why Johnny Bradley had come to him in the white light, to let him know that burial wasn't much to worry about.

Bart did notice that it was no longer so bright, and it occurred to him that he now could make out sounds. The executive officer and his first mate came into the sick bay.

"Casualty, sir," the pharmacist's mate reported. "Off one of *Renegade's* Higgins boats. Got killed on the beach."

"Killed? How?" the executive officer asked. Bart was surprised that he knew that the executive officer, Lieutenant Commander Hobbes, a man he had never seen before or heard of, was a twenty-eight-year-old college graduate who had been commissioned into the Navy without a day of nautical experience. Bart wondered if that was part of being in the white light, knowing things he wouldn't ordinarily know.

"Don't know how he was killed, sir," the medics answered. "Nothing obvious like a wound or a burn. Name's Sullivan. Soon as you sign off we'll get graves registration to take him away."

Bart could see that the executive officer was repelled by the sight of Bart's dead body. Bart watched as Mister Hobbes gave the orders to his first mate.

"Okay. Get him out of here as soon as you can. I'll sign right now. And send a signal to *Renegade.*"

"Aye aye, sir."

"Set up a BOI," Hobbes continued.

"A BOI?"

"A board of inquiry. Try to find out how he got killed. I need *Renegade* to send over Sullivan's crew chief, his Higgins boat crew...that's probably enough witnesses."

"Aye aye, sir. What about Sullivan's sea bag?"

Bart's spirits were jolted at the mention of his sea bag.

*They can't get in my sea bag. A sailor's sea bag is his castle.*

"Tomorrow, first light, before we get underway."

"Underway, sir?"

*Underway?* Bart wondered.

"Your ears only, skipper. We're not headed back to Pearl Harbor. Training's over. As soon as all the soldiers are back on their troopships and the Higgins boats are stowed, we're underway. We'll resupply and refuel at sea. You've got about twenty-four hours to get your crews ready."

*Underway? Refuel at sea? Those bastards. They are going to dump me over-board! And they're going to open up my sea bag.*

And suddenly being dead wasn't quite such a good thing anymore. Bart remembered what he had glimpsed through the window and felt a pain in his chest that equaled the pain in his head that he now felt for the first time, the pain where Olafson had bashed his head with Bart's machine gun.

"Any word where to, sir?" Bart heard them ask.

"I don't know where we're going," Hobbes said, "but it ain't gonna be Miami Beach. MacArthur's headed for the Philippines. Halsey's attacking a chain of little islands that stretch all the way to Japan. Training's over. This is the real thing. Anyway, let's set up the inquest on Sullivan for tomorrow first light and get this body out of the way."

"Aye aye, sir."

Hobbes had had enough of the sick bay, and the body. He nodded at the men and left.

Bart's white light began to fade. He heard the roar of gunfire from the training battle. He smelled the sick bay. Bart groaned.

"Unhh."

"Did you say something?" the pharmacist's mate called over to the medics, who stood on the other side of the table where Bart lay.

Bart now was having trouble hovering above the flagship. The view down into the sick bay was very dim and he couldn't see the bridge or the main deck at all.

"Me? No," both medics answered.

"I thought I heard something."

"Unnnnhhhhhhh."

Everyone in the sick bay stopped moving.

"Oh, it's just the corpse." The pharmacist's mate hovered over Bart, whose fading spirit watched him pry open Bart's eyes to prove that he was dead. "Body's organs shutting down, sir. It's kind of spooky when the air comes out. He's dead." The mate pulled out a lancet and poked Bart's foot.

The white light became the glare of a light bulb just above Bart's face. The medic poked the sharp lancet again.

"Jesus Christ, sir! Look!"

He poked again. Bart's foot jerked. Bart's mouth said, "Unnhhhhh." Everyone in the sick bay jumped.

"This corpse ain't dead!"

Then the white light was gone. Purgatory, limbo, Johnny Bradley and Eddie Toliver and the dim window where Bart had seen what was going to happen in the future, gone. All of it was gone.

But Bart Sullivan wasn't gone, not entirely, not yet.

# Chapter 3

*Diary, September 21, 1944: A brief inquiry, and a visit from the chaplain.*

The launch that carried Bart's crew to the flagship arrived at 0700 the next morning. The board of inquiry commenced at 0715. Lieutenant Commander Hobbes began by asking Chief Petty Officer Olafson if he had noticed Seaman Sullivan missing when they were in the jungle. Olafson said no. Hobbes then told the startled crew that Bart wasn't dead after all.

"We thought he was dead. No pulse, heart wasn't beating. Eyes, nothing, didn't move a bit. He was dead as a rock. Almost a whole day went by, so you can imagine what it was like down in the sick bay when Sullivan gasped and his eyes suddenly popped open." The crew stared, eyes open, mouths slack. "Medic stuck a needle in Sullivan's foot, and then he groaned and kicked his foot a bit. Scared everybody half to death. Sure enough, he's alive. Sort of. Can't talk, at least not yet. Can't move. Anyway, Sullivan's not dead." Hobbes smiled at the shocked looks on the faces of Bart's crew mates when they heard this surprising turn of events. "So, head back to your ship, men. The convoy's getting underway in a half hour. Dismissed."

By 0730 Olafson, Barker, Hantsel, and Smith were on the way back to *Renegade*. The only thing said in the boat was when Smith muttered, "He was dead, I swear it." Barker, who they considered to be retarded, said, "Don't mean he's actually alive. Probably just a hant." Olafson told them to shut up.

At 0800 the convoy steamed out into the vast Pacific.

As for Bart not being dead, this now was more or less correct. He made another series of sounds when the pharmacist's mate and then the ship's surgeon began to coax him back to the land of the living. However, most of his sounds were of the 'unhhh' variety. At some point during the second dog watch, when the sick bay was dark, the pharmacist's mate on duty heard Sullivan say 'gorp.' He entered it on the sick bay log, 'gorp,' at around six bells and, again, shortly after watch change. As far as reporting his progress to Mr. Hobbes before the inquiry, the surgeon had said only that Sullivan still wasn't dead but he also wasn't talking.

It was not until a day or two later, when the chaplain made his rounds of the sick bay, that Bart tried to say something.

"Well, sailor, how ya doin'?" the chaplain asked. "You're quite a story. Everybody's buzzing about the Higgins boat man who came back from the dead," he smiled. He put his hand on Bart's shoulder to let Bart know, if Bart was cognitive, that Bart was in good hands. "I'm Lieutenant Snopes. The chaplain. I'm here to let you know that if I can comfort you in any way, I will." Snopes looked into Bart's dulled eyes to see if they blinked or if his mouth changed shape, anything to let Snopes know that Bart was in there. "Anything at all."

Snopes reached for Bart's dog tags. "'C,' eh. What does 'c' stand for? Christian? Catholic? You know, when we went through chaplain school you could tell a man by his dog tags. Baptist, Catholic, Methodist, that sort of thing. Not anymore; these new dog tags aren't very clear." He waited for Bart again. Bart did nothing. "Calvinist, maybe? You know, we had some Calvinists on our last convoy, stood right on the bow of the ship singing *Onward Christian Soldiers*.' We landed them in Palau. Not very good gospel singers, I'll say that, but they sure would stand right up on the beach under fire when things got hot. Not afraid to die. Very good men. Are you a Calvinist?"

"Gorp." Bart seemed to have turned his head slightly, to face Lieutenant Snopes, but it might have been nothing more than the ship rolling with the waves. "Gorp."

Bart's left hand also flopped free, lolling alongside his cramped berth. Snopes took it as a sign.

"Are you trying to talk to me, sailor? It's all right, you don't have to say anything. I'm right here. God's right here. God will comfort you. Do you want to tell me something?"

Bart did want to tell him some things. He wanted to tell about the white light. He liked the glow, and the quiet, and where instead of being in trouble, Bart had been at peace. He wanted to tell the chaplain about the visits from dead people he had known as a boy. He wanted to say to Snopes that he had seen his past, both the good parts, such as riding his bicycle and learning how to make wickedly strong peach brandy, and the bad parts, such as learning how to use his father's old printing press to make counterfeit ration coupons, from which he had made a lot of money before he was drafted, and such as getting Johnny Bradley and Hoyt Carter in trouble, for which he seemed to have been forgiven.

. Unfortunately, Bart also remembered the present. His throbbing brain was muddled about some things but he remembered being temporarily assigned to the clerk's office in Pearl Harbor, where he had used the mimeograph machine to counterfeit the phony orders he had tried to hand Olafson on the beach. He also remembered making up a lot of fake dance cards for the Black Cat Club in Honolulu, which he had used to trick Gretel, Smith, Barker and a whole lot of others into giving him their pay right before the *Renegade* shoved off to sea.

Even more unfortunately, Bart also had looked through the dim window of the future. He had seen vague images of an explosion, of fire and water, men tumbling onto the sand, mighty winds, none of the scenes clearly, with one exception: Bart had seen *Renegade* disappearing in a turbulent ocean, at night, the waves tossing him one way and the ship another. Bart believed he had seen fate, his fate or the ship's, or both, and it scared him. For the first time in his life, Bart Sullivan wanted to talk to a chaplain. In short, Bart wanted Snopes to talk with God about a general pardon. He opened his mouth.

"Bnnnnggg...."

"Nnnnngggg?" Snopes asked. "Did you say 'nnnnggg'?" He gripped Bart's flopping hand, made the sign of the cross, and tried to gaze into Bart's mostly closed eyes. "What's 'nnnnggg'?"

"Bnnnnngggg," Bart uttered. *Bnnnngggg? Bart wondered. What's Bnnnngggg? I want to say 'white light.'* "Bnnnnggggo." *Bingo? What's Bingo?*

Then he remembered his sea bag. Something about it was coming back to him.

"Bnnnnggggo."

Snopes patted his hand, held up a bible, and stood up.

"You're a brave young man, Sullivan. I can see you're tired. I'll come check on you pretty often. Get some rest." Snopes turned to leave the sick bay, then turned back to ask Bart one last question. "You're from Texas, right?" Maybe Bart nodded, maybe he didn't. "I'll be back, hear?"

---

At more or less the same time, a few miles away on *Renegade*, there were others who also were thinking about Bart's death and resurrection. Chief Olafson sagged against a bench in the petty officers' mess, digesting the heady fumes of torpedo juice and rolling with the sway of the ship as *Renegade* sloughed through the troughs and crests of a moderate storm en route to Eniwetok atoll, the convoy's first refueling stop at sea.

"Dumn him," Olafson said, "dumn him and his dumned smart mouth. 'No combat for me, Chief.'" The memory of Bart Sullivan flopping to the ground and lighting a cigarette under a palm tree still made Olafson's pink face turn beet red. The torpedo juice was unusually strong and moderately toxic, which didn't trouble Olafson; he had three hours to kill before going on watch and, regardless, he could handle any moonshine that Cookie could brew on board the ship. "'I've got my orders,' he says. Dumn him!"

"What'd the XO ask you?" Cookie wanted to know.

The executive officer's board of inquiry into Sullivan's death had scared the wits out of Olafson. Fully expecting to be charged with murder, Olafson had sat in the launch on the way over to the flagship, practicing his story. He had been prepared to swear that he had never touched Sullivan, that he had no idea what happened to him, that the Higgins boat crew, Barker, Smith, and Hantsel, were all liars, and that Sullivan was a general all around goldbricker who tried to desert during battle.

"But the old man, Hobbes, he never actually asked me what happened. He just pops off that Sullivan ain't dead after all." Olafson told Cookie what happened next.

"He then asks us all if we seen the little bastard after the crew joined the soldiers in the training assault in the jungle. And 'I say *after* the men go into the jungle?' And he says 'Yes,' and I say 'No, sir, we last seen him back by the beach,' and the old man says 'Guess he was left standing guard on the Higgins boat' and I don't say anything." Olafson let this fine line of disingenuous lying sink in, then took another swig of torpedo juice. "And then he asks 'when did I first see Sullivan was missing?' and I say 'after the training was finished up and we got back to the Higgins boat to take the soldiers back out to the ship. Sullivan wasn't at the beach no more. Sir.'"

Olafson, who knew a thing or two about sea lawyering, had not lied, not exactly. He had not seen Sullivan *after* they ran into the jungle; everything had happened before then. And, they didn't know that Sullivan was *missing* until after the training because they didn't know that the beachmaster and the medics had taken Sullivan's inert body out to the flagship. As for Sullivan guarding the Higgins boat, Olafson had waited for Mr. Hobbes to turn it into a question, but Hobbes had not. Olafson hadn't given a false answer to any of Lieutenant Commander Hobbes' questions, not exactly.

Gretel, Smith, and Barker all had stood at attention while Hobbes breezed through his questioning of Olafson, their eyes wide and mouths shut. Then, when Hobbes announced that not only was Sullivan alive but would be sent back to *Renegade* after he recovered, the XO had glanced at the three Higgins boatmen and asked almost casually if they wanted to add anything; they had not wanted to.

"What'd they tell him?"

"Nothin.' Criminy, Cookie, what'd you put in this torpedo juice?" Olafson's red face was now burning. Sweat boiled down his cheeks and onto his uniform.

That particular batch of torpedo juice wasn't Cookie's best product. Cookie usually filtered the ethanol out of the torpedo fuel by pouring it through loaves of bread before mixing in the pineapple juice.

"Bad yeast in the stores, Chief. Turned my last round of bread into hard slabs. They did't filter so good." The resulting moonshine that Cookie had traded to Olafson for cigarettes was stiffer than a dead cat and twice as toxic. "So, it's over?"

"I don't know," Olafson answered. "The XO, he just says to us 'Well, it all worked out, men. Sullivan's down in the sick bay. Once his head's cleared up we'll get him back to your ship. Dismissed.' So, I don't know."

Olafson's head was spinning. He had been in trouble before: his first arrest when he burglarized the brewery in New Ulm, his bar fight in Minneapolis that propelled him into the Navy, a dozen Navy charges here and there with promotions and demotions. But, Olafson had never been in this much trouble. Cookie was asking something else.

"What're you gonna do when Sullivan's head clears up, Chief?"

"I don't know."

"But so far, Sullivan, he ain't said nothing?" Cookie asked.

"Not yet."

---

As the convoy sailed on, Bart improved. For the first few days he lay on his berth in the flagship's sick bay, taking a little soup, a compress to his head, and acetylsalicylic acid tablets to tamp down the bonfires inside his head while the ships tossed and rolled and changed course every few hours. The medics, the galley orderlies who brought his food, the men who came in for treatment of their rope burns and sea sickness stopped by his berth to stare at him while he gazed dully at the gray metal ceiling or kept his eyes closed; each of them reminded Bart that he was a celebrity of sorts, the Higgins boat man who had come back from the dead.

But, as the swelling in Bart's brain went down, his anxiety went back up. He had played his best card to get out of combat and instead he had been killed. Now, here he was, alive again, and on a warship, going to war. He saw no way out of it. Snopes came back one afternoon.

"Hello, Sullivan. I hear that you're going to get up and around soon, on your feet. Great progress." Bart nodded; yes, the pharmacist's mate had told Bart it was time to get off his back and try walking around. "Say, about Texas. Did you live out in the country?" Bart nodded again. "Texas is full of snakes, rattlesnakes, diamondbacks. You ever see any?"

Bart began to wonder if the white light had come back on. He didn't have much experience with clergy; even at home he had gone to church because his father had made him go, not because he listened to the sermons. But yes, he had seen snakes in Texas.

Snopes looked again at Bart's dog tag and gave a knowing smile.

"The 'c' means "Church of God, right? You're in the Church of God." Snopes winked. He was pretty sure he remembered there being fellow believers in Texas. "I'm from Stone Creek Cove. Tennessee. You do know about Stone Creek Cove, don't you?"

Bart had never heard of Stone Creek Cove or, not precisely, the Church of God either. His hometown was a Baptist-Methodist-Catholic hometown. He closed his eyes.

"You did say you're from Texas, didn't you?" Bart nodded. "Snakes? Book of Mark? Chapter 16?" Snopes had made his way to Bart's cot and whispered in his ear. Bart was not quite clear what that meant. "'They will pick up snakes with their hands.'" Snopes made a little waving motion with his hands and arms, like a magician, and waited to see if Bart reacted. "Did you ever pick up snakes with your hands?"

At that moment, Bart began to suspect that Lieutenant Snopes might be a nut. He tried to tell him he needed some sleep. It came out wrong.

"Bnnnnggggo."

"Bingo?" Snopes asked. Did you say 'Bingo?'"

And then Bart remembered some more: his sea bag was full of Bingo cards. He had stolen them out of one of the offices at Pearl Harbor with a view to making a little money off the soldiers and his fellow sailors on *Renegade* just in case he got stuck going to sea with them. And there had been a code book. Bingo cards and a code book. A sailing code book. The code book had something to do with typhoons. But the code book, he couldn't remember if the code book was in the bag or not. Olafson had the code book once, but Bart couldn't remember what became of it.

*Oh, shit! I've got to get to the captain and tell him about the typhoon.* His next thought was a bit more selfish. *And get back to Renegade and get rid of all that Bingo stuff before anybody finds it.* Either way, he had to come back to life enough to get out of the sick bay.

He took his hand away from Snopes, closed his eyes, and rolled to face the hull of the ship.

"Gorp," he said. It was time for Snopes to go.

# Chapter 4

A few days later, Snopes asked Bart if he wanted to try walking on the main deck. He helped Bart off his sick berth and led him to the gangway. After a few comments about saltwater and sea air being good for the constitution, Snopes made Bart an offer.

"How's the head, Sullivan? Able to talk yet?"

Bart stumbled and shook his head no. He might have been able to say 'yes,' or 'no,' or perhaps even something with two syllables, but Bart suspected that Snopes had something in mind more than 'yes' or 'no.'

"I've been thinking. I need an assistant. I was going to get one of the Calvinist boys to help me, but they didn't seem to know much about snakes. What do you think?" Snopes waited. "Your head injury could be lucky in the end. It's enough to keep you here, working for me. What do you say?"

If Bart was going to say something, it was going to be to the commander, not Snopes, and something important, not snake talk. Bart turned around and began to stumble back toward his bunk.

Bart had spent days with his eyes closed, thinking about what had happened to him and, for the first time, he had been visited by his conscience. He had genuinely loved being in the white light. But, he suspected, if he ever wanted to see the white light again, he had to change course, to make some amends. The path back to the white light lay not in his lucky head injury or in carrying communion cups for a potty chaplain but, rather, back on the *Renegade*, and on his Higgins boat. His problem wasn't Snopes, he thought, but doing the right thing.

And, he realized that somehow he knew some things that no one else knew, things about the future, and the future was bad. He had to get word to the commander before it was too late to change course.

But, back in Pearl Harbor, other things began to percolate to the surface.

---

The Third Fleet's convoy group Welfare and Morale officer had no particular coordination with any of the other fleet offices in Pearl Harbor. He did not, for instance, read the lists of arriving and departing sailors, soldiers, and Marines or read the secret orders that set up and deployed the convoys. He, instead, booked cheap bands to play the USO clubs around Honolulu and set up screenings of 'Fight Syphilis' films for the troops, thereby implementing the fleet's delusion that men would rather risk combat with the Japanese than risk unlucky sex with whores in Honolulu.

Lieutenant Beach certainly didn't see the irony in Welfare and Morale's arrangement with The Black Cat lounge, for whose dance cards his office paid $5.00 each. Welfare and Morale bought a dozen or so cards each week, paid from a pool of unit welfare funds, and sent them off to subordinate units to award to lucky sailors who had been named sailor of the week. Beach was surprised, then, when Madame Rochelle came in person to his office to ask him to pay for two hundred forty Black Cat dance cards.

"Twelve hundred dollars?" he asked. "Are you crazy?"

"No, sweetie. Here they are." She handed Beach a packet of Black Cat dance cards, each numbered, each punched to show it had been used. "If I had enough working girls it would have been two thousand. We turned sailors away for three nights. Half the girls threatened to quit. So, I'm here to collect."

Beach's dance card fund contained sixty dollars. He passed the buck.

"There's some mistake, Miss Roach. These didn't come from us."

"It's *Rochelle*, sweetie."

"Miss Rochelle, pardon me. There's a mistake. Welfare and Morale never bought more than a dozen cards, ever." That was not exactly true; Beach had a private arrangement with a strictly Hawaiian lady who sent him a kickback for every officer that Beach directed to her discrete Wahia Lounge, earning him another fifty or seventy-five dollars a week on the side.

"That's all the money we get allotted. And, there's not even enough units in the convoy to give away two hundred and forty dance cards. These must have been your own cards, not ones we bought."

Madame Rochelle politely explained the difference in the dance cards she sold to the Navy, printed on thick cheap white paper with a black cat purring, and her own cards, sold at the door, printed on thick sea blue paper with a black cat purring. These were thick and white; there was no mistake.

"But I can't pay you, Miss Rochelle," he stuttered. "We don't have the allotment."

"It's *Madame*," she corrected him. She gave him a warning smile, turned on her heel, and left.

The next day Beach found himself standing at attention before the commander of the Third Fleet service group, who read Beach a news article in the Honolulu *Star-Bulletin*: "Navy Cheats Working Girls." Exactly twenty-seven seconds later Lieutenant Beach promised the commander that he would find out 'where the hell all the extra dance cards came from.' Until then, all leave into Honolulu was canceled for all sailors in the Third Fleet convoys.

––––––––––

The Third Fleet's planning and operations office also worked in isolation, at least from the Welfare and Morale office.

"There's a new operational order in Bingo," Commander Black announced to Lieutenant Commander Grey. "The new signal is 'I-69.'"

"'I-69,'" Grey replied. "What's the new operational order for I-69?"

"Warships who get the signal break off for Code Zulu." Code Zulu was in the Philippines.

"Yes, sir. And the support ships?"

"They proceed to Code Zebra." Zebra was out in the ocean, away from the task force. "Get the signal out to the fleet."

"Yes, sir."

Grey was back before his superior in ten minutes.

"Sir?" He waited. "Sir, there's a problem." He waited. "It may be nothing. One Bingo code book is missing."

"Say again, Grey. What the hell do you mean one book is missing?"

There were fifty vessels in the convoy—destroyers, cruisers, amphibious troop carriers such as the *Renegade*, landing ships, and four submarines to escort them. Each ship had a matching code book with its own signals link to Pearl Harbor.

"One code book, sir. It's a set of sailing orders, sir. And a whole raft of Bingo cards." He let the news sink in, then continued. "I've done some investigation, sir. All the code books were sent over to the fleet unit clerk's office for distribution to the convoy. Right before the last convoy went over to the Big Island for training. It's probably still at one of the unit clerk offices."

Commander Black thought it over and decided it probably didn't matter.

"First, the Japs can't break the code. If they did hear anything, even if they read the code books, it would just sound like a bunch of guys playing Bingo."

"Yes, sir. Except there is no I-69 in real Bingo." Such was the trickery that CincPac played on the Japanese.

"Second, the Japs don't have enough subs to follow all the boats if the fleet changes. They'd have to surface, pick up the signal, break the code, and then decide who to follow. Destroyers would pick them off before they get that far."

"Yes, sir. But, if one ship misses the signal and goes off on its own, a Jap sub could sink it, easy.

"They wouldn't need the code book to sink a troop carrier. They'd just torpedo it and disappear."

That sounded more serious than stumping the Japanese code breakers.

"You're right, Grey. Send a signal to the convoy. All Bingo signals are to be confirmed by visual shipboard signal."

"Yes, sir."

"And make a few phone calls. See if you can find the code book."

"Yes, sir. By the way, what do you think really happened to the code book?"

"Oh, somewhere there's a bunch of sailors trying to play Bingo. I really think that's the worst that could happen."

It wasn't.

———————

The clerks in the Fleet Convoy office didn't have time to coordinate with anyone, especially not Planning and Operations or Morale and Welfare. The Convoy office desk clerk shouted into the telephone at the Planning and Operations clerk.

"You want me to find some Bingo cards? And a rule book? Are you nuts? Do you have any idea how many sailors there are in fifty ships?" The clerk slammed down the telephone and shouted at the room in general. "We've got a week to process twenty thousand sets of orders," he yelled. "And Planning and Ops wants me to find some Bingo cards? Why would they send Bingo cards over here, anyway?"

"Because it's not a rule book and they're not real Bingo cards, you idiot," the chief clerk answered. "They're operational sailing orders. In code. We got them from Planning and Ops to deliver to the troop carriers on the last convoy. And we did deliver them. Here. Take a look at this."

The chief clerk stuffed a wrinkled page of orders and an inky mimeograph stencil into his subordinate's hands.

"The ensign was policing the trash and found these. Says he can't find no order pulling this guy off the convoy."

"What guy?"

"Some asshole sailor named Sullivan is wanted by some asshole congressman named Wirtle back in Texas." The ink-stained order stated that Seaman Second Class Sullivan was to be withheld from training, combat, and sea duty pending posting back to the States. "But the ensign, he can't find no order actually pulling Sullivan out of the convoy and sending him home. So, what direction does shit run?" the chief demanded. It was a stupid question; everyone in the Navy knew that shit runs downhill. He made the clerk take the ink-stained stencils and the order. "And this time it runs down to you. Go find whatever it is the ensign wants."

"The sailor?" the clerk asked. "Or the order pulling him off a ship and sending him home?"

"Both. Now."

The clerk went off to look. An hour later he came back, announcing that he hadn't found the sailor but he had found even more orders for Sullivan. He handed them to the chief clerk.

"Found these in a trash can, Chief," the clerk reported. "Damnedest things I ever saw." He handed his own set of inky stencils to the chief, along with more stained and messy orders. "They're the same orders for Sullivan that you've got, but the dates are changed to October and November. They want him back, for sure. But the ensign's right; there ain't no orders actually pulling Sullivan off a ship out at sea or sending him back to the States."

The chief thought about the ensign, who in his view was a twerp, and about the congressman who, like all congressmen, was a pain in the ass, and made a decision: he would cut Sullivan's orders himself, pulling Sullivan off the convoy. Whether Sullivan was actually found or sent home was not his problem. Two hours later, he delivered new phony orders to the ensign who nodded, then put them in the stack of communications to be sent from Third Fleet out into the great ocean in search of Bart Sullivan.

*So I rigged up some orders for some sailor who gets pulled out of the war and sent home,* he thought. *What's the worst thing that could happen?*

On the same day that Lieutenant Beach was being told that he and he alone was responsible for screwing up the shore leave for the next convoy, and while Black and Grey were looking for Bingo cards, and where the Fleet Convoy office was sending phony orders out to get Bart Sullivan off his ship in order to carry out Bart's own phony orders, the ordnance office made a discovery of its own:

CincPacBuOrd
NS Pearl Harbor, Hawaii

SECRET
Subject: Missing ordnance

1. On the CincPac Training Command inventory of 17September44, a large number of M5 detonator devices were missing from stock.
2. They are determined to be stolen.
3. The detonators are activated by a hidden hinge-spring-release. Improperly used, such devices could disable and damage a vessel.

Action:
1. All commanders are to search and interrogate all personnel who were in ComThirdFleet training on/before 17 September.
2. All guilty personnel will be court martialed. This office will strongly recommend immediate maximum punishment.

Signed:

Calvin Pastis, Captain, for CincPacBuOrd

That was getting close to being the worst thing that could happen.

# Chapter 5

*Diary, October 2, 1944: A snake, a blast, and a cloud of smoke*

B art saw rings of clouds in the distance. *That'll be Eniwetok*, he realized. The destroyers had begun to reposition themselves on the western side of the convoy. *They're setting up to protect the fleet when we stop to refuel. We must be getting close.*

For the first time in Bart Sullivan's life, his heart was moving toward the right place. His body, however, was still on the convoy's flagship, where Bart stood against the port rail gazing at the blue Pacific. Apart from a dent in his forehead and a headache of biblical proportions, he had recovered nicely between Pearl Harbor and Eniwetok. He had gradually become able to go up on deck to fish, to watch dolphins race the ship, and to decide his future.

He had begun to form words and speak, just "yes, sir," and "no, sir." Anything with more than one syllable came out garbled. As a result, he had spent most of his dolphin-watching days in silence, considering how to tell the convoy commander what he had seen when he was dead.

*Sir*, he wanted to say, *do not follow Operation Bingo.* Bart wasn't entirely clear if Operation Bingo was a secret sailing order or if it was a plan for assault on some island, but either way Bart was certain that it would lead the convoy into a typhoon. *A storm, sir, so huge that it'll wreck the fleet. But we can avoid it if we....*

When he practiced, the word 'storm' came out as 'scone,' 'typhoon' was 'tycoon,' and Bart never even saw the convoy commander. He was forced to consider lesser corrections, things he might control.

*First, when we get to Eniwetok, I've got to get back to the Renegade, he* thought. Next, he wanted to tell Olafson that he forgave him. *And I promise, Chief, that from this day forward, I, Bart Sullivan, will be the best and most fearless sternman in Higgins boat history.*

And, of course, Bart knew that he had to face his crew mates, Hantsel, who hated being called Gretel, Smith, and Barker. *It wasn't much, but I've got to fix things up with them, too.*

He also had figured out that settling things with Olafson and his crew mates would be the easy part. The rest would be harder, so much so that Bart was tempted to ask the pharmacist's mate to keep him on sick leave, even to try to put him on one of the Catalina flying boats back to Pearl Harbor.

*No, he concluded. That's not right. I've got to do the right thing. I just got pocket money from Gretel and Smith. But all those soldiers I fleeced at Pearl—I've got to pay them back, too.* He sighed, wondering how he had got himself into so much trouble. *I just hope nobody gets into my sea bag.*

---

A couple of miles across the sea on the *Renegade*, where Olafson and Cookie huddled in a corner of the ship's galley, Bart's future was the same topic. Cookie went first.

"Chief, I been thinking. This guy could be trouble, yeah?"

Olafson agreed; if Sullivan talked there would be big trouble. Bashing a sailor to death on the beach wasn't like getting into drunken fights with the shore patrol or paying a swabbie to cheat for him on Olafson's written promotion tests.

"And if he's comin' along, you know, comin' to, gettin' fit for duty, they might send him back over here soon as we refuel at Eniwetok," Cookie added. Olafson shuddered at what might happen if Sullivan did come to. "So, I been thinkin'. There's only two ways Sullivan can cause trouble, Chief. What he says and what he does." He let that sink in. "First, for what he says, it'll be his word against yours, right? And the brass always side with a chief over some swabbie. Right?" Olafson agreed. "So, in order for Sullivan to do somethin', not just say somethin', he's got to have proof. He can't do nothin' if he ain't got no proof." Olafson was getting fired up over the idea of Sullivan having no proof, forgetting that Sullivan had a lot of proof. "So where would his proof be?" Cookie asked. Olafson had no idea. "In his sea bag."

Olafson began to see light. Every sailor had something in his sea bag.

"So maybe you better see what's in Sullivan's sea bag. If there ain't no proof in his sea bag, it'll just be his word against yours, right?" The ray of light just got brighter. "So, you fix him before he fixes you."

Olafson stood up to go right then and steal Bart's sea bag. Cookie grabbed his arm and pulled him back to the bench.

"But don't you do it. No way do you want them catching you with Sullivan's sea bag. Send the crew. If anybody gets caught with Sullivan's stuff, better them than you."

---

The next afternoon, Barker, Hantsel, and Smith swiped Bart's sea bag and made their way with it through the dark passages of *Renegade*'s lowest decks.

Smith and Hantsel always deferred to Barker on matters to do with navigating their Higgins boat, but otherwise assumed that Barker was retarded. Barker, from a family of Louisiana swamp traders, rarely spoke. He hadn't said a word when Olafson conked Bart to death on the beach, nor on the way to the board of inquiry into Sullivan's death, nor during the inquiry itself, even when the executive officer pronounced Bart to be alive again. They had ignored Barker's comment, made on their way back to the *Renegade*, that Bart might be a hant.

They were accordingly startled when Barker now said, "The old man didn't ask what happened with Sullivan's machine gun."

"What do you mean?" Gretel asked. "What happened with Sullivan's machine gun?"

"What happened was Olafson picked it up. On the beach. But the XO, he didn't ask about it."

Neither Gretel nor Smith had thought about the fact of Olafson having taken Bart's machine gun with him after having used it to bash Bart on the head.

"I don't getcha," Gretel followed up. "So what?"

"The old man," Barker went on, "asked us if we wanted to add anything to what the chief told him. You didn't tell him it was Olafson that conks Sullivan to death. Then you didn't tell him that Olafson takes that machine gun that Sullivan brung off the Higgins boat and then chases us into the jungle to join up with the Army."

"Hell no I didn't tell him," Smith snapped back, "and neither did you. If I would'a said one word to the XO, Olafson would'a bashed me in the head, too."

Gretel listened to them. None of them cared if Olafson got tossed in the brig. However, none of them wanted Olafson to bash them in the head either, which was more than idle talk since Olafson had just ordered them to bring Bart's sea bag to him.

"So what?" Gretel asked. "What difference does it make? The XO held a mast, Olafson got off, and nobody asked us anything. So what if the XO didn't ask about Sullivan's machine gun?"

Barker didn't answer. They picked their way along the companionways and ladders of the troops' quarters, but when they got close to Olafson's nook in the petty officers' mess, Barker put his finger to his lips to shush them.

"Where're we going?" Gretel asked.

"We're gonna see why Olafson wants Sullivan's sea bag, that's where." He led them aft through a series of watertight bulkheads and into the *Renegade*'s Higgins boat maintenance deck.

Their boat was stacked on top of two other Higgins boats along the *Renegade*'s starboard hull. Barker was the first one up a rope ladder and over the side. The others followed, then they all hunched down to hide from anyone who might glance up at them.

"So here's the thing," Barker started up again. "Olafson kills Sullivan. Sullivan's spirit don't die. Sullivan's comin' back here. Now Olafson wants—"

"What do you mean 'Sullivan's spirit don't die?'"

"He's a hant. I told you that comin' back from the flagship," Barker snapped. "Don't you listen? So now Olafson wants—"

"What's a hant?"

Barker looked at Smith in disbelief.

"He means 'haunt,'" Gretel said.

"What's a haunt?"

"Didn't you learn nothin' back in Kansas? Christ. A hant is when the body gets killed but they don't kill the spirit. So it comes back."

Smith and Gretel both snorted; this was the most the retarded bowman had ever said at once, and it was about ghosts.

"I seen it lots of times. Christ!" Barker muttered. He was tired of having to explain everything to them. "Anyway, Olafson sends us off to get his bag because when Sullivan gets out of sick bay it ain't long before he tells somebody..."

"...before he tells somebody that Olafson tried to club him to death on the beach, then left him for dead and took off into the jungle with his machine gun." Gretel began to understand. "The old man thought Olafson left Sullivan to guard the beach, but if he did, Sullivan would of kept his machine gun with him. But he didn't—Olafson took it into the jungle with him. And we never said a word. When that comes out, it'll look like we're in on it."

Even Smith could figure out the rest: if Sullivan started talking, it wouldn't be just Olafson who would wind up in the brig. There was more.

"So, here's the thing," Barker continued. "His machine gun ain't all that was picked up." Barker dug into his blue shirt and fished out a crumpled piece of paper. When he unfolded it, beach sand fell onto the deck. The paper was stained with sweat and saltwater, but otherwise legible, a testament to the high quality of paper that Bart had stolen in Pearl Harbor. "Remember what Sullivan says to the chief right before Olafson smashes that machine gun on his head? He says 'No combat for me.' Then he flops down on his butt, lights a smoke, and tries to hand this to Olafson." Barker showed them Bart's order. "I picked it up off the beach, thought it might come in handy."

Barker proceeded to read parts of it out to them in his slow Cajun drawl:

20 September 1947

SECRET
Subject: Seaman Second Class Bart Sullivan number this and so on

1. Subject enlisted personal to be withheld from all combat training pending re-posting as essential war personal per request of Congressman Wirtle of Texas.
2. Subject enlisted personal not to be deployed at sea.

"So, Sullivan hands this to Olafson an' blows a smoke ring. Then Olafson bashes him over the head." Barker handed the order to Smith.

"Lucky bastard," Smith mumbled. "No combat, going home. Well, maybe not so lucky—he got murdered. Well, not murdered, exactly. But they're reposting him as central war personnel. What's central war personal?" Smith passed the order to Gretel.

Gretel studied it.

"Not 'central,' idiot. 'Essential.' Or is he? This is dated 1947." He read some more. "And 'personnel' is misspelled. Hmmm. Somethin's fishy here."

Barker nodded, then added, "Listen. Chief knows Sullivan ain't dead, and the chief wants Sullivan's sea bag." He let it sink in. "So, why does Chief want Sullivan's sea bag?"

It began to register on Gretel and Smith that Barker wasn't as retarded as they thought. They dumped the contents of Bart's sea bag onto the wooden deck.

Denim jeans. Blue chambray shirts. Dixie cap. Tee shirts. Skivvies. Fatigue jacket. Fatigue pants. Pea coat. Socks. Bingo cards. Letter from Michael Sullivan, Tierra, Texas. Second letter from Michael Sulllivan, Tierra, Texas. Letter from Matthew Gulliver c/o YMCA, Lubbock, Texas. Handwritten recipe for peach brandy. Dance cards.

"Look at that," Smith whelped. "Where'd he get all the dance cards?" There were dozens of printed paper cards, each of which admitted the bearer to one taxi dance at the Black Cat Club, Honolulu, Hawaii, equal to five dollars. "How'd he get so many passes to the Black Cat?"

Barker had another question: "How many Black Cat dance cards did Sullivan sell you?"

Gretel admitted that Bart had sold him a dozen dance tickets at half price. Smith confessed to having given Bart six dollars for ten cards the night before they boarded the ship.

"And I'm guessin' maybe that ain't all Sullivan got off you..." Barker looked his crew mates right in the eyes; they looked away. "How much?"

Bart had borrowed another twenty dollars from Gretel. Smith, whose father ran a dry goods store, had lent Bart thirty dollars, at interest.

"Sullivan didn't get any liberty in Pearl," Gretel mumbled. "And they put him on shore duty at the personnel office, so he wasn't around for pay day either."

"He needed to send money home," Smith added.

"So, tell me: if he didn't get any liberty, and he didn't get any pay, how come Sullivan had so many dance cards for the Black Cat?"

Barker was turning out to be pretty smart for a swamp dweller.

The slowly grinding gears in Smith's and Gretel's heads calculated that Sullivan had borrowed money from them before pay day, when Bart had been detailed to the fleet clerk's office for the whole week, and sold dance cards to them right up until the night before the ship left Pearl Harbor.

"He said he'd pay me back when we got on board," Smith said in self-defense.

"Which would be after pay day," Gretel pointed out. It was becoming pretty clear that Sullivan had clipped Smith for his pay.

"And which, according to this," Barker said, taking back the grimy order, "would have been a week after Bart Sullivan was long gone back to the States and the rest of us were at sea."

They dug into Bart's sea bag with a vengeance. Underneath the dance cards there was a manila envelope, which Gretel opened to find Bart's Navy papers. On top was Bart's assignment to boot camp at San Diego, his promotion to seaman second class after boot camp, his assignment with the rest of the men in boot camp to the bureau of naval personnel in Pearl Harbor, his transport order to Pearl Harbor, and—

"What's this?" Gretel fished an order out of a brown manila envelope.

'This' was an exact copy of the same order, but was dated October 3, 1947.

"October 3? That's today!"

There were dozens of similar orders neatly stacked inside the envelope, each authorizing Bart's transportation back to Pearl Harbor by the first available means. Each was misspelled. As Gretel read one set he passed it to Barker or to Smith to study in the dim light of the maintenance bay.

"How come they got different dates?" Gretel asked. "This one's October 11. Here's October 20. Huh!" The orders were dated well into December. "And how'd he get these orders, anyway?"

They waited for the swamp dweller to spell it out.

"Sullivan typed 'em all up himself, while he's on duty in the clerk's office. They're counterfeit, like the dance cards. Somehow he figured out all the days when the fleet would stop out in the Pacific to refuel, then m made up orders sendin' himself home from ever one of 'em. Then he starts sellin' dance cards and borrowin' money, and once he's got your money he's got all sorts of orders to go home."

"So he faked 'em? That's why it says 1947. And the spelling mistakes."

"Every counterfeiter makes a mistake somewhere," Barker sniffed.

Smith and Gretel found their money stuffed inside one of the letters that Bart's father had written to him. There were sixty-two one dollar bills folded inside a written note that said, "Take heart. Powerful people are working to bring you home."

"And he made out enough fake orders for himself to get away from us no matter where the convoy is. He robbed us!"

"He's a thief!" Smith shouted. "I'll kill that sonofabitch!"

"Shush," Barker clamped his hand over Smith's mouth. He jerked a thumb in the direction of the sailors doing maintenance work just outside of the Higgins boat. "You want them to hear you?"

"He robbed me! I trusted that little bastard and he robbed me."

"It was just business. Some day you just rob him back."

But Gretel wasn't satisfied. He continued to dig around in the sea bag. Under the clothes and letters and orders, he found a false bottom of thick canvas to hide more underneath.

"Look at this, men."

He jerked the false bottom out, lifted it for them to see, and grinned. "Oh, shit."

---

Bart stood amidships on the flagship's main deck, dangling a fishing line over the side. A sea snake wiggled through the water in search of an eel, then chased some angelfish into a ledge of broken coral and pecked at them with its head. While he fished, Bart watched the whaleboat navigate across the lagoon, passing between the troopships, oilers, destroyers, and cruisers, dodging the combat-damaged ships that were under repair at Eniwetok's floating dry docks. When the whaleboat arrived alongside the flagship a small crane swiveled down from the flagship's deck and dropped a hook to the whaleboat.

The whaleboat, Bart knew, would take him back to the *Renegade*. The scuttlebutt was that in a couple of hours the convoy would up anchor and set a westward course. Bart tried to drift his fish hook over the snake. He thought about how he would get down into the whaleboat.

*I wonder if they'll hook me onto that hook or put me in a bosun's chair or what?*

The snake, a long banded black and white krait, glided above the wreckage of a Higgins boat that was broken in two, twenty or thirty feet down on the sea floor. Debris from the battle for Eniwetok two months ago—shell-shot airplane wings, tank tracks, sunken road graders, propellers, helmets, and rifles—littered the ocean bottom.

*I wonder if I can do this,* he worried, staring at a demolished tank sixty feet below. *All I have to do is fake like I'm fainting on the deck, tell them my head hurts or I'm going blind, and they'll put me on that hospital ship and send me back to Pearl.*

A few minutes later the hook latched on to a rope net full of canvas bags down in the whaleboat, then was hoisted back up. Hundreds of orders, signals, communiques, changes, bulletins, and naval scraps of every kind packed into the canvas bags were lifted up, then dropped onto the deck of the flagship, not fifty feet from where Bart was angling for the sea snake.

"Sullivan?" Lieutenant Snopes wandered up alongside him.

"Sir."

"The offer's still open. I need a chaplain's assistant. I've already cleared it with the CO."

Snopes had visited Bart every day while he convalesced. He had talked sometimes about men going down to the sea in ships, other times discussing the glory of going into battle against the Philistines. He once asked if Bart spoke any tongues, or actually had been bitten by a rattlesnake, laboring under the hope that, as one who both knew rattlesnakes and who had come back from the dead, Bart was a closet Pentecostal.

"It'll keep you out of direct combat," Snopes added, hopefully.

The krait backed out of the broken coral and saw Bart's hook. It bit.

"NOW HEAR THIS." The ship's loudspeakers carried the sound across the entire lagoon. During the convoy's refuel and refit Bart had watched the maintenance crews tear shattered panels off battle-scarred destroyers, saw them remove the wrecked gun mounts from a cruiser, welding and bolting and painting day and night. Mostly, he had looked at the hospital ships linger as hundreds of wounded men were transferred to them from ships that had been in battle, loaded one litter at a time to be taken back to Pearl Harbor. He knew that more fierce battle was coming, and it frightened him. He could still say his head was bad, that his vision was off or he couldn't put words together, and get out of it all. "WHALEBOAT STANDING BY TO CAST OFF."

"Thank you, sir." Bart's fleeting thought of escaping battle came and went. Helping a mildly delusional chaplain to conduct church services he didn't much believe in seemed like not much improvement over going back to the *Renegade*. More than anything, Bart wanted to believe he might go back to the white light, and he had seen enough of the future to know that meant he had to face the music on *Renegade*. "But, no. I'll go on back to my ship. My crew is over there. I've got to get back to them."

Bart saluted Snopes, then felt the tug of his fishing line.

"This is for you." Bart reeled the krait in and lifted the wiggling snake over the side, then put the pole in Snope's hands and stepped back.

"Goodbye, Sir."

"It's like a sign, Sullivan." Snopes was delighted with the snake. He pulled it up close to him in case one of the other officers tried to take it away or throw it back in the water. "It's a good one, for sure. Thank you."

Bart nodded, then marched over to the officer of the deck.

"Sullivan, sir. Reporting to go aboard the whaleboat. Back to *Renegade*, sir. Permission to, uh, board? To get in the whaleboat, sir?"

"Permission granted, Sullivan. Don't fall in the water, for God's sake." He clamped Bart's fingers onto the rope net and signaled to hoist away; Bart was officially off the temporary crew roster of the flagship and restored to the permanent crew roster of the *Renegade*. The whaleboat crew grabbed the net, and Bart, lowered him into the open cockpit, and motored away toward his ship.

The little boat was halfway across when thunder erupted across the lagoon.

WHOMP!!! came a booming noise across the water.

A moment later a puff of smoke floated up from *Renegade*'s aft deck, where the Higgins boats were launched.

"Christ, what was that?" the sailor on the tiller shouted over the roar of the whaleboat's engine.

*Well*, Bart thought. *It looks like Olafson just got into my sea bag.* He wondered, fleetingly, if it was too late to fake something about his head, or even to accept Snope's offer, anything just to not go back to the *Renegade*. But, Bart had seen the future, so said nothing as the whaleboat motored on toward *Renegade*.

Bart Sullivan was about to begin the do-over of his life.

# Chapter 6

T he explosion shredded Bart's sea bag but not the money he had stuffed in the false bottom underneath the detonator. Barker, a swamp thief, knew to never be the first thief to open anything, and wisely had chosen to hide behind the machine gun mount when he saw Gretel pull the false bottom out of Bart's bag. Gretel, however, was blown over the side of the Higgins boat, clutching nothing but the piece of canvas. Smith, with Black Cat dance cards in one hand and $62.00 in the other, was knocked backward against the engine well. They were found within minutes.

---

Four Marines stood at the *Renegade*'s quarterdeck, rifles aimed at the whaleboat as it motored up alongside. The watch commander and the Marines' squad leader stood next to the deck rail while two sailors unrolled a rope ladder over the side.

"Ahoy, *Renegade*. Permission to send seaman aboard."

"Stand by," the officer of the deck called down over the side. He saw a single sailor, armed with a sheet of typed orders, trying to stand up in the whaleboat while grabbing at the fluttering rope ladder as the two vessels bobbed in the ocean. The whaleboat appeared to have nothing to do with the explosion below *Renegade*'s aft deck so he told the Marines to stand down. "Permission granted. Make it quick."

Bart, looking up at *Renegade*, saw almost exactly the same view that he had seen from his Higgins boat two weeks before when he had tried to scuttle up a rope ladder to flee from combat and instead ended up dead on the beach. He climbed up the rope ladder, slipped on the last rung, nearly fell head first into the Pacific, and was hauled on board by a Marine and a sailor. He saluted the colors, then the officer of the deck, and handed over Hobbes' order sending him back to *Renegade*.

"Permission to come aboard, sir? Sullivan, seaman second class, sir."

"Granted." The officer of the deck read the single page of hand-typed orders. "Welcome aboard, Sullivan. Report to the skipper, now."

"Aye, aye, sir." Bart saluted and made his way over to the ladder amidships that led to the wardroom.

"Not there, sailor. The bridge."

"Aye, aye, sir."

Bart had no clear sense of exactly how to find the bridge. He stumbled around, working from the general notion that it would be high up and somewhat forward. He had no doubt that the sailors scurrying back and forth had as much to do with preparations for the ship to get underway as with the explosion he had heard while on his way to the ship. He mentally practiced one last time what he had prepared to tell Captain Hull.

*Sir*, he would say, *Seaman Bart Sullivan reporting for duty. And I have a confession to make.*

He would tell the commander how he had fleeced the men back in Pearl Harbor with fake dance cards, confess to counterfeiting orders to get him off the ship, and admit to his efforts to flee his post during the training exercises. He would declare his willingness to accept his punishment, take up his post on the Higgins boat, and offer to do extra duty at sea to get up to speed. And then he would say:

*Sir, this is going to sound crazy, but there's a typhoon forming in the ocean and the convoy is headed right for it. I'm not sure when it will blow, but if we change course now we can save the convoy.* He was sure the commander would laugh at him, so then he would tell the skipper what else he had learned during his soul-floating stint while dead. *Sir, I don't know how to explain it, but I know that the convoy is headed to Peleliu. That's top secret, so how could I know this? Because I was dead, sir, and when I was dead, I saw the future. With my own two eyes.* The skipper would realize that no lowly sailor could possibly know about the convoy's secret sailing orders, so Sullivan would have to be telling the truth. *The convoy's going to land these troops at Peleliu and we're going to lose some*

*Higgins boats on run-ups to the beach. But we can prevent that, too, if....* That's what Bart wanted to say to the skipper.

*Renegade*'s junior officer of the day was standing at the door to the bridge.

"Welcome back, Sullivan. Captain Hull's waiting inside. Enter, stand at attention, and wait until you're spoken to."

"Aye, aye, sir."

The officer knocked, opened the door, and announced that seaman Sullivan was safely on board, and was ready and present. He stood aside. Bart walked in, stood at attention, and almost fainted.

"At ease, Sullivan. Welcome back." The skipper was almost forty, clear of eye and square of jaw, and was extending his hand for Bart to shake. Bart got the shakes.

"Sullivan," the skipper went on. "That's quite a story the CO sent over. Report says they found you dead on the beach there at the Big Island, took your body back to the flagship, and were about to bury you at sea when some pharmacist's mate heard you make some sounds. They sent us a signal every day or so about you getting your head back on straight. You're the most famous sailor in Convoy Three. Welcome back."

Bart only heard about every fifth word the skipper said because, immediately behind the skipper, stood Olafson, at attention, smiling at Sullivan in a way that left no doubt that Bart's second life might be just temporary.

"I intended to put you on light duty on board for a couple of days while we get underway, but no. There's some bad news. There was an explosion on your Higgins boat. Some damned fools swiped a detonator and it exploded right in front of the engine hatch. We're about to get underway and it's gonna be up to you to get your boat shipshape for combat. Chief here will take you down to her. You boys have to get to work."

"Permission to speak, sir?" The skipper nodded. "Well, sir, I wanted to ask if I could have a word with you, sir."

"What about, Sullivan? We're on the move." The deck beneath their feet was in motion; *Renegade* was getting under way.

Bart sneaked a glance at Olafson. This was not the time to tell the skipper about impending typhoons and island landings. It also wasn't the place to tell the skipper that he had expected to find Olafson locked up in the brig for murder, or attempted murder, whatever it was.

43

"Then it's time for me to get to my duties, sir. Aye, aye, sir."

"Good man, Sullivan. But that's not all the bad news. The reason there was an explosion on your Higgins boat is because somebody tried to steal your sea bag. They took it to the boat and tried to get into it but you must have had it dogged down pretty good because they set a det charge to blow your bag open, and destroyed it. All your gear was shredded. Your personal papers blew out the back of the ship's deck. All you've got left is this."

'This' was a pack of Bingo cards, a recipe for pecan brandy, some now-singed Black Cat dance tickets, and over a thousand dollars in one dollar bills, all stuffed into a new sea bag. There were a few shreds of his forged orders and the singed flap of his old sea bag, 'Sullivan' stenciled on it. But, as for anything he had ever owned being legible, there was nothing.

Bart's good intentions began to crumble. *I can't very well confess to forging orders to get me off the ship if there aren't any forged orders left for me to confess to,* he realized. And, in a very queasy realization, Bart also grasped that he wasn't quite as ready to confess when the only other evidence of his Fagan-esque past was a wad of cash that the captain seemed to think was Bart's. He wondered whether purging his soul should wait for a more opportune moment.

"I think we got all your money back," Hull went on. "You can count it. To be honest, Sullivan, if you're going to carry that much cash around you should lock it up in here until you get some liberty. Anyway, the chief here will take you down to the ship's stores to draw new duds. They're waiting for you."

"Yes, sir."

"That's it. Dismissed."

Bart stood at attention, stiffened, did an about face, and walked back through the companionway.

Olafson came out behind him, squeezed past the waiting junior officer of the deck, then led Bart toward the ship's stores. They turned past the chiefs' mess and found themselves in a tiny space between two watertight doors. Bart thought it was a good time to at least sort things out with Olafson.

"Chief, I know you killed me, but I just want to...."

Olafson slammed the door behind them and jammed down the locking lever to the door in front of them. With one meaty palm he grabbed Bart by the neck and pinned him against the steel walls of the impromptu cage. Bart's eyes bulged and his aspirated voice sounded much as it had when he had come back to life in the flagship's sick bay—"*Errqqqhhh.*"

"I know about you, Sullivan. I know ever thing," Olafson hissed toward Bart's rapidly-aspirating mouth. "And where you're goin' you ain't gonna be spending that cash you stole." Olafson dropped Bart to the deck.

"Where," Bart gasped, "am I going?"

"You're goin' to the fishes, Sullivan. Soon's we fix up the boat, you're goin' over the side. Maybe tonight. Maybe tomorrow. I ain't decided when exactly, but what you done to those tree is nothin' compared to what I'm going to do to you."

"What," Bart struggled to blurt out, "did I do to what tree? Three?"

"Your mates, Sullivan. They was trying to save you. Hantsel, and Smith, and that got dumned Cajun. They're trying to make it right with you comin' back to the ship, but they got screwed when you booby trapped your sea bag. It blew up. So now they're in the brig."

"The brig?"

"Locked up 'til we get to port. Then they're going to get shot. 'Sabotage in time of war,' the skipper says. Sabotage of the ship."

Bart was trying to understand not only why Hantsel and Barker and Smith had gotten into his sea bag in the first place but also how he could add to his list of confessions that it was he, not they, who had put the detonator in the sea bag, without getting himself shot for sabotage. All of that was flowing through his suddenly-oxygenated brain when Olafson released his grip, swung open the forward hatch, and threw Bart into the ship's stores room, where he tripped on the threshold and landed face first on the supply desk, breaking his nose.

It would be a difficult voyage.

# Chapter 7

*Diary, October 10, 1944: Coding messages*

Except for the bars, the brig wasn't much different from the rest of the *Renegade*. Gretel, Smith, and Barker were the first three sailors who had ever been confined to the brig for more than a few hours and the only ones to have been jailed at sea. The ship's master at arms also was the ship's fire control officer; he designated three of his gunnery mates to rotate as jailers, a job they performed by playing solitaire on the deck outside the bars. For most of October, the prisoners huddled against the hull, whispering what they would do if Olafson or, better still, Bart suddenly materialized inside the cell while the lights were out.

"I'll kill the sonofabitch," Smith hissed. "I'll rip his guts out," Gretel seconded him.

"We've got a way of dealin' with 'em in the swamp," Barker hinted. Even so, Barker was not as restless or loud as the other two. "But maybe you shouldn't be saying things you don't want heard when the time comes." The time, they knew, was the court martial that would be waiting for them when the convoy made port. "You think that swabbie's just outside playin' solitaire, but for all you know he's hearin' every word we say and tellin' the skipper. Just sayin'."

Now and then the ship lurched violently onto a new course, slamming them across the cell and against the bars. At those sudden course changes the men collapsed in heaps on the deck, their heads banging the bars, cursing the jolt, the jail, the war.

"Ship's zig-zagging. Maybe it's a sub," Gretel panicked.

"Maybe."

"What're we gonna do if it's a sub? What if it torpedoes us? We're trapped."

"Then we're gonna die."

"It's not right. I demand to get out of here. Hey, swabbie!" Smith yelled at the guard. "What if we get torpedoed? What? Huh? What?"

The guard sat on the deck, rolling with the ship's motion, arranging stacks of hearts and clubs between his legs. The fourth or fifth time Gretel yelled at him he turned his back on them. Thus was their grim existence as the convoy sailed west across the Pacific Ocean.

Then one day a note appeared in Barker's plate of navy beans. He plucked the slimy paper out of his mouth, spread it open with his fingers, and read it.

"*Od ton erapsed,*" it read.

He didn't mention the note to Gretel or Smith. It might have been just a wad of paper someone dropped in the beans. However, the next day a second note appeared.

"*Od ton erapsed,*" it repeated. "*Ouy evah llufrewop sdneirf.*"

It took Barker three days to figure out that the messages were written in swamp code, spelled backwards, but with mistakes.

On the fifth day a message arrived in the beans that said, decoded, "Tap on the bars so I know you got the messages." Barker waited until the cook's swabbie came to pick up their mess trays. As he handed his own mess kit back through the opening in the bars, he raked his metal cup back and forth across the bars a few times, then banged it on the door itself.

"Pipe down!" the guard yelled at him. "We're running silent."

"Runnin' silent with eight boilers and two turbine engines?" Barker answered.

"Runnin' silent with a black five to a red four. Pipe down."

The cook's swabbie shuffled away with the prisoners' dirty mess kits. Barker saw him turn at the companionway, nod imperceptibly, and disappear.

That same day, when the first dog watch was handed over to the second dog watch, a mimeographed sheet from the ship's clerk appeared in the executive officer's reports box.

Ordinance Officer's report of investigation of exploding sea bag:

To the Captain:

1. No weapon system on this ship is equipped with detonators like the ones the prisoners used to blow open Seaman Sullivan's sea bag.
2. The only place where such items could be found would be at CincPac in Pearl Harbor, at the Third Fleet armory.

There was an unintelligible ink signature over the typed line 'for the Ordinance Officer.' The executive officer read it, scratched his head, and took it to the captain.

"Ordnance delivered this report, sir. No-go on the detonators. Thought you'd want to see it."

"Thanks," the skipper answered. He didn't lower his binoculars from his scan of the rest of the convoy, spread out over the wide Pacific, and his search for signs of a periscope. "Good job."

The executive officer assumed the skipper had ordered the ordnance investigation; the skipper assumed the executive officer had ordered it. Each was satisfied.

Two days later another message was fished out of the beans. Barker read it.

"Lett eht rippiks taht navilluS dias ouy dlouc evah sih aes gab fi eh tog dellik." "Tell the skipper that Sullivan said you could have his sea bag if he got killed."

"Hey," Barker hissed. The jail birds huddled in the corner. "Look at this." He slipped the note to Gretel and Smith. Smith couldn't figure out the code, so he explained it. "It's sayin' for us to tell the skipper that Sullivan said we could have whatever was in his sea bag."

"How do we tell him?" Gretel whispered. "I don't think the skipper's coming to visit."

Barker wanted to slap him. Gretel wouldn't have survived in the swamps for a week, maybe not even a day. Smith was so stupid he would have tried to hand feed an alligator.

"You idiots," he hissed. "Why would we tell the skipper that Sullivan gave us his sea bag?"

"To get out of the brig?" Gretel suggested.

"So we could have Sullivan's money?" Smith always hoped to be rich but, until now, didn't have a plan to make it so.

"No, you numbskulls. Who was it told us to get Sullivan's sea bag in the first place?"

Slowly but surely it began to dawn on them that only one person on the ship knew that they had been told to get Bart's bag out of the crew quarters.

"Uh, Chief Olafson?"

"And why would Chief Olafson send us to get Sullivan's sea bag?"

"He wanted the money for himself?" Smith suggested.

"You're dumber'n a bag o' rocks, Smith, you know that? Who you think's been sendin' us these notes?"

Olafson was not known for reading or writing. While it wasn't one hundred percent certain that he was behind it all, there was no other good candidate.

"It's Olafson who whacks Sullivan on the beach. It's Olafson who tells us on the whaleboat goin' over to the flagship to keep our mouth shut when the XO is about to find out it was Olafson who killed Sullivan. And it's Olafson who hears the XO say that Sullivan ain't dead. So Olafson's goose ain't cooked, but if Olafson thinks his goose still might get cooked, who does he think could do the cooking?" Barker let it sink in. "Us, that's who. So, then it's Olafson who sends us to get Sullivan's bag."

Slowly but surely, through huddled talks in the corner of the cell, they figured out that Olafson wanted them to get caught getting into Sullivan's sea bag.

"So, if we got caught with Sullivan's money, Olafson could claim we were the ones who had a motive to kill Sullivan back on the beach," Gretel whispered. "And now," he added, holding up the coded note, "he's trying to get us to tell the skipper that Sullivan gave us whatever was in his bag because the skipper would never believe us. It'd look even worse for us."

"It's like a swamp light," Barker told them. "We put a light out in the swamp so the revenuers who's out lookin' for us sees the light and think they found us. Then they run their boat over to the light and piles it up on the bank while we're watchin' from the trees. Then we go scot-free while they're stuck in the swamp. No way are we sendin' word to the skipper that we had a right to dig around in Sullivan's bag. That's what Olafson wants us to do, so we stick our own heads in the noose with such a sorry alibi. So, we ain't tellin' the skipper nothin'. 'Specially nothin' about Sullivan's sea bag."

Something else had been nagging at Gretel's mind.

"Hey, Barker," Gretel whispered. "Why'd Olafson try to kill Sullivan anyway?"

But even Barker had not figured that out.

Nor did they have a good plan of how to keep their heads out of the noose. They might have rested more easily if they had known that someone else had a plan; another mimeographed report had made its way to the executive officer's wardrobe. It appeared the next day.

Ordinance Officer's second report of investigation:

To the Captain:
1. Maintenance chief reported to this officer to come down to the weather deck to inspect readiness of LCP (Higgins boats). Chief ordered all personnel out of the weather deck and then showed this officer the hatch on one of the landing craft. Inside the hatch was an emergency tool kit with a box of spare gaskets. Inside the gasket box was an M5 detonator.
2. He then showed me another landing craft hatch; there was another M5 detonator inside its emergency tool kit. In fact, there was a detonator inside all of the Higgins boats. The chief now has them locked up inside the landing craft ordnance locker.
3. It is possible that the detonator that went off in the sea bag when this vessel was anchored at Eniwetok somehow got jostled around and just exploded without anyone knowing it was there.
4. So, the prisoners may not be guilty of intentionally sabotaging the boat.

There was an illegible ink signature over the typed line 'for the Ordinance Officer.'

Neither the executive officer nor the skipper were suspicious when, the following day, Seaman Sullivan appeared on the bridge shortly before the first dog watch and asked permission to speak to the *Renegade's* captain.

"Granted. At ease, Sullivan. What is it?"

Bart's familiarity with the bridge was limited. He had been in the ship's sick bay, repeatedly, to see the pharmacist's mate. That medic had sewn up a cut on Bart's leg, salved a black eye, buffed the edges off a broken tooth, and put gentian violet on a bruise that ran from his hip to his shoulder blade. The medic also told Bart there wasn't much he could do about repeat cases of night horrors.

Bart also had been busy on the maintenance deck, working double shifts to get his Higgins boat back to readiness before the invasion that everyone knew was coming. Except for the unfocused moments when he had reported back on board, he had never been on the bridge or anywhere else high enough to see the horizon, yet found it strangely familiar.

"We're about three hours before raising Yap, sir. Aren't we?"

"How would you know that?" the skipper answered. He looked at Sullivan, then out to the horizon, then back at the lowly and banged up sailor who stood at ease while the ship rolled. He lifted his binoculars again, scanned the horizon, and saw nothing, no evidence of land, no birds, no airplanes, nothing. Yap was nowhere in sight. How, he wondered, would Sullivan know that?

"I can't exactly say, sir. Since my, uh, the thing back at Hawaii where, you know, I was, uh, dead..."

"You weren't very dead, Sullivan. The convoy commander cleared you for duty."

"Yes, sir. But, like I said, it's hard to explain. I saw things. Future things, that still haven't happened yet. And I still do. So, I just know kind of where we are. That's all. And I'm ready for what's next, sir. We've got our boat ready to go, sir."

"Good. What do you want, seaman?"

"It's the crew, sir. The Higgins boat crew. Boat can't make shore runs without them, sir. I wanted to ask if there was some way they could come back to duty."

The captain was prepared to remind Sullivan that the crew was in the brig for trying to blow up the ship while robbing Sullivan, but he remembered that the ordnance officer had just reported that maybe Seamen Hantsel, Smith, and Barker hadn't been trying to explode the detonator. He instead reminded Bart that the crew was in the brig for robbery of Sullivan's personal effects and "...quite a lot of money. That's hundreds of dollars, Sullivan."

"Well, yes, sir. But they didn't know about the money, sir. They're good mates, sir. I told them back at Pearl that if anything happened to me, for them to get in my sea bag and send letters to my family back home. Anything else in there they could divide. I didn't know they was in any trouble until Chief Olafson told me what happened."

The skipper was beginning to suspect there was more to the story than that. He was about to ask Sullivan if he knew anything about booby traps when the quartermaster shouted at him.

"Convoy's turning, sir." Sure enough, ahead of them, every vessel in Convoy Three turned hard to starboard. Three destroyers broke ranks and raced to the port side of the group and began to patrol the flank. "Could be a sub, sir."

He forgot about Sullivan, but the next day a final mimeographed order was posted, this time to the master at arms. The jailer told the men.

"You're free. Out you go." He unlocked the iron bars, opened the door, and stepped back.

"What's up?" Barker wanted to know.

"Case dropped, the master told me. Get out of here before he changes his mind."

"Why?"

"Don't know, but it may not matter. Scuttlebutt is, wherever we're going, tomorrow's the day."

They passed by the galley on the way back to their berths. None of them noticed the startled look on Cookie's face as he watched the three freed men walking down the companionway. What they did notice was that the ship was running all hands on. Something big was about to take place.

# Chapter 8

*Diary, October 30, 1944: Into battle*

They survived their first real combat, a landing under Japanese fire on Peleliu. But, when they got back to the ship Barker told Smith and Hantsel, who they still called Gretel, that he believed more than ever that Bart was a hant.

"What exactly is a haunt?"

"A hant? Don't you know nothin'? It's a hant." Barker had thought a lot about what was in Bart's sea bag while he was in the brig, but this was the first time he had thought about Bart himself. "You kill somebody, but you don't kill his spirit, he comes back, he's a hant. They don't look dead, not to us, but they don't look right, either. For chrissake, just look at him."

Bart, never large, did indeed look ghostly. Being dead for a few days had cost him twenty pounds and, even though he was alive again, being at sea did not particularly agree with his appetite. If Barker had claimed that Bart was a rail, Smith and Gretel would have agreed. But, when he instead said that Bart was a hant, Smith and Gretel did not agree, not entirely. Barker laid out his facts.

"I seen plenty of 'em in the swamp." That wasn't strictly true, since he had never seen a hant in the swamp. But, Barker had heard about them, mostly from his swamp trading family when he was a little boy. "You go out at night an' they're in the cypresses, floatin' around. Sometimes they come up to your pirogue while you're asleep, or you're doin' somethin' on shore, an' they mess with your stuff. Or you see their lights in the trees, flickerin', all green, an' then they disappear. When they do that they're lookin' for a soul, somebody who's about to die. Stay away from them green lights."

"Chief didn't kill Bart under a green swamp light," Gretel reminded them. "He didn't kill Bart at all. He's not a ghost. He's just..." Gretel didn't know what Bart was. In truth, he did think that Bart might actually be back from the spirit world, a place he had heard about where people died and went to a great white light and then came back to life. "Sullivan's got a body. He's just different. He's not a haunt."

"Hants've got bodies. Unless you kill one. Course, if you kill a hant, it just becomes a shade. But Sullivan's not a shade. He's a hant."

Barker let the distinction sink in. Smith was ready to believe anything. Gretel rolled his eyes.

"Okay," Barker said. "Think about this a bit. We see him in Hawaya, climbin' out of the Higgins boat like a big coward. Then he tells Olafson he ain't gonna do combat an' shows him those orders that we seen in his bag. Then Olafson kills him on the beach. You seen it. I seen it. Sullivan was dead. And now? He's alive again." He let that settle in.

"So?"

"So, did you see him today? Completely different. Wasn't afraid of nothin'. He didn't climb out of no boat, hell no. Well, he did, but not like in Hawaya. Not like he was runnin' away. He wasn't afraid of nothin'. And nothin' touched 'im." Then Barker went back over everything that happened on their first day in combat.

---

"Steer toward Amber Beach," Bart had called out. "To evacuate some wounded." Bart stood over the Higgins boat's machine gun and read the signal flags from the *Renegade*, acknowledged with his own signal flag, and called out to Smith to change course to the west.

"What?" Smith yelled back at him.

"Ship's signaling us," Bart answered. "They're sending us on a run in to Amber Beach. To take off some wounded. Hard to port." Bart waited for Smith to move the wheel. The nose of the Higgins boat turned to the west to go around the tip of Peleliu. "It's going to be a hot beach," he added.

Their little landing boat steered away from the echelon of Higgins boats that were on a run to Scarlet Beach. Soon the four sailors were all alone, bobbing toward the blind side of the island.

Smith looked toward Peleliu while he steered. The crew's first four landings had been scary but safe, more or less. Every transport in Convoy Three had sent their Higgins boats onto the war-torn island, first to deliver all the soldiers on board the troop ships, then to bring back troops from the island who were being relieved after six weeks of brutal combat. The waves of landing craft had motored up to Peleliu through channels that were already cleared for them on Scarlet Beach. They had dropped their ramps, let their soldiers out, picked up the men being relieved, and roared back to their ships. They had been scared to death on the first run and wary on the second, but by the last two trips they had realized that their landings were protected not only by aircraft roaring overhead to strafe the Japanese but also by the shape of the island; the beaches were protected from Japanese fire by a ridge of Mount Umurgrogol on that side of Peleliu.

But Amber Beach was not protected. The Japanese had been counter-attacking the Americans with mortars and point-blank machine guns hidden from view. Whole regiments were pinned down. That side of Peleliu was exposed and under fire.

As they changed course, Mount Umurbrogol loomed high in front of them. Airplanes from the Navy's carriers roared low over the water, climbed, bombed the mountain, circled, and returned to sea. From off to the right, somewhere near the airfield, artillery rounds boomed away and hit the side of Umurbrogol. Tiny tanks, visible through the shattered trees and rocks, clanked their way up the side of the mountain toward the Japanese. Flames billowed up, both from the bombs and from hidden Japanese artillery that ravaged the thousands of men dug in on the mountain, the advance elements of the soldiers the men were sent to relieve. And, down on Amber Beach, Japanese fire raked the sand and the reefs in front of their landing craft.

"HARD TO STARBOARD," Bart screamed. Without thinking, Smith wrenched the rudder to the right. The boat's hull scraped across a wrecked gun mount from an amphibious tank that had been shot up and sunk weeks before. A screech of steel against their wooden hull scared them out of their wits; if they had waited ten more seconds before jerking the boat away the bottom of their Higgins boat would have been torn out. They would have drowned a hundred yards from shore.

"APORT!" he yelled again, and Smith jerked the craft hard back to the left. A Japanese mortar round blew up in the water, twenty yards ahead on the course they would have been on if Smith hadn't followed Bart's orders. "BARKER," he yelled. "Look out ahead! There's wrecks all over here."

No one else on the landing craft had seen any of them. They zigzagged back and forth until the Higgins boat crested the last ripple of surf, then made for the beach.

"Thirty yards," Barker called out. "Twenty-five."

"Ten knots," Hantsel yelled. "Eight knots." The craft slowed.

"Twenty yards." Barker and Hantsel released the ramp locks and stood to the winches.

"Idle."

"DUCK!" Bart yelled. "DOWN!"

A hail of machine gun bullets ripped across the bow of the Higgins boat, striking the ramp and Hantsel's winch. Hantsel flopped to the deck and peed his pants. Bart unleashed a burst from the boat's machine gun, a futility burst since the Japanese were so far away that he had nothing in particular to aim at.

"Fifteen yards. Ten. Five. Down ramp!"

Hantsel lay curled on the deck, terrified that he had been shot. Bart thumped Smith on the shoulder. "Coming through." Bart took the machine gun off the mount and climbed over the engine well and toward the bow. Smith leaned over the helm as far as he could to let Bart crawl forward. "I've got the winch. Let's get the ramp down!" Bart could tell that Smith also thought that Hantsel had been shot, but if they didn't let the ramp down evenly, if the ramp dropped and dug into the sand and they let the Higgins boat run up sideways, they would all be sitting targets for the Japanese machine gun.

The boat scuffed up onto the sand. The ramp dropped. From out of the ragged trees and shell-cratered draws of Peleliu a dozen medics ran toward them, bearing litters of wounded men. Bart stood at Gretel's winch, his machine gun propped onto the boat's plywood coping, and aimed generally toward Mount Umurbrogol. Despite the urgency, he knew without knowing how he knew that they wouldn't be shot.

The medics loaded the wounded onto the little craft, then jogged back to the relative safety of the trees and waited while another dozen Marines brought three more litters. Eventually the exposed Higgins boat was crammed with wounded men. Bart made way for them, then jumped into the surf and yelled at Hantsel to crawl back to the machine gun mount behind the engine well.

"You're okay, Gretel. You're not hit. Swap places with me," he insisted. "For now."

Bart stood alongside in the surf and dragged Gretel to the aft machine gun well, then passed the machine gun up to Smith at the helm, who helped the shaken Hantsel attach it to the mount. Bart then turned and jogged onto the beach. His shipmates gaped while Bart dodged another round of machine gun fire, then disappeared into the trees. He reappeared a few minutes later, jogging back with the last of the medics, helping to transport a final litter onto the ramp.

"That's it! Ramp up! Go, go, go!" he yelled. He hadn't taken command of the craft so much as he had perceived that Smith, Hantsel, and even Barker were just staring at him as he climbed on board with the last wounded man. "Ramp! Reverse! Let's get out of here!"

Smith shoved on the throttle and the wooden scow backed out into the surf, then turned toward the open ocean. Another round of bullets fell short. Bart pointed left, then right, then straight out to sea, and the little Higgins boat dodged another mortar shell. Hantsel, Smith, and Barker continued to stare at him as their boat bounced on the swell, racing back toward the *Renegade*. When they were half-way back to the ship and the water was smooth, Barker broke the silence.

"Hey! Sullivan! How'd you know all that?" Barker shouted at him.

"Know all what?" Bart answered. The engine rumbled and the wounded men on their cots moaned each time the hull slapped the water and bounced.

Barker persisted.

"How'd you know that there was a tank sunk underwater, about to rip our hull out? Huh? Or how about those machine gun bullets headed toward us? How'd you know when to tell Smith to helm this way an' that way so we don't get hit? Huh? How'd you know what to do?"

---

Later, back on *Renegade*, the three of them huddled over their work, patching up the Higgins boat after the last run of the day. Bart had taken the machine gun away to clean it in the ship's armory. All of them knew that something had happened at the beach but none of them, not even Barker, was quite sure what.

"So, what'd he say?" Barker insisted. "Remember what he said?"

"'Sometimes I just know things.' That's what he said," Gretel answered.

"Sometimes he just knows things," Barker snapped. "So, he just knew there's a tank sunk under our keel. He just knew there's a mortar round comin' at us. He just knew exactly where on the beach the medics is hidin' in the trees?" And, Barker thought, *he knew we was goin' to burgle his sea bag, so he booby trapped it. How'd he know that?*

Not a day had gone by that Barker hadn't thought about the wad of money that he had seen stashed in Bart's sea bag just before the detonator blew it up.

"How does he 'just know things' before they happen? I'll tell ya how. We seen with our own two eyes him dead on the beach back in Hawaya. And we seen with our own two eyes that he ain't dead now.

"How come? I've told ya how come; 'cause he's a hant, that's how come."

"Maybe he just has good eyes," Gretel answered. "Maybe he sees better than the rest of us." Gretel was grateful that Bart had pulled him off the deck and put him at the back of the Higgins boat, and for not making a big deal out of Gretel's peeing his pants.

"You know why he's a hant? He proved it hisself. What do hants do?"

Neither Smith nor Gretel had ever seen a hant, much less a shade or a ghost, nor even the little green lights that followed them around in the swamp.

"They hant places 'cause they're disturbed. Why're they disturbed? 'Cause the reason they're hants in the first place is 'cause they were killed! Killed instead of dyin', you know? Like murdered."

"Bart wasn't murdered, Barker. He was conked on the head. Then he came to."

Barker ignored him.

"An' when they've been killed, they're restless, so they go hantin'. An' where do they go?"

"I don't know. Where do they go?"

"They go lookin' for the place where they was killed. They hant places 'til they find it. Hant here, hant there, 'til they find the place. Restless. So, we're on the beach, right? Our orders is to stay with the boat and get her off when we're loaded up, right? But Sullivan, he jumps in the water, and then what does he do?" He let them think about it before telling them. "He runs up on the beach and into the trees, right?"

That was right.

"And where was Sullivan killed?"

"Back in Hawaii."

"On the beach."

"In the trees."

"'That's right. On the beach. In the trees. So there on Amber, Sullivan runs up on the beach, in the trees, dodgin' Jap bullets with nary a hit, an' he looks around. But he doesn't find the place where he was killed, so he comes back." No one could deny that. "An' I'll tell you one more thing. He's gonna keep lookin'. Trust me."

There was no explanation for how Bart had foreseen every single disaster that would be in their path. There was no way he could have known exactly where on Amber the medics were hiding or where the mortars were landing or the wrecks were sunk on a reef they had never been to. Gretel and Smith wavered. Maybe Bart was a ghost.

"Not a ghost. A hant. Completely different."

At that moment there was the rattle of a chain, clanking its way toward them, banging on the deck plate of the steel companion way. The hatch opened. They held their breath. Bart walked in, dangling the security chain of the Higgins boat's machine gun.

Barker raised his eyebrows and whispered. "Now you believe me?"

"So, what do we do?" Gretel asked. Smith nodded.

"We prove he's a hant, that's what."

"How do we do that?"

"By putting him at peace," Barker answered.

Barker then told them the four ways to kill a hant.

# Chapter 9

*Diary, November 2, 1944: They think I'm a ghost....*

The crew were heroes. There even was talk of them being awarded medals. But, the exorcism failed.

Hantsel had drawn the short straw. He talked Bart into going to see the ship's chaplain to give thanks to God for getting them off Amber Beach and, three days later, off Peleliu itself. Hantsel told the chaplain that he felt as if they were in the grip of an evil spirit and would the padre pray to cast it out.

Bart had said nothing, not until the chaplain asked Bart if he had any special requests.

"Have you got a snake?" Bart had answered. The startled priest had asked again, to be sure he had heard correctly. Bart repeated himself. "A snake. I met this other chaplain on the flagship. He liked snakes. I thought maybe there was some connection between the Lord and snake-handling."

The priest had backed away, said a quick Lord's Prayer, and fled down the number two passageway to the officers' heads. Bart had shrugged and headed back to his berth. "I've got second dog watch tonight. See you at chow."

Hantsel returned to the hiding place underneath the aft gun mount, where Barker and Smith were waiting for news.

Hantsel and Smith had agreed to kill Sullivan, or his ghost, but only on the condition that they do so in a way that would ease Bart's passage to Heaven, such as with a priest. Barker did not himself believe in exorcisms. He had, however, seen at least three different swamp children taken away to New Orleans for priest treatment and, after they were returned to the swamps, the children were very changed and frightened, so he had decided it was worth a try. Thus the news of the failed exorcism wasn't a surprise to Barker, but the question of priestly snake-handling was an unforeseen bonus.

"A snake?" Barker crowed. "Only a hant would ask a padre if he liked snakes." He rubbed his hands together and peered up the ladder to make sure no one overheard. "That proves Sullivan's a spirit." Hantsel wasn't so sure.

"He didn't exactly ask if the chaplain would *like* a snake; it was more like 'Have you got one?' Either way, it don't prove Sullivan's a ghost. It just proves the padre don't like snakes."

"It don't matter," Barker answered. "It might not a worked anyway; it takes the right kind of priest to exorcise a hant so, even if the chaplain had a tried, it might not of killed Sullivan. But it does prove that Sullivan's a hant. That's what you wanted, wasn't it? Proof?" He didn't give Hantsel time to argue. "So we move on. Here's the next plan. It's called fire an' salt. Or salt an' fire. Same thing. So, here's what we do."

For the next three messes Bart found himself to be the focus of saline attacks. At breakfast, Smith spilled salt on Bart's forearm, which Bart brushed on to his powdered eggs, which he then ate. Barker then knocked over a metal salt shaker at lunch, dumping a couple of tablespoons onto Bart's leg, which he brushed off. Neither were able to get their Zippos out and apply a flame to Bart's salted skin before Bart brushed the salt away. At supper mess Hantsel went so far as to send Bart to the kitchen stores for a whole can of salt, then dumped it on him. Barker had his Zippo lit and waiting but still was too late to set fire to Bart's encrusted feet, arms, hands, or legs. At this point Bart asked what was going on.

"Nothing."

"Nothing."

"Let me see your arm." Barker looked at Bart's arm. There was no fleshly evidence of a shrinking ghost nor even so much as a sulfurous burn. He stared away, out the galley companionway.

"We're just messing with you." Hantsel couldn't make up lies as easily as Barker, nor could he pick fights, so he tried to make everyone feel good. "You know, locker room stuff."

Bart had never been in a locker room in his life. He had no friends back in Texas, nobody with whom he had snapped towels or traded insults. Being messed with was awkward.

"You know, the salt and stuff. Just horsing around."

"Why?" It was out before Bart could stop from saying it. "Why salt? Hell, we're in the ocean. Pour something on me I like, like ice cream. Or peach brandy."

"Because Barker thinks maybe you're...." Saying it sounded even dumber than thinking it. Smith, however, was dumb and couldn't think of anything else. "He thinks you're a ghost. You know, 'salt on a ghost,' that kind of thing."

Bart had never been called a ghost, either, so had even less of an idea what to say than Smith, who continued.

"It was that thing on the beach, you know? Turning the boat right before it hit something in the water. Dodging out of the way of the mortar shell. It was like you knew what was coming."

"That and running through the bullets," Hantsel added. "They went right through you. Like a ..."

"A ghost?" Bart had seen many things in his future but had not seen that his crew would think he was a spirit. "The bullets—they didn't go through me; they just never hit me." But, at that instant, a note of doubt crept into Bart's mind. Yes, he had known in advance that he would not be shot on the beach, because back in September he had seen it through his window in the sky. He began to wonder if coming back to life might have some strings attached. "And why salt?"

Like a fart in church, the crew mess hall had suddenly become utterly silent. Men at every table looked up. Sailors in the crowded galley stopped to listen. No one budged until Cookie walked up and told them to move along, to make space for the men coming off the first dog watch. The four of them stood up and began to scrape the spam gelatin and bean scraps off their trays to dump in the scrap cans.

"It's more'n that, Sullivan. We seen you. You was dead!" Barker hissed. "We seen you on the beach in Hawaii, deader'n a doorknob. An' now you ain't."

Cookie told them again to make way for the crew coming off the dog watch. They headed to the starboard passageway that led to the crew quarters.

"I just got hit in the head," Bart said. He and Barker bumped each other in the passageway. "I wasn't dead; I was just knocked out." They bumped again, hard, and it occurred to Bart that Barker was seeing whether

Bart was corporeal.

"Tell me this, then," Barker demanded. "Howdja know where those things were in the water. An' the incomings. And back in Hawaya you was gutless. Now you're a he-man. That's what Smith called you when you took that gun and run up on the beach and run back. 'Sullivan's like a he-man,' he said. 'He ain't afraid of nothin.' You're a different man from Hawaii, Sullivan. Not a mortal man. Thats what I'm sayin'."

Bart had no experience in telling people that in fact he had been dead for a while, albeit dead with strings attached. Barker waited. Smith waited. Hantsel waited.

"Sometimes I just, know things."

"What do you know, Sullivan? Huh? What exactly do you know? You knew someone was goin' to get in your sea bag so you rigged it to blow up? Howdja know that?" Barker bristled at the memory of stealing Bart's sea bag, only to watch it explode before he could get his hands on the money inside it.

"I didn't know that. I was just being safe."

"An' you knew we were gonna get tossed in the brig, too? Huh? You knew that too, didn'ja? You may not be a hant, Sullivan, but you ain't human. Get out of my way." Barker pushed past him and walked away. "Sometimes you jus' know things," he muttered under his breath. "Spook!"

Bart also knew that he had gotten them *out* of the brig, but explaining how he had done that would make it worse, not better. The others stood aside. Bart went topside to report for the second dog watch. None of them had noticed Cookie, listening through a ventilation grille.

---

Cookie had a particular interest in Bart Sullivan.

Although Cookie didn't know about the detonators and the Bingo code book, he did know about the Black Cat dance cards, although strictly at the consumer level. While *Renegade* was being outfitted at Pearl Harbor, Cookie had gotten four shore passes. He used the first at the Lucky Club, where he was turned down by a girl from Cincinnati, got drunk, and slept it off on the beach at the base of a tree. During his second pass he found the Black Cat Club, where he spent one dance card on Hualani Mahai'ai. Hualani danced close and bumped Cookie's middle a few times and he asked for more dances. He then spent his third shore leave, and most of his pay, on Hualani, who gave him about a half-hour of frenzied delight in a hotel room one block from the Black Cat, then returned to work, inviting Cookie to return the next night. But Cookie was out of money. Olafson told him it was not a problem.

"I've got this swabbie," Olafson had said to him, "who can make up anything. I get you some Black Cat dance cards."

Olafson knew the swabbie because he had chosen Bart Sullivan for temporary shore duty in the fleet's clerical office, Bart being the only volunteer on *Renegade*'s unassigned crew who could type. Olafson quickly discovered that not only could his swabbie type, he could print, a discovery Olafson made after barging through a small crowd of jarheads outside the clerk's office who were handing money to his swabbie in exchange for wads of Black Cat dance cards.

Among the agreements Olafson then made in Pearl Harbor with Bart Sullivan, his swabbie clerk typist printer, was that in exchange for letting Bart have another twenty-four hours at his profitable temporary duty at the clerk's office, the swabbie would give Olafson as many Black Cat cards as Olafson wanted. That number was twenty, of which ten went to Cookie, who consumed them on Hualani during his fourth and final shore pass. Olafson used the other ten for himself, which he spent for the favor of the private company of Hualani's friend and fellow night worker, Suzy Kapuli, whom he concluded was a decent girl and for whose favors he would gladly help her out with a favor himself.

Cookie's interest in Olafson's helpful swabbie increased several days later, after Olafson had spent more nights and one morning with Suzy. The base morning report revealed that the shore patrol and Honolulu police had raided a hotel one block from the Black Cat Club and detained two night workers, whose first names were Hualani and Suzy but whose last names, instead of being Mahai'ai and Kapuli, were actually Nakajima and Mazuka. Each of the two were reported to have a surprising amount of dollars in their possession, and a few other things were found in Suzy's apartment.

Unbeknown to Cookie, Olafson's swabbie soon offered to Olafson to modify the terms of their agreement: in exchange for the swabbie not being sent back to sea or to combat, the swabbie would not remember anything about Olafson's unfortunate love interest. Olafson declined the generous offer and physically removed the swabbie from the clerk's office, then man-handled him back aboard *Renegade*, where he remained under Olafson's eye until the ship cast off for war. When Cookie asked what the swabbie knew, Olafson said, "You don' wanna know."

It was enough for Cookie that the swabbie knew more about him and Hualani than the Navy did. Accordingly, Cookie did his best to explain to Olafson that the swabbie's crew mates believed Bart was a ghost and that his shipmates were trying to kill him.

*Yumpin Yehosaphat,* Olafson thought. He had arranged for Bart and the crew to die for America by volunteering them to make the run to Amber Beach; he considered them cowards for not having had the decency to get killed there. *Now the li'l fokers is goin' to get medals.* He also figured that the li'l fokers would be protected by the fame of their rescue at Peleliu and tell someone what actually had happened on the beach in Hawaii. Worse, Bart might let out what had happened even before that, when he had forged a requisition slip for Olafson to get some detonators at the armory in Pearl Harbor. *I got to do somethin' fast or my goose is cooked.*

Cookie continued.

"It was somethin' about salt, Chief, salt and fire." Olafson was stumped. "They was pourin' it all over him. One of 'em tried to light his leg with a Zippo."

"Why?"

"To kill him, they said. Or prove he's a ghost. Apparently that's how you do it."

Olafson hadn't heard of killing anyone with salt before, but it seemed reasonable. He left Cookie's scullery and headed for the galley's dry storage where fifty-pound bags of bulk salt were stacked. He left the storage and walked up to the boat deck to watch Bart make his dog watch rounds on foot. He hid behind a life raft and watched Bart patrol the deck, walking from the radio room amidships, aft to the stern gun tub, across the stern, and back along the other side.

*Dat li'l foker don't deserve a medal. He deserve a rope, dat's what he deserves.*

There were plenty of ropes on board, ropes to secure the landing boats to the deck, ropes to secure their tarps, ropes to hoist the booms that lowered the landing boats into the water, and endless coils of rope that would work just fine to hang Bart if Olafson could only find a convenient way to get Sullivan to pass below one of them so that Olafson could drop it over his neck. Bart walked past.

"Evening, Chief," he said.

"Hmmphh, Sullivan. You pay attention to your watch, hear?"

Bart nodded and moved on to the completion of his rounds. Olafson heard Bart make his report to the junior officer of the deck—no men overboard, no ships, no planes, no fires, no sabotage. The ship rolled with the sea and plowed onward. Olafson studied the booms that lowered the Higgins boats to the sea and the cranes that hoisted them up and down.

He went back to the galley storage locker and hauled a bag of salt out and up the companionway to the boat deck. He waited for Bart and the junior deck officer to walk out of sight, then attached the bag to one of the ropes on the hoists. After one more pass he winched the bag high above the deck, then waited while Bart made his rounds. At eight bells Bart finished his watch and reported to the junior officer of the deck, then made his way along the deck to the crew ladder. Olafson centered the bag of salt above Bart's descending head, aimed, and dropped it.

Three tubes poked up out of the water, five hundred yards aft. A communications mast. An oxygen intake. A periscope.

*Renegade* rolled, then lurched hard to port. Olafson saw the torpedo wake emerge on the surface of the water, a growing wide path headed straight toward him. He forgot about the bag of salt and slammed the nearest alarm. Loudspeakers immediately sounded general quarters. An explosion sent a fireball across the dark blue sea.

# Chapter 10

*Diary, November 19, 1944: Ectoplasm, force fields, and Hollandia—I'm coming home.*

Hobbes, executive officer of Convoy 3, studied the ships from his seat in a motor launch that was weaving its way through Hollandia Harbor. After three days in port, most of Convoy 3 was refitted and ready to get underway, with one exception. The troop transports were docked bow-to against the temporary docks, waiting for the soldiers who would fill them, who they would transport to the next battle, which Hobbes believed would be in the Philippines. The exception, *Renegade*, was anchored a quarter mile out in the harbor. It was toward *Renegade* that Hobbes directed the whaleboat.

He ignored the clouds of flies and honey-buzzards that swarmed above the ship, but the stench was more than he could disregard. The breeze carried an overwhelming stink, so powerful that Hobbes wouldn't have been surprised if the smell alone stopped the boat dead in the water. From the water, Hobbes could see *Renegade's* sailors swarming the decks with brushes, brooms, buckets, anything they could find in what appeared to be a vain task to clean the ship.

The boat drew up to *Renegade* and threw a line. Hobbes made his way up the ladder, saluted the quarterdeck, and asked the nervous officer of the deck for permission to board. He was escorted to the wardroom where, even with all portholes opened, the air was so foul that Hobbes wondered how the crew had breathed during the rough crossing from Peleliu to Hollandia. Hull, the *Renegade's* skipper, and the officers who had been on watch the night the torpedo was fired, all stood at attention, waiting for the convoy's

67

hangman to investigate how they had let a Japanese mini-submarine get within several hundred yards and take a point-blank shot.

"Well, gentlemen, there doesn't appear to be much structural damage. That's something."

"Yes, sir," Hull answered. "The principal thing is the blubber. When the torpedo hit that whale the explosion caused the blubber to catch on fire. Hell of a burn—whale oil burns worse than gasoline. God-awful stink everywhere." He paused to retch. "But, yes, sir, as far as damage is concerned, we were pretty lucky. Here's the ship's report."

*Structural: The whale's head, about half its body, and some fins and flippers hit the ship above the waterline, knocking Renegade sideways. One landing boat boom was dislodged from the aft mast, dropping Higgins boat #21-08 onto the 40 mm gun director housing and damaging its bow ramp and winches. It also knocked loose the aft mounts of the radar and radio antennas. Three life rafts were unmoored, retrieved, and their restraining latches under repair.*

*Other: Charred whale parts (no precise description) and hot oozing blubber coated most of the aft deck, flowed down number 4 and 5 hatches and from there throughout the carpenter shop, sick bay, mental ward, and aft troop quarters. Cleaning details report that 'whale guts' flowed everywhere. Burning whale blubber scorched into the bulkheads, ladders, ventilators, hatches, decks, and lockers throughout the aft starboard quarter of the ship.*

*Injury report: Ensign Lanier has shell shock. S2C Sullivan's shoulder dislocated. 114 crew treated for nausea and vomiting from whale blubber stench; the sick bay and treatment deck are directly under the number 4 hatch and flooded with rotting whale parts so most of the sick preferred to go topside to help cleanup.*

*Note: Debris from the Japanese Kaiten periscope and cockpit, heavily damaged, was found in the water near the life rafts and retrieved. No sign of the suicide pilot.*

The name Sullivan rang a bell to Hobbes.

"Sullivan was on deck patrol for the second dog watch," Hull told him. "He reported the whale sounding off the starboard quarter a few times during the watch patrol. He'd just come off watch when the whale blew up and caught fire. It's in the watch log."

"Where's Sullivan now?" Hobbes asked. The bell was ringing louder.

"Sullivan, sir? He's swabbing decks in the sick bay."

"Have him report."

Seaman second class Sullivan was on his knees in the sick bay, a bristle brush in his right hand, his left shoulder done up in a sling. He rubbed away at rotted and charred whale blubber on the deck, the bulkheads, the water tight door, the examining tables, the lights, and the dressing cabinets, swabbing along, dwelling on the past to avoid thinking about the future.

Bart happily remembered how much he had loved being the postmaster in Tierra before he was drafted. He had genuinely delighted in opening the town's personal mail, reading who had cancer or who was financially strapped, whose son was missing in action or who desperately needed something. Everyone came to the post office to gossip, making it the ideal place to sell the counterfeit ration coupons that he printed up at night on his father's newspaper press. Those had been good times, simple times.

He was swabbing and humming when the bosun in charge of the work detail came in.

"Avast, Sullivan. Scrub yourself, put on your topside blues. Report to the bridge. Now."

Bart looked up. *Topside blues?* He wondered why he was going ashore; had the Black Cat cards and detonators caught up with him? "And, no, you're not going ashore. No one is. But the XO's on board and he wants you topside, now. Skipper said dress up. You've got five minutes."

Bart made his way past the officers' mess, down the portside crew ladder, wedged past Barker and Hantsel who were scrubbing the maintenance deck, and headed toward the aft crew quarters. Barker glared at him; Bart ignored him. Bart had decided that there was no point in continuing to try to be a buddy to the crew. He had tricked them in Pearl Harbor, not by much, just $62.00 and some dance cards, and booby trapped them, also not by much, with a detonator in his sea bag, which landed them, not him, in the brig. He also had got them out of the brig, which they didn't acknowledge, and saved them on Peleliu, which they also didn't acknowledge. Now they were trying to kill him.

The more complicated part was that he had seen the future and the future was now. Knowing that he had only a few days to live anyway, Bart had decided to go it alone from here on. He pulled off his stinking dungarees and tee shirt and concentrated on the past.

The thumb on the scale of Bart's past was pretty heavy. He had especially enjoyed reading his sister's, Virginia's, forlorn correspondence with Will Hastings, who Bart detested. He realized that he could no longer remember why he detested Virginia, apart from the fact that Virginia loved Will Hastings, which made life hell on Bart because Shirley Fleming also had been in love with Will Hastings and thus spent every waking day of her life ignoring Bart. Will had shipped out for England in 1943. After Virginia turned up pregnant, Bart had taken special delight in stealing their letters; Will had no idea that Virginia was pregnant and Virginia didn't know that Will thought she had abandoned him, to Bart's delight. Now Bart wondered what kind of baby Virginia had, girl or boy, and whether Will had ever found out about it. He dug out his topside blues, plucked some loose threads and buffed up the piping, and dressed. Smith, loitering in the companionway when Bart left to go topside, nodded. Bart nodded back and made his way to the bridge. Smith reported to Barker and Hantsel.

---

"Okay, so this dead whale shit is the best thing we coulda asked for," Barker whispered. He had huddled Hantsel, still called Gretel, and Smith behind the damaged Higgins boat down in the maintenance deck. The maintenance deck smelled like an unventilated slaughterhouse. Bilious fat coated the work benches, the tool cabinets, the hoists, and especially the deck itself where full loads of gelled whale oozed through the ship's interior. Hantsel and Smith weren't clear how scrubbing rank whale was the best thing that they could ask for. "'Cause it's all ectoplasm."

"What are you talking about, Barker?" Hantsel had begun to show some signs of resistance to killing their ghost.

"Ectoplasm. It's what hants is made of. This whale blubber is the same stuff. Slimy. Wet. Rubbery. Stinks. All it needs is a charge." He waited for them to agree; they didn't. "A force field electric charge. Best way to kill a hant there is. Didn't bring it up before; never dreamed there'd be any ectoplasm. Now we got enough to kill all the hants in Hell. All we need is a force field."

*Renegade* was full of force fields. Radios could be dialed, fan wires and battery chargers plugged into power outlets, light bulbs part-way unscrewed, battery cables jumped. The possibilities were endless.

"Force field? Ectoplasm? Are you crazy?"

"Nah. It's perfect. We've just got to get Sullivan to enter the force field. Here's what we do."

---

Bart waited outside the wardroom. The five minutes he had been given to present himself became ten minutes, then a half hour. Officers came and went. He stood to attention; they ignored him. He gazed toward Hollandia.

The base was a sweltering beehive. Cranes loaded and unloaded ships. On shore, swarms of trucks and tractors hummed around a huge supply yard. An endless stream of troop trucks, supply trucks, ambulances, and jeeps inched backward and forward on the docks. The beaches were carved up with busy roads that led to Quonset huts and to a permanent airfield several miles inland. Airplanes patrolled overhead, guarding the approaches to New Guinea and far out to sea.

Neither Bart nor any of the officers onboard noticed the Catalina PBY descend out of the low lying clouds, glide down to the water, land, and taxi to the dock. It was too far away, there were too many other ships in the harbor, and everyone on *Renegade* was too busy to see Lieutenant J.G. Beach, formerly Lieutenant Commander Beach, crawl out of the plane, drop to the dock, and puke out everything he had kept bottled inside his stomach for two days while the Catalina island hopped from the safety of Pearl Harbor to the war in New Guinea. Bart was reflecting on Hoyt Carter and Johnny Bradley when the wardroom door opened and he was ordered to report.

---

"Yes, sir," he told the room full of officers. "First time I saw the whale it was abeam starboard. I'd never seen a whale before so I looked at it pretty good for a few minutes. I'm guessing it was a hundred yards from the ship. Then it kind of flipped and dived down. I saw it two or three more times during my watch."

"Anything else?" Hobbes asked.

Bart knew that 'anything else' meant anything like a periscope or a torpedo, which he had not seen. He could have answered 'Yes, Chief Olafson rigged a crane to drop a bag of salt on my head to try to kill me,' but then he would have to come up with a reason why he hadn't mentioned Olafson to the watch officer.

He came up with a half-truth.

"I saw the rest of the convoy across the water. And the whale. No lights. Nothing in the sea."

The light at sea that night had been very bright, bright like the night back in Tierra when he had ratted to Sheriff Hoskins that Will and Johnny Bradley and Hoyt Carter were drinking a quart of peach brandy out by the cemetery, without mentioning that he had made it and sold it to them. Will got away but the sheriff arrested Johnny and Hoyt and scared the wits out of them; Hoskins had them in the Army the next day. Hoyt somehow escaped from Bataan. Johnny Bradley didn't escape, and was dead. It had been that kind of night.

"How bad's your shoulder, Sullivan?" Hobbes' bell had begun to connect the dots. "You're the sailor we thought was dead back in Hawaii, aren't you?" Bart admitted that he was. "You know, we nearly buried you at sea on the way to Eniwetok. You are one lucky sailor, Sullivan." He noticed that the lucky sailor turned white as a sheet when he mentioned burial at sea.

"That's probably what brought me to, sir," Bart answered. "Being buried at sea scares me, real bad."

"At ease. You're in good hands here on *Renegade*. So, you didn't see anything out there in the ocean on the dog watch except this whale, is that it?"

"Yes, sir."

"Let me tell, you, Commander," Captain Hull chimed in, "if there had been anything to see, Sullivan would have seen it. Do you know what he did on Peleliu? His chief volunteered Sullivan to pick up some wounded Marines on a suicide run in to the hottest beach on the island. He zigzagged that Higgins boat around reefs and wrecks and mortar shells and God only knows what else. Perfect seamanship, like he was looking at it all through a big window. It was the best job any crew did on Peleliu, sir, getting in, getting out, and saving lives. I've put him and the crew in for a medal."

Then Hobbes remembered what it was that he was supposed to do with Seaman Sullivan.

"How'd you like shore duty, Sullivan?"

"Sir?"

"I just remembered—some congressman thinks you're essential to the war. Your orders came in back at Eniwetok but it was too late to do anything there. You're supposed to detach here and go back to the States. How'd you like that?"

The thumb on Bart's scale seemed to lighten.

Bart couldn't believe it. So much had happened since he had forged those phony orders back in Pearl Harbor, since he had tried to hand them to Olafson on the beach and the enraged chief had clubbed Bart to death with his machine gun. All he really remembered from being dead was floating high above the jungle, looking through a window in the sky into the future, and everything he had seen had come true. Now, all that remained of his future was to die somewhere out in the Pacific Ocean, and that was coming due in a few days. But now? Maybe his destiny had changed.

*He's sending me home!* Bart hadn't spent much time in Bible study and, despite the evidence to the contrary, he didn't believe in miracles. *No more Olafson trying to kill me. No more Barker trying to get Gretel and Smith to kill me. No more landing wooden boats on Jap beaches under fire. No being lost at sea.* It took less than ten seconds for Bart's worse angels to fly down and land on his shoulder.

"Yes, sir. I'd like that."

With every breath in and breath out, Bart now saw a different future. Instead of dying at sea he saw himself back in Tierra, a war hero, selling more counterfeit gas and tire and sugar ration coupons than ever before, making money hand over fist. In another vision, equally fleeting, Bart was in Washington D. C., on Congressman Wirtle's staff. *That's where the real money is. I could get my hands on some war contracts, sell favors to lobbyists.* That was a very good vision. *And I'll fix that god damned Olafson if it's the last thing I do. And Barker.*

"Congressman Wirtle says you're essential to the war effort, Sullivan. But what's more essential than getting men on and off the beach and winning this war? You're the kind of sailor we need to keep." Bart's angel panicked.

"Congressman Wirtle's in charge of the farm production committee, sir. Food for the troops. I worked for him in his Texas office, did his printing and typesetting bulletins and reports to congress and farmers. His work keeps the whole Navy fed, sir. And the Army."

Bart was pleased at how easily lying came back to him. He had left Tierra in the back seat of a government car after four men had walked into the post office, grabbed his arms, and led him into a kangaroo medical examination where a Mexican doctor from Clovis pronounced him fit for service. His last view of home had been driving past Nona's Café and onto the Lubbock highway. They had laughed and bundled him onto a train bound for San Diego Naval Training Center. *I'll get those four bastards, too.*

The worm was about to turn. Bart was dismissed.

It was Bart's best day in the Navy, by far. He left the wardroom and went aft to the bridge ladder where, once back out in the open, he could at least breathe salt air. He took comfort in the fact that Olafson and Barker, Smith, and Hantsel would still be breathing whale stink while he was going to USO shows and drinking cold beer and hopping a plane back to Hawaii. Life was good. He had no idea that a force field was about to surround him.

---

"Okay, here's how it works," Barker said. "The force field is that string of electric wires up there. The radio boys hooked 'em up between the aft crane and the foremast to liven up the loran and the radar antennas. That's the force field. Got it?" Hantsel nodded; Smith looked at Hantsel, then nodded as well. "So, when the energy of a force field hits a hant's ectoplasm, the blast kills the hant. Got it?" They did. "So, soon's Sullivan enters the force field, we cover him in ectoplasm. The force field will break it down and he can't survive. Got it?" They understood. "You ready?"

They lugged six buckets of ectoplasm up into a Higgins boat that was suspended from the middeck crane, then hid in the boat. They peered over the gunwales and gripped the buckets.

Bart stepped down from the bridge, walked directly under them and into the force field, and stopped. They rose as one, buckets in hand, just as the radio room sent out a test signal and the antenna wires overhead crackled with energy. They tipped the buckets of whale gut ectoplasm over the side, directly toward Bart's head. Bart stepped back. The whale guts crashed to the deck without so much as a splatter on his pants leg. Bart stared at them and laughed.

"Hey, Barker, listen, you stupid Cajun," Bart sneered. "And you too, you dumb-ass soda jerks!" he yelled. The three men looked down at the poltergeist that had gotten away. "I've seen every single stupid thing you tried to do to me, from dragging me to a priest to salting my arm and trying to set fire to my leg. I saw that dumb son of a bitch Olafson try to drop a bag of salt on my head. I saw it because all of you guys are dumber than a carpet full of rug beaters. So listen to this. When you're back out at sea and headed to the Philippines and you're landing on a hot beach somewhere, you're going to be on your own, because I've been transferred. I'm shipping out. I'm going home. I'm going to the States. And you guys are not. You're probably going to get shot up somewhere on the way to Japan and I'm not going to be there to save you. So, kiss my ass and adios." He shot them a finger, then headed down the ladder toward the crew quarters. "And I'm not a ghost."

Bart was home free. All he had to do was pack his sea bag, get his cash out of the skipper's safe, and wait for Hobbes to send over his orders, then go ashore. Life was good.

---

That same afternoon Lieutenant J.G., formerly Lieutenant Commander, Beach, presented himself to the convoy personnel office, where a boat was found to take him out to *Renegade* to report for duty. He steadied himself, gripped the gangplank's rail, and lugged his sea bag up to the deck, made a miserable showing of a salute, and stepped aboard what by anyone's standards was the most foul-smelling ship in the ocean. The officer of the deck led him amidships, past three sailors who were swabbing up a mountain of whale blubber immediately beneath a Higgins boat. Beach mounted the bridge ladder, went to the ship's administrative office, and told the duty yeoman his business, where he learned that not only was the skipper aboard but, by coincidence, so was the convoy's executive officer. He waited a half hour, then was escorted to the skipper.

"Lieutenant Sonny Beach, sir. Reporting." He stiffened to attention and waited.

"Welcome aboard, Beach. Stand easy." They shook hands.

They read his orders and personnel file, then explained to Beach about the whale. Captain Hull decided that Beach would replace Ensign Lanier in charge of a section of Higgins boats. His own executive officer said that they would find Beach a berth once things were sorted out.

And Hull asked him "What's that you've got there?"

"This?" Beach answered. "Just a newspaper, sir. Honolulu. Two days old."

"Well, Beach, we don't see many newspapers out here. When you're finished would you mind if I took a look?"

Even across the skipper's table Hull could read the headline:

"Honolulu prostitutes convicted in spy ring."

"Not at all, sir," Beach answered. "Take it now."

Hull took the paper. A smaller headline announced that an office building in Washington had been renamed for a congressman who had died the year before.

"Thanks, lieutenant. It'll be good to catch up on the news."

# Chapter 11

*Diary, November 14, 1944: What is destiny? It's watch duty in the middle of the night at the back of the boat, that's what.*

As soon as he had his money, his orders, and a boat to take him ashore, Bart's days as a Higgins boat crewman were over.

"You can go in, Sullivan," the duty yeoman announced. Bart sensed an unfriendly glare at his back as he entered. Not one sailor on board would have lifted a finger for Bart after word made the ship's rounds of his gleeful taunt about him being shipped home. He couldn't get off the ship fast enough for his sake or for theirs.

All the cash that Barker, Hantsel, who was still called Gretel, and Smith had tried to steal from Bart's sea bag had been kept in the ship's safe. A stack of dollar bills now stood neatly on the skipper's desk, along with a paper bag and a receipt book. Bart stiffened to attention; Hull told him to stand easy.

Bart spread his ankles apart, put his hands behind his back, and waited for freedom.

"Well, Sullivan, congratulations," Hull announced. "You're the only sailor in the Pacific who's going home not in a body bag. We'll miss you. Not too late to say you'll stick around for the war."

"Thank you, sir. No, sir, I'll go on home. Congressman Wirtle needs me there. The war effort."

"Thought so. Hoped you'd stay and teach the new lieutenant the ropes. Guess he'll learn on the job."

"Yes, sir." Bart already had seen Lieutenant Beach, wobbling on deck, waiting to meet the landing boat crews that he was about to command. Beach looked sea sick, even though *Renegade* was at anchor in a flat bay. Bart had ducked into a locker, both to skip a meeting that no longer concerned him and to avoid laughing at the suckers who would be stuck on the ship long after he was gone.

The skipper counted out the money that had been blown all over the maintenance deck when Barker, Smith, and Hantsel triggered the booby trap detonator during their robbery attempt. Bart signed a receipt and put the money away.

"And this is yours too, Sullivan." He handed the paper bag to Bart. "Check to see that it's all there." The contents spilled out on the desk.

'This' was the rest of the debris from Bart's exploded sea bag. It consisted of a recipe for peach brandy, a pack of Bingo cards, a few shreds of his forged orders and the singed flap of his old sea bag, the name 'Sullivan' stenciled on it. There also were a dozen unused dance cards from the Black Cat Club in Honolulu. Bart turned beet red.

"Your buddies had these when they blew your bag up." Bart held his breath, waiting for Hull to figure out the other possibility, that they actually had been Bart's dance cards and had been inside his bag, not outside, before Hantsel triggered the detonator. "You might as well take 'em. You'll see Honolulu before we do." He handed the cards to Bart.

"And the Bingo cards?" Hull beamed at Bart. "What do you say we keep those? The troops can play Bingo, get their minds off where they're headed. Sign here."

Something hazy floated through Bart's mind, something about the Bingo cards. Was it something he had seen while he floated in limbo? Something during the white light? Something he noticed as he stole the Bingo cards from the clerk's office back in Pearl Harbor? Maybe it was nothing. He couldn't sort it out, other than the only thing standing between him and the boat home was his signature. Bart signed.

The money, the dance cards, the scraps, all went into Bart's new sea bag.

"One last chance, Sullivan. You're a good sailor, damned good Higgins boat man. Wish you'd stay on board. No? Well, good luck." He stiffened, Bart stiffened at attention, and Bart was dismissed. A steward who had been serving coffee to the skipper stood aside to let Bart leave.

Bart made his way down to the main deck to wait for the whaleboat to take him to shore. The other troopships, the cruisers, destroyers, and oilers had taken up their positions to depart. Bart's last official act on *Renegade* had been to help board a very frightened Army infantry battalion into its packed quarters below decks. Everyone understood that they were bound for the battle raging in the Philippines.

Lieutenant Beach stood on deck in front of the Higgins boat crews. It was obvious that he had no idea what he was doing. Bart felt a twinge of guilt that all the crews, not just Hantsel, Smith, and Barker, but all of the Higgins boat crews would be expected to go into combat under an officer as green as Beach.

As for those three, they ignored Beach and turned hostile stares directly at Bart. Bart felt the hatred of their collective gaze. He had escaped them; they had lost. He was going home; they were not.

He thought about laughing at them, but for once he didn't feel the joy of getting away with something.

"Are you the sailor going home?" a gentle voice asked at his elbow. Bart turned around to see the chaplain standing next to him. He, too, had his sea bag packed. "I'm supposed to ride with him, with you I guess, on this boat that's headed our way." Sure enough, a small motor launch came out from behind one of the ships in the convoy and headed directly toward them.

"Yes, sir," Bart answered. "Got my orders home." He recognized the chaplain from Hantsel's short-lived attempt to have Bart exorcised. Neither he nor the chaplain noticed the ship's steward make his way through the crews on deck and whisper something to Chief Olafson, or that Olafson changed color.

"I'm transferring over to the flagship," the chaplain added. "I've been promoted, or demoted, I'm not sure which. Didn't you come to see me back at Peleliu? You and another sailor?"

"Yes, sir. My friend was pretty shook up after we made some landings. Thanks for helping him get over it."

The launch was moving slowly toward them.

"You're welcome," the chaplain continued. He gazed up to where he assumed Heaven to be, then sighed. "Fact is, I'm going ashore with you first. I've got to conduct a burial service for Chaplain Snopes. He was on the flagship but, well, he's dead. Strangest thing—it was a snake bite. They found a krait slithering around in his communion chest." He gave a melancholy smile, one that said you never know when your time has come. "Can't imagine how a snake like that got on board a ship."

For the first time in his life Bart Sullivan realized that he had gone too far. Back in Eniwetok, Snopes had pestered Bart about signs from God and serpents, so much so that Bart had decided to risk Olafson's wrath on the *Renegade* rather than stay on the flagship as altar boy to a deranged preacher. But Snopes also had been at Bart's side in the sick bay on the flagship, when Bart had re-emerged from the white light and from his plate glass window in the sky and his fear of being buried at sea. Snopes had comforted Bart's re-entry into the land of the living and helped nurse him back to fitness. Bart shouldn't have fished out the sea snake swimming in the reef at Eniwetok, and he shouldn't have handed it to the delighted Snopes as if it was Halloween candy. Snopes had just tried to help, and now his snake had bit him. Bart's escape from the war would involve riding to the beach alongside chaplain Snopes' dead body. He knew he had gone too far.

"That's what we all do," the chaplain continued. "Help where we can, in our own little way."

Then it hit him: 'help where we can. There was no 'where,' not for Bart. No one back home ever wanted to see him again. Congressman Wirtle wouldn't know him if he walked in leading a brass band. Virginia, his sister, hated him. Even his father, Poppy Sullivan, had gone into hiding. Bart had no place in the world. Then there was the word 'help'.

Bart tried to remember one single time in his life when he had been happy and, apart from being in the white light, when he was dead, there was only one: saving Hantsel's life on Amber Beach. Hantsel had been seized with fear when a Japanese machine gun ripped at their landing boat. Bart had pulled Hantsel out of the way, taken over his position, and saved their little Higgins boat. Because of him, they had completed the mission. He had saved someone and something bigger than himself, and it had felt good. That was it, just that one thing.

The rest of his life had been crap, crap hating his sister and crap reading other people's mail, crap selling black market ration coupons, and crap printing phony dance cards to sell in Hawaii. *And that other thing, with Olafson, that was the worst*, he thought. Saving lives felt good. Cheating people felt bad. It was so simple that he was ashamed he hadn't seen it before.

"Excuse me, sir," he said to the chaplain. The motor launch had arrived and was tying up to the gangway. From up on deck, Bart could look down and see Snopes' body in a bag on the deck of the launch. It was now or never. "Excuse me, sir," he said again, and picked up his sea bag. He hoisted it over his shoulder, then made for the ship's bridge, trundling himself and what little he owned up the ladder. He asked for permission to see the captain on a matter of some urgency.

"I've changed my mind, sir," he reported. "If it's not too late. I'll stay. My place is here, not back in the States."

Captain Hull was delighted. "Good man, Sullivan. Glad to have you back." He flashed a smile. "Let's get this ship underway."

Bart wasn't quite ready to leave. He brought out his forged orders and handed them to the skipper.

"Sir," he began. "About my orders. They're..." *Their fakes,* he wanted to say. *I forged them myself at the clerk's office back in Pearl, the same night I forged all the Black Cat dance cards. As far as being essential to Congressman Wirtle, I don't even know him. He doesn't know me.* These confessions and more ran through his head; Bart was prepared to confess to everything, forging his orders, selling his counterfeit dance cards, that business with Olafson and the detonators. *Should I tell him about Olafson?*

It was one thing, he thought, for him to forgive Olafson for killing him. It was something else to rat on Olafson. While he was hesitating, the skipper was laughing at Bart's orders.

"1947!" That's hilarious, Sullivan. These orders are for 1947, not 1944. Just another typo in the personnel office. You can still go home, Sullivan. I'll initial the orders for you. No? Good man. Well, I've got to get this ship underway."

"Sir?" Bart tried to say. "Sir, I need to tell you about..." *Bingo.* It was still hazy, but there was something about the men playing Bingo that seemed connected to something bad happening to the ship. It was too late.

"Not now. Take up your duty station. Dismissed."

The skipper waved him away. The yeoman led Bart out. No confession. No atonement. Not even time to give the money and the dance cards back to the skipper for safekeeping. But, on the bright side, Bart was back in the fold. He was a new man. He was going to be a hero. On his way out the door an ensign made his way in and asked permission to deliver a dispatch case.

"I'm from the launch, sir, from the flagship." He waited for acknowledgment, then handed Hull a canvas dispatch bag.

"The chaplain's already aboard. I'm waiting for one sailor." Hull told the ensign that the sailor was staying. "Shall I wait for your reply to the dispatch, sir?" There was no reply. "Then the whaleboat's away, sir."

An hour later the flagship signaled the convoy to weigh anchors. The warships motored away from Hollandia and out into the vast Pacific.

———————

As soon as *Renegade* was on course Olafson left the deck and found Cookie.

"What the hell, Cookie!" he said. "What the hell! You hear what happened?" Cookie had only heard what the steward had told him. "The skipper found Black Cat dance cards in that got dumb Sullivan's stuff! He thought they belonged to the got dumb crew, to Hantsel and Smith and Barker. You know why?" Cookie didn't know why. "Because them dance cards was found when they blew up Sullivan's got dumb bag and the skipper thinks they was theirs. You know what else?"

Cookie didn't know what else.

"We got this new lieutenant, Beach. You know why? The Black Cat. Yes, the Black Cat. Beach is as green as green can be, so when he asks me to show him the ropes, Beach tells me his story. You know his story? He says 'Oh, Chief, I was screwed by the brass. I was the morale officer in Pearl Harbor and they demoted me because I was the officer who gives the men some dance cards now and then for morale. Then this madame turns up and says there's hundreds of dance cards that nobody paid for. Black Cat dance cards. And so this madame goes to the newspapers and tells them that I gave away a thousand dollars' worth of dance cards but I didn't pay her for them, so the brass stops shore leave and I get demoted.'"

Olafson had to stop to catch his breath.

"Then Beach says that a few days later a couple of girls gets arrested. Black Cat girls. For spying. You understand? Black Cat girls? Eh? Spies? Eh?" Olafson had almost stopped breathing; Cookie wasn't taking in much air either. "'So the brass in the welfare office,' Beach says, 'ships me out here to get me out of the way.' And here he is." Olafson was almost deathly sick by that point in his report. "What you think about that?"

Cookie was beginning to quiver.

"And there's something else. This morning, when the skipper sends Sullivan to shore, he gives that got dumb Sullivan the Black Cat dance cards and he hands him a thousand dollars. It was all in Sullivan's sea bag when that got dumb crew got caught robbing it."

Olafson had to sit down. Cookie handed him a coffee cup full of torpedo juice. Olafson drank it off in one gulp, wiped his mouth, and took a deep breath.

"That got dumbed Sullivan had all the money in his sea bag that Beach lost on dance cards, Cookie. What are we going to do?"

"What do you mean, do?" Cookie answered.

"What are we going to say? If that lieutenant gets wind of that got dumb Sullivan and his Black Cat dance cards and that thousand dollars, he's going to ask some pretty hard questions. Do you want to answer some hard questions?"

"What do you mean, we?" Cookie saw his fair weather friendship turning foul.

"We? I tell you who we is. We is the sailors that Sullivan gave out dance cards to go see Suzy and Hualani at the Black Cat," Olafson said, poking a finger into Cookie's chest. "And Suzy and Hualani is the same girls who the Navy says is Japanese spies." Cookie's skin had become the same yellowish color as the artificial eggs that he served in the mess deck. "And the Sullivan that gave us the dance cards to take a couple of Japanese spies to the hotel is the same Sullivan that I clubbed on the head under the palm trees and left him for dead. And Barker and Hantsel and Smith is the same sailors who watched me club Sullivan on the head." He let Cookie stew for a moment over the ever-expanding list of witnesses against them. "And we're the same sailors that told Barker and Hantsel and Smith to go bring us Sullivan's sea bag. And Sullivan's sea bag is the same sea bag that had all the Black Cat dance cards in it. And a thousand dollars." He let sink in the implications of someone connecting all those dots, then continued. "And exploded. Now do you remember who *we* is?"

Olafson wasn't sure whether Cookie, in his heaving, sweating, and rutting with Hualani had overheard Suzi promise to Olafson unlimited acts of sexual delight if he could bring her some hard to get items, like detonators, for Suzy to take to her family for a traditional family celebration. He decided not to bring that up, just in case Cookie also decided to turn on him.

As for Cookie, his heart began to race. His pulse bounded. His eyes lost focus. He filled a second cup full of torpedo juice and drank it himself.

"You know what else?" Olafson hissed. Cookie had collapsed into a steel chair. "That got dumb Sullivan ain't leaving *Renegade* after all. He told the skipper he wants to be a hero. He's staying on the ship."

Olafson didn't need to spell it out—there was one person who could get him and Cookie hanged from a yardarm for giving stolen Navy detonators to Japanese spies, and instead of being dead on some beach back in Hawaii, he was walking around the ship with a sea bag full of hard evidence.

---

Bart was not the only one who could get them hanged. Their Higgins boat was back on deck, ready for action under the aft hoist and with nothing between it and the deep blue sea but a flimsy set of ropes to keep careless sailors from falling overboard. The crew climbed into the boat and ducked down to avoid being seen. Barker started.

"You see Sullivan go back up to the bridge?" Hantsel, who still was called Gretel, and Smith had seen him. "You see him come down?" They had not. "You see him get on the launch and leave the ship?" They had not. "You hear the scuttlebutt?" They had. "Scuttlebutt is that Sullivan didn't go ashore. He stayed on the ship." They knew it. "That's the same Sullivan that called us assholes and said without him we'd be dyin' on some beach." Barker was riled, Smith was riled, and even Hantsel had decided that Bart was a jerk after jeering about not being around to save them next time.

"It's the same Sullivan," a voice said from behind them. Bart rose up out of the Higgins boat's portside machine gun well and looked at them. "I did stay. I'm in for the duration."

"So, you still here, asshole? We thought you're supposed to be drinkin' beer an' watchin' USO shows on the beach. We was glad you's gone." Smith, and even Hantsel, mumbled complete agreement. "Why're you still here? Huh?"

"Amber Beach," Bart answered. "You said it yourself, Barker, that I was like a different man on Amber Beach, getting us in and out under fire.

Saving you. Completing the mission. It felt good to do the right thing. I decided to stay, be a part of the crew. It's what I'm supposed to do."

"You ain't part of the crew, Sullivan," Barker snarled. "We don't want you."

Bart had expected resistance, so he tried to tell them that they had been right all along.

"Okay, here's what really happened on Hawaii. Olafson really did club me to death under that palm tree." That stopped even Barker. "And while I was dead, I was in this..." he searched for words, "this *perfect* place. I could see my past, and the present, and the future. I saw you all watch Olafson pick up the machine gun and head off into the jungle. I saw all three of you were getting ready to lie to the XO about what happened to me because Olafson said he'd kill you if you told the truth. I saw all three of you were going to get into my sea bag and trigger the detonator. And when we got to Amber Beach, I already knew exactly where to steer us clear of the reefs and the Japs because I had already seen it, when I was dead. I saved you all, especially you, Gretel." Hantsel believed him. Smith wasn't as sure. Barker knew that he had to get rid of Bart.

"That's how I knew you were trying to kill me," Bart went on. "The exorcism, salt, ectoplasm, radio waves. All that stuff." He let it sink in. "And, I forgive you."

"You forgive us?"

"Well, I forgive you, Smith, and you, Gretel. You were just doing what Barker was telling you to do. As for you, Barker, you were going to screw everybody. You used Smith and Gretel to try to get rid of me just so you could steal the money out of my sea bag."

Barker lurched at Bart, as much as one can lurch on the deck of a Higgins boat that was hanging on cables above the deck of a rolling ship, but Bart was beyond his reach.

"And, yes, I forgive you, too, Barker. Nothing you did really hurt me. The money's back in my sea bag if you want it. It's under my bunk. I don't care."

"You could of killed us, you bastard, what with that detonator an' all."

"And I could've let you rot in the brig, Barker. They thought it was your detonator, not mine. Skipper even thinks the Black Cat cards were yours, not mine."

"How'd you get us out of the brig, Bart?" Hantsel wanted to know.

"I made it look like your blowing my bag up was an accident. There's other detonators hidden around the ship. I just made sure the XO found them."

"How'd you know there is other detonators?"

"You don't want to know," Bart answered. "Let me just say, I'm not your enemy. Ask yourself—who stands to gain if you're not around to tell the XO what really happened back in Hawaii?" Bart was surprised that the XO hadn't thought to ask any of them how Bart's machine gun made it back to the ship if Bart, the machine gunner, was dead. "And who volunteered us to go on a suicide mission to Amber Beach?"

Bart saw their twitching eyebrows and furrowed faces and realized that he had just given them a better reason to kill him than to blab on Olafson. If Bart disappeared, everybody gained. Then there would be no need for cover-ups. No witnesses. No explanations. And, yes, Bart had practically handed them a thousand dollars. But it didn't matter; Bart already had seen his fate.

Even so, he was disappointed. He hadn't really expected Barker to accept him—Barker was a swamp trader, and with him it was just business. And Smith? He was just stupid. But Gretel? Gretel only looked away. "You on watch tonight, Sullivan?"

"I am."

Bart reported for the middle watch, midnight to 0400.

———————

Captain Hull was too busy running the ship to open the dispatch case before dark. It contained the convoy's order of departure, followed by the convoy codes for the routes and rendezvous points. There was a standing order of signals for general quarters and signals for identifying aircraft. There was a reference to the command briefing. And, on the bottom, there was the *Honolulu Star*. Hobbes, the convoy's executive officer, had circled two items. Hull looked at them.

### Office Building renamed for Statesman

Officials and dignitaries turned out for the ribbon cutting to dedicate a new congressional building as the Wirtle Building, named in honor of late Texas

Congressman Arleigh Wirtle, former head of the agriculture production committee. Wirtle, who died in 1943, was noted for his close ties to Texas farmers and ranchers....

Hull was dismayed at the bad news.

*Poor Sullivan,* he thought. *He must not have known.* He pondered how best to tell Sullivan that his congressman had died. *Sullivan really liked working for Wirtle, doing his printing and all that. And Wirtle must have liked him, too, what with him requesting the Navy to send Sulllivan back as essential to the war effort.* It would be hard on the young man, especially after he had turned down a transfer to go back and work for him. He would send a steward to find Sullivan so that he could give him the bad news.

Hull read the other article that Hobbes had circled.

### Honolulu prostitutes convicted in spy ring

Honolulu: November 1, 1944: A military judge has convicted two Japanese women of espionage and attempted sabotage. Prostitutes Hualani Nakajima a/k/a Mahai'ai, and Suzy Mazuka, a/k/a Kapuli, prostitutes from the Black Cat Dance Club, were caught in September with stolen copies of the sailing orders of Convoy 3. Mazuka also obtained some explosive devices from a sailor. Black Cat Dance Club owner Madamoiselle Rochelle testified that the two had collected more than a thousand dollars from cashing in dance cards taken from two unidentified sailors, which led her to report the women to the authorities. They confessed. Sentencing has been delayed while the authorities search for the identities of the two sailors.

*Well,* Hull thought, *that's two men I need to talk to.* Sullivan, with his congressman dying, and Lieutenant Beach, who had gotten such a raw deal over his accounting problem with the Black Cat. *Beach'll be glad to know they've fixed that crooked place once and for all. Too late for him, but that's something.* He sent for Beach.

One reason why Lieutenant, formerly Lieutenant Commander, Beach had been demoted was that he had not come up with the money to repay Madame Rochelle for all the Black Cat dance cards that Olafson and Cookie had spent on Suzy and Hualani; Madame Rochelle made a stink in the newspapers, and the Navy does not like stink. A second reason was that Lieutenant Beach was stupid, at least too stupid to investigate where all the

Black Cat dance cards had come from before he was demoted and sent to the war. Captain Hull helped him figure it out.

"Look at this story, Beach," the skipper told him. "I thought you'd like to know a little bit more about it, what with your fitness report saying you got demoted over a bunch of dance cards that you couldn't pay for."

He handed the *Honolulu Times* to Beach who, despite his dull wits, could read. It finally registered on Beach that while one part of the Navy brass was humiliating him over accounting for Black Cat dance cards and pressuring him to come up with the cash to pay for them, another part of the Navy brass knew exactly who had used the dance cards, which would have led to the missing cash. Beach's career, his nice, safe job, all had gone down the crapper because different parts of the brass didn't bother to talk to each other. Steam came out of his ears.

"Come on, Beach, don't take it too bad," the skipper consoled him. "Nothing like being in combat to get promoted. You get out on those Higgins boats and do a great job and you'll get your rank back in no time." Beach didn't seem consoled by the idea that being inside a plywood boat under Japanese machine gun fire might get him promoted. "In fact, this is why I said you'd probably like to know a little bit more about it," the skipper continued. "You're not going to believe this but some of your own Higgins boat men here on board had a bunch of those dance cards, lots of them. A sailor named Sullivan has 'em now. He's a real hero—you'll like Sullivan." The skipper saw Beach's mousy little ears perk up. "I'll tell you what—go find Sullivan, bring him up here to me. We'll figure out what he knows. Maybe you can put that whole thing behind you."

"Aye, aye, skipper. I'll go right now."

Beach didn't know Sullivan, but he did know Olafson. Olafson knew the story.

"Why, yes, Lieutenant. It was like a miracle to us. We thought he was dead. When they checked what was in his sea bag, there was a bunch of those dance cards. And a thousand dollars."

*I'll kill the sonofabitch,* Beach thought. *I'll kill him.*

"I'll help you find him," Olafson finished. Olafson led Beach to the crew. The crew led him to Bart.

---

## SPLASH

---

"Sir?" One hour before daylight the oncoming officer of the deck tapped on the skipper's stateroom door. "Sir? There's a problem."

Hull bolted awake and demanded a report: "Attack? How many submarines? Airplanes? Sound general quarters!"

"No, sir, no submarines, no attack. It's—one of the crew is missing."

"Missing? Christ, how do you know someone's missing? There's over a thousand men on board."

"It's one of the Higgins boat men, sir. Sullivan. The guy who turned down his transfer home. He was standing watch, deck patrol aft of the bridge. The duty officer said he made his rounds right up until the watch changed, sir." He was panicked; he had never lost anyone who was standing watch. "And then, sir, then he disappeared."

"Disappeared?"

"Yes, sir. I asked the junior officer of the watch if anything happened. He said just one thing. He thought he might have heard someone say 'Et tu, Gretel?' But it didn't make any sense and, for that matter, he isn't really sure that's what he heard. Then, when it was time for Sullivan to hand over the watch, he was gone. Just gone." The officer had trouble breathing.

*Overboard,* the skipper thought. *Poor guy. And he was a damned fine sailor.* It seemed like there was something he meant to talk to Sullivan about, but couldn't remember what it was.

*Renegade* was a large ship. It had a crew of hundreds and transported more than a thousand soldiers. There were ladders, cabins, holds, quarters, and storage lockers tucked into thousands of places.

Sullivan might be anywhere, but for some reason, Captain Hull doubted it.

"Sound the man overboard drill, lieutenant. Then search the ship. Start with his crew and his chief, then all duty stations. Then the holds and then the troop quarters. Report every quarter hour but don't stop until you've searched every inch of the ship." He told the junior grade to roust out the executive officer and all the watch officers and brief them, too. "And get a signal out to the ships following us in the convoy to be on watch for a man in the water." He waited for the lieutenant to acknowledge.

The one thing Hull didn't say was what they would do if Sullivan was not found. Everyone knew that there would be no turning back to search the ocean, not for just one sailor, not in time of war.

"Sullivan was a hell of a sailor, Lieutenant. The best we had. I'd hate to lose him."

———————

The following day, *Renegade* sent a signal to the flagship, which sent a message to Pearl Harbor. When Third Fleet received the message it sent a form to the Secretary of the Navy. The Secretary of the Navy sent a telegram to the family of Bart Sullivan, telling them that he had been lost at sea aboard *U.S.S. Renegade*, on November 14, 1944.

# Part II

Footprints in the Sand

# Chapter 12

The very thing that scared him the most is probably what saved him. He had floated no more than a few hundred yards from the ship when the wind whipped up and the flat Pacific Ocean had begun to swell. The convoy was already spread apart to avoid the ships crashing in to one another in what was forecast as a 'blow' but what every old sailor on board feared would turn into a typhoon. The barometers had dropped, the wind began to back out of the southwest and clock to the north, and in the darkness of the submarine blackout, no one was exactly sure where any other ship was in the water.

Instead of crashing into one of the other ships, his life ring bounced on the peaks, surfed down into the troughs, and spun like a top as the breakers crashed and the storm began to blow in earnest. His last view of the fleet was a ship, probably *Renegade* but perhaps one of the other troopships or destroyers or oilers that had been in the convoy; it was pitching up and down and listing heavily to starboard, then rolling all the way over to port so that its rudder and propellers were out of the water, then disappearing in a trough of water. He assumed he was dead, summoned up some memories from days before the war and the Navy, dwelt on them, and waited to be plunged into the depths, there to be eaten by fish.

Inexplicably, like straws found driven through pieces of steel after a tornado, like a dozen eggs that survive intact inside a cement mixer, the life preserver didn't break apart, nor did the flimsy rope to which he clung rot in two. After being thrown across the waves, through the air, and across endless bounding seas in torrential rain and lightning, after surrendering and waiting for death, he awoke one calm day to find his face crusted with salt, his tongue swollen twice its size, his fingers unable to bend or clench, his ankles dangling in the sea, and the bodies of dead fish and live sharks eddying about him.

He had survived a typhoon in a life ring. The easy part was over.

The remnants of Typhoon Cobra rounded the tip of Irian Jaya, crossed the equator, and dropped down into the Banda Sea. The typhoon's tail continued to whisper like the end of a whip. It whirled around, crossed back over Jaya at the bird's neck of an isthmus, and pushed the life ring back and forth across the ocean, first back out into the Pacific, then pulled it back toward land.

Instead of torrential rain he now had no water at all. He hadn't stolen anything from the galley, no M & Ms or gum or even a bit of spam to chew on, and he was starved. His knife had disappeared somewhere in the typhoon, along with his shoes, his Navy ring, and his cap.

Watching the sharks as they surfaced to snatch at dead fish, then live ones, then turtles, he carefully took off his dungarees. He buttoned them through the button holes, then tied the ankles and fashioned a make-shift bag. He dragged it through the shoals of fish and, now and then, caught one. However, when he tried to scrape the scales off he lost his grip on the pants and the life ring. When he gripped the life ring too hard the fish got away. Eventually he just began to bite down on them, but when he found the fish to be bitter he gave in and chomped down hard on their white bellies, bit off what he could, and threw the rest as far away as possible before the sharks got to him. The fish guts made him sick. Days passed.

He watched the sun. The life ring didn't seem to be drifting with any particular current but the sun continued to rise up out of the ocean on the east, cross over the midday sky, burn to a crisp the skin on his face and hands and the tops of his feet, then sink into the ocean on the other side. He was dying of thirst.

At night he watched the stars. Like every sailor, he knew Centaurus and Vela but not where they should be in the sky over New Guinea or the Philippines or wherever he had been blown to. Now and then he thought he saw airplanes flying across the night sky, hundreds of them, or maybe none, all too far away, too dark, to be sure. It occurred to him that maybe he was going crazy, no food, no water, no hope, and that maybe the only way he had survived a typhoon was to be already dead.

Then, after he had lost count of the days, he saw the bottom of the ocean.

It was a beautiful bottom, ripples of light casting shadows onto fan coral, pink fingered coral, white coral, and thousands of fish. Yellow fish, white ones, blues ones, fat ones, tiny ones, fish so iridescent that they hurt his eyes to stare at them, and fish so clumsy and slow that he knew if he could only reach them he could have them. He gazed and gazed and gripped the rope on the life ring and allowed himself to sink down into the water, only to discover that the coral was much deeper than he had expected. The fish paid no attention to him, schools parting on either side of his drifting body, rejoining as they swam around him, moving on to the deep. A shark swam by twenty or thirty yards away, looked at him, swam on, and a trigger of barracuda darted past in the opposite direction. He ran out of breath.

When he surfaced he pulled on the rope, drew in the life ring, and found that he was so exhausted that he was afraid that he wouldn't be able to get it over his head and past his shoulders. When he did, he flipped over, bobbed below the surface with his head down, and nearly drowned. When he righted himself and got his bearings, he saw trees.

Palm trees. Ficus. Mangium.

A rumble of surf, a reef, separated the trees from the ocean but he thought that by kicking and swimming with his arms he could make it to whatever land they were on. He was wrong. The harder he kicked, the smaller the trees became. After an hour, the foaming surf had disappeared and only the tops of the trees could be made out. Another hour passed and he saw nothing. He began to blubber.

After dark, the ocean began to rush again, pulling him along at a speed that could not possibly be the wind. He kicked against it, turned around, and the trees reappeared, but far behind him. He had passed the island. The sun was gone, the moon was high, a point of light shone from the island directly to him in the water, and something hit him.

*Shark!*

Something else hit him, something steel and hard and much bigger than he.

*Boat!*

And again.

*Tree!*

When he kicked around he found himself being pulled along by a current littered with ocean trash. There were crushed boxes, marine rope nets like those he had climbed up and down to the Higgins boats, driftwood, and so many pieces of cardboard and tin and rubber that he couldn't tell what they had been. There were long, looping strands of seaweed, conifer branches, sea turtles, and an old tire. A bit of barbed wire cut his arm, a rusted oil drum rose and sank, and a platform that might once have been part of a dock but might also have been the planks of a tent floor or the deck of a wooden fishing dock, all floated over and around him. He climbed onto the planks. The current rushed onward.

The pink dawn began to rise but, for the first time, it rose over land, real land, not a mile distant. The current flowed toward the shore and the shore was a beach, a sandy beach, a beach that arced and curved like a gentle horseshoe like the little hidden beaches he had known in Hawaii. The trees came into focus and, when he blinked his eyes to get rid of the salt crust, he saw that the trees were a lot like him, battered and parched.

The typhoon had blown more down than it left standing. Palm trees had been ripped from their roots and flung into a thick forest of razor grasses and tangled brush. The brush became a rainforest that grew from the beach toward a ridge. The ridge, perhaps a mile inland, ran parallel to the beach and, toward the north, led to the foothills of a mountain. From the beach it looked as if the mountain was rock and cliff on the side facing the ocean but rainforest on the western side. He rode his precarious raft to the shore and landed on a beach covered with rotted shoes and boxes and oil drums, driftwood and seaweed, dead fish and thrashing turtles trying to waddle back to the water. The sun came up. He was alive.

It took a long time for him to be able to stand up. His legs were covered with scabs from the sun and saltwater. The skin on the tops of his feet had burned so badly that they were swollen and painful. His hands hurt as well, hurt from gripping the rope, gripping the side of the life ring, gripping his sailor's denim pants. He began to untie the ankles of his dungarees, unsure if he could do it, or even if he could put them back on because his skin was so burned. Even so, he was aware that oil drums and barbed wire and boxes meant that somewhere on the ocean, maybe right there on the island, the typhoon had found other people and ripped them apart as well. He might not be alone.

The saltwater had eaten off any markings there might have been on the boxes and the oil drums. The boxes themselves were so waterlogged that he couldn't decide if they had been American or Australian or Dutch or Japanese. The oil drums seemed like any other oil drums, which he thought meant American or Dutch but, if Dutch, the Japanese might have captured them. Even the barbed wire was so ordinary it could have come from anywhere, and the tires. If he was not alone he had either sailed into some island paradise, a typhoon-battered paradise, or into the far reaches of the war, or into Japanese captivity. A loud, screeching roar came ringing over the tops of the trees. He ducked down behind the oil drum and looked.

Nothing.

Another roar.

Nothing in sight. No one was there, not on the beach, not in the brush. It was possible that someone could be up on the ridge, or even up in the trees, and had seen him. He looked out once more over the oil drum, peered as best he could from one side of the lagoon, all along the beach and the tree line, and all the way to the other side of the lagoon at the end of the beach.

Nothing.

It was fifty yards to the tree line, seventy-five at most, and he stood up. It was hard to stagger, hard on his feet, hard on his legs, and especially hard in the powdered sand. He struggled across the beach to the first line of palm trees and flopped back down to catch his breath.

The typhoon had wrecked Shangri-la. Most of the palm trees were blown over, supported only by shrubs and other palm trees that also were blown over. Beneath the wrecked palm fronds and jumbled in with the palm bark there were green coconuts littering the sand, tangled up in the thick razor grass that cut at his hands. He tried to peel away the coconut husk with his fingers, and failed, and tried to scrape it off with bark, and failed again.

A way could be made through the trees off the beach, toward the interior, a more or less opening between the palms and the ficus and razor grass. He carried his coconut and began to pick his way into the forest. His feet burned with every step, brush and branches hacking at his legs and arms, the sharp grasses cutting what the burning sand and palm bark had not already wounded.

Another roar, a deep, gargling, angry animal sound.

He stopped, listened, and tried to tell where it came from. He thought it was far ahead of him and to the left. He went right. Birds burst out from the cover of the trees. A thick green snake coiled itself around a branch. He picked his way forward under the battered trees and thick brush until he stumbled onto a rocky outcrop of the ridge line he had seen from the beach. He tried to break the coconut with a rock and found that it was tougher than he was. If he didn't find food soon, he would die.

Step by step he began to climb, bare stones burning his feet and cutting at his toes. The path up the ridge continued for several hundred yards, at which point a gap in the rocks was too large for him to climb further. He had to make a decision.

*Should I turn right, back down into the jungle toward the beach*, he thought, *or left, to the other side of the ridge?* He climbed the last few feet to a ledge and peered over. Below him, toward the ocean, he could see the beach where he had washed ashore. The oil drum, some dead fish, his raft, all were there. His footprints in the sand were plainly visible, staggering from the water's edge toward the trees. He had come no more than a mile and, worse, had found nothing he could put in his mouth. He turned left.

On the west side of the ridge the rocks quickly gave way to rainforest. It had been in the lee of the storm and was less battered but harder to walk through. Insects stung him, nettles burned him, and every sound startled him, but he struggled on until he heard a roar of rushing water, like a river. Rivers meant fish. Rivers might mean fruit, bananas, berries, something. Rivers also might mean a village. He pushed his way through the trees toward the river and soon came out into a mangrove swamp.

Looking across the swamp, he saw a cataract of water rushing down the side of a mountain, pushing the rainforest apart, and flowing directly into another bay, a flat bay no more than a half mile away. There was no beach there, just a mud flat where the water of the bay oozed toward the mangroves. As he worked around the mangrove swamp he saw that it, too, had been battered by the typhoon.

The wreckage of dugout fishing boats, shredded nets, and a mountain of bamboo littered the mud flats. He saw the jumbled remnants of a bamboo dock and a wide delta where the river rushed out of the trees and into the bay, backing into the mangrove swamp. Somewhere here there were people. Humans. Food. He was saved! He turned around slowly, taking it in, looking for people, someone, anyone in the dark trees and turbid water where something caught his attention and then RRRRRAAARRGHHHOOOOAAARRRRAAARRGHHHH!!!!!!!!!!!!!! shrieked into his ear, not twenty feet behind him.

*"Ningen!"* someone shouted. Humans. Voices. *"Ningen!"* There were people! He was saved!

*"NINGEN!!!!"*

And then he saw it. A crocodile thrashed through the swamp, roaring and tearing at something in the water. A dozen small wooden arrows stuck out of its hide but appeared to do nothing to slow the monster down. It clawed and twisted in the murky swamp and jerked its way up out of the water, reaching for the air.

He gasped.

The crocodile was being eaten by a dragon. Its huge jaws had clamped onto the reptile's stomach, tearing at it with dozens of teeth, whipping it back and forth in a death throe. The croc's long head twisted down at the dragon, snapping at its thick neck. Blood flew out in streams and both beasts roared.

"GOT DUMB!" he yelled. "What the foke...?" he panicked.

He turned to flee, took one step, and a vine rope snare trapped his ankles and snatched him feet first, high into the air with such force that it almost broke his neck. In just seconds he found himself dangling by the legs above the swamp, his head down, arms thrashing, and blood rushing to his brain. Below him were a dozen tiny aboriginals with spears and bows, naked except for bone necklaces and cassowary feathers, scrambling and shouting: *"NINGEN!"* they yelled, scrambling away from the thrashing monsters in the swamp. *"NINGEN! KOMODO! NINGEN!"*

As the light in his eyes began to dim, Chief Olafson watched the dinosaur sink its jaws into the crocodile's neck and jerk, blood exploding into the water. There was a feral, primal roar as the crocodile ripped itself free and clamped its jaws onto the Komodo dragon. Olafson swung slowly, head down, feet in the air, dog tags dangling below his chin, swaying side to side, the tiny aboriginals fleeing into the forest.

The last thing Olafson saw was a tall person, not brown, not quite, not naked, not quite, a person with straight hair and long slender arms, looking up at him. She took her knife and held it to the vines that had snared Olafson by the ankles, glanced up at him, nodded, and cut them away. He began to fall.

Another roar, and he blacked out.

# Chapter 13

Saya sat cross-legged on the floor of the tree hut, watching Olafson scratch at a thorny devil walking stick that had jammed its mandible into Olafson's left ankle. He was having trouble scratching it because Saya had tied his hands with vines and strapped them behind his head to the bamboo slats that formed the wall of the tree hut, limiting him to the use of the toes of his right foot. The bug bites were red and deep and eventually would wake Olafson up. In the meantime, however, she studied him.

He was, by her standards, quite tall and, by anyone's standards, big. He was more or less bald, the wispy blond hair that he had brought with him into the Navy by now almost gone from sun, salt, and receding hairline so that now he had little more than pitiful tufts of hair feathers above his ears. Saya thought his face was ugly as well, somewhat long and round, jowly, and with wide-set eyes and a long nose beneath a high forehead. His chest and stomach were fleshy, his hands and arms crusted from peeling sunburn scabs. There was a blemished tattoo on his left arm, some kind of bird clutching arrows. She was grateful that he wore pants of some kind, the remnants of his Navy pants, to cover his ugly legs, but his red, cut, sunburned feet stuck out and displayed ugly hairy toes. He was perfect in every way, and had cost her a small pig to keep the cannibals from eating him.

Her negotiations for ownership of Olafson had not been simple. Saya had been shadowing the cannibals, lesser Sawi from the rainforest on the river basin, partially to make certain that they didn't try to raid her redoubt and partially to see for herself how badly the typhoon had damaged the bay.

The typhoon hadn't wrecked much of the Sawi *tanahland*, at least not the main villages in the lee of the mountain. It had, however, churned up the river and choked it with trees and rocks rushing down to the bay. The farming plots, mostly taro and yam roots, had been ravaged and most of the chickens and pigs scattered, so the men had gone downstream to the inland bay to gather fish. They found the fishing village wrecked, and the docks and dugouts broken up and floating free.

Saya had quietly watched them from the cover of a thicket of mangium trees near the mangrove swamp. They had stalked through the scattered remnants of bamboo docks, thatched palms, and broken canoes, turning over the debris and filling their baskets with still-live fish and turtles when, to their delight, a crocodile rushed up from the slough of the delta and charged at them. The men set about to kill it, good crocodiles yielding more meat than pigs, but without the religious or political disputes. They quickly put twenty or thirty arrows into it, then chased it as it headed into the mangroves. Neither they nor she had been prepared for what happened next: a Komodo dragon leapt out of the murky water and bit the crocodile's neck.

Even the cannibals had been unnerved by the dragon. Komodos were known to be *bad ningen*, negative gods that ate the souls of Sawi ancestors before the Sawis could eat the newly deceased ancestors personally. None of the Sawis on this island had actually seen a Komodo before but they all knew that the local water monitors were descendants of ancestral Komodos; they accepted without question that this time one had been delivered to their island by the wind gods. Saya had watched them scatter before the Komodo could finish off the crocodile and start in on them. After the dragon gave up on the crocodile it floundered back to the deck hatch of a demolished Dihatsu merchant ship on which it had floated into the bay during the typhoon.

When the Komodo was a mile away Saya cut Olafson down and tied him up, then waited while the Sawi finished off the crocodile. It took her another hour to negotiate with them for finders keepers: the Sawi could keep all of the crocodile except for a modest portion of the tail; she kept Olafson, who the Sawi correctly claimed to have been similar to the Dutch colonists who had been rounded up by the Japanese up in the island's plantations and, thus, would be good for barter. She agreed to give them one male pig, in their eyes a concession of bargaining weakness on her part, but in her eyes an easy way to get them to carry Olafson to her redoubt. They numbed him with a small dose of pitohui feather toxins and lugged him two miles up into the rainforest. When he was safely tied up in the treehouse, she discretely disappeared into the jungle and came back with a smallish pig. The cannibals shook their heads and bows at her, took the pig, and left. Now, two days later, she watched Olafson emerge from his pitohui-induced anesthesia and begin to scratch.

"Got dumnit, that hurts like—what the hell?" He lurched against the vines that bound his wrists, and failed.

She didn't understand his words, not precisely. They were neither the toothy Dutch of the Manokwari traders nor the shrieking Papuan Austronesian of the other islanders. She watched his eyes to see if they would make more sense.

"Untie these got dumbed ropes," he moaned. He waved his hands around to the extent the vines permitted, and doubled his knees to his chest in an effort to bring the itching ankle into range. The first thing he saw was the thorny devil and, shrieked. That she understood. The thorny devil left its eggs and most of its head in Olafson's ankle and died. Saya flicked it off his leg.

The second thing Olafson saw, then, was her.

"Lemme go," he shouted, shaking his wrists. He shivered and struggled, then stared straight at her, heaving for breath. Saya stood up and walked across the room, picked up a coconut bowl, and brought it back. "You—cut these fokin' ropes!"

He struggled a bit, thrashing his legs around, and tried to stand up before discovering that his bonds would not let him do so even if he could have gotten his feet and legs underneath him to make the attempt. All the while, Saya watched him. When he finally accepted defeat, she edged around to his shoulders and held out the coconut.

"*Drinken?*" she asked. She held the coconut close to his lips, poured a bit of coconut milk on them, and watched him lick it. She poured another sip onto his lips, then opened her own mouth a bit wider and made a drinking motion. "*Dringim?*" His eyes darted from left to right, but he parted his lips. She poured a small measure directly into his mouth, and he swallowed it. She stepped back out of reach, waited for him to swallow, and poured another bit of coconut milk into Olafson's mouth. His teeth were better than the Sawi and even, she thought, the Japanese, but not as good as the Dutch. Maybe he was Australian; there had been Australians on the islands before the Japanese caught them all. She gave him a few minutes to let the coconut milk settle into his system, then offered him a bit of coconut copra meat.

"*Eten?*" she asked. His eyes brightened at the word. "*Makan?*" His eyes dulled. "*Eten,*" she tried again. She put the copra onto his lips, he opened his mouth, and took it. He chewed it, coughed, and chewed some more.

"*Eten?*" he said. It was dull, the way he said it, more like the word *eaten* than the word *eten*, but he had figured out that he wasn't going anywhere and he was hungry. "*Eten?*" She gave him more to eat. He chewed the coconut meat for a while, swallowed it, and tried another word. "Where am I?"

"*Waar?*" *Waar* was almost the same as 'where', especially on the island. "Where?"

"*Eiland.*" She concluded that he was sort of Dutch, but stupid Dutch. It should have been obvious that he was on an island; he had floated up to it after the tyhoon.

"Island? What island?" Olafson concluded that if he spoke slowly and loudly she would understand English. "WHAT ISLAND?"

She smiled but didn't answer. It didn't matter what island, as far as she was concerned. He was what she needed, and if he knew what island he was on he might try to escape. Then she would have to recapture him before the Sawis found him, it being understood that if her part of the bargain got free he was fair game, just as her pig would have been subject to her taking it back if it got away from the Sawis. It was also likely that he would simply die in the jungle, what with the snakes, the pitohuis, and the thousands of snares and pits that everyone who lived in the rainforest used to trap food. Her biggest fear, however, was neither the Sawis nor the rainforest but the Japanese.

They mostly stayed on Ambon but, every now and then, some ambitious Japanese officer would send a few dozen men over to the island, where they crashed through the rainforest, along the cliffs and the ridge line, and up and down the coast on patrols, searching for the few elusive Dutch resistance fighters who had got away when the Japanese captured the Molucca islands.

The last Japanese patrol had come through more than a month ago. They had discovered a few steel fish hooks in the dugout fishing canoes. The natives had used steel fish hooks for more than fifty years, the Dutch having handed them out freely along the coast in exchange for the right to explore for oil and to cut logs. The Japanese had never noticed them before, believed that the natives were not only primitive but sneaky, and tortured several of them in full view of the bamboo fishing docks.

When they went inland a few days later, both the Sawi and Saya personally had thrashed around in the jungle to imitate the noise made by the Dutch resistance fighters, causing the Japanese to chase them so that several soldiers were snatched up in foot snares, where they were filled with arrows shot from unseen bows. The Japanese made their way back to the bay, beheaded two old men, and left.

They would be back and, given the debris that the typhoon had washed ashore, they again would accuse the Sawi of hiding Dutch resistance fighters. If the Japanese found Olafson wandering around lost in the rainforest, they would probably cut his head off on the spot, thwarting her plans. Olafson didn't need to know any of this. She smiled at him, picked up a piece of dried crocodile meat, pulled out her knife, cut off two small cubes, and held them out to Olafson's mouth.

"*Eten?*" she asked.

He opened his mouth and, when she popped one in, ate it greedily.

*He'll do fine*, she thought.

She would give Olafson a few days to become meek, then begin to train him to get caught. He was exactly what the Japanese were looking for.

# Chapter 14

Saya had not decided whether to let Olafson see Ambon. She left him tied up in a water-filled pit that was lined with bamboo spears, not so much as a test but merely to keep him occupied for a few hours. He stared at her, wild-eyed with fear, and she disappeared into the rainforest.

She had not visited the spice plantation for more than two weeks, not since the day she had taken possession of Olafson. The home where she had grown up, what was left of it, was much higher upland than the cannibal hamlets and the hidden *kamp* where Saya now slept. She made her way between the trees, through the brush, past her clearing, the Sawi village and the four sacred cannibal grounds, then came out onto the remnants of the road. From there she turned west and followed the old trade route as it wound across the island.

Saya returned to her family plantation now and then, just to smell the spices, to remember helping her mother catch songbirds and tend the pigs. Her family had farmed near the center of the island for as many generations as her parents and grandparents and their grandparents could recount. They were smallholders, growing nutmeg and cloves. Her grandfather had attempted to grow coffee but the plantation was too low on the island for the soil to support java.

The road had been adequate to get their wagons back and forth to Bintuni Village and, twice each year, all the way to Port Haru. Just before the war, Ford trucks appeared on the road. The first trucks came to the plantations to collect the clove and nutmeg harvests and to leave off bags of meal and boxes of chicks and canned coffee and tobacco. Saya's first ride in a motor was in the back of a Ford truck loaded with all the cloves that the farm had harvested. When they delivered the cloves to Port Haru that time,

Saya was told that she looked more like her grandfather and her own father than like her grandmother and her mother and her brothers.

"*Ho, Piet,*" the men at the docks had called out to her grandfather. "Did you come in that truck from Batavia?" Batavia was across the ocean. None of them had ever been to Batavia. "You've got a hitchhiker." They laughed and smiled and told her grandfather that Saya was whiter than a *vaderlander* girl, which had made her grandfather proud. It had not occurred to Saya before then that it might matter that her skin was more white, like a *vaderlander*, than dark, like an islander.

Her grandfather taught her how to catch fish and to set snares for birds, which snakes to avoid and which plants to eat and not eat. Her father taught her how to build with bamboo and which Sawis might eat her. It was not until she was on her own that Saya had learned how to become invisible.

While she walked she listened for snapped branches, for a flight of birds, anything that would tell her that someone was watching her, or following her. She moved deeper into the trees, away from the overgrown road. The road led past several abandoned plantations, small holdings of her former neighbors, and she avoided walking across them.

Unfortunately, the road that had been adequate for the trucks to take their clove and nutmeg to Port Haru also had been adequate for the Japanese to bring soldiers from Port Haru. Their farm, the market village, the neighboring farms, all fell in one day. When the soldiers marched onto their plantation her father hid Saya and her mother. The soldiers lined him, her two brothers and the Malays who helped with the harvest, up in front of the house.

"I am Tanaka Rikugun-Chui!" the officer had announced. A half-dozen soldiers pointed rifles at her family. "This is no longer your plantation. You are now prisoners of the Empire." A Malay from Port Haru translated. "For as long as you are good subjects of the Emperor, he grants you the privilege to remain on this farm. You may sleep in that house," pointing to what had been their house, "and care for the Emperor's crops and livestock. You may harvest his nutmeg and cloves and raise the Emperor's chickens and pigs and grow his yams and peppers. You may eat what the Emperor does not need. Be grateful. Be good subjects of the Emperor. *Wakuru? Ha!*" Then the Japanese wrote their names on a form, counted the clove and nutmeg trees, the garden plants, the chickens and pigs, and their pens and coops. They filled her family's wagons with her family's tools and furniture and took away everything the Emperor wanted.

The next time that Saya saw Bantuni Village the school was closed, the post office was closed, the clinic was closed, the telegraph was operated by two Japanese and one Malay, and the church doors and windows were nailed shut and covered over with wood. She also learned that the Hemaha plantation, west of her family's, and the Boer plantation, to the east, had a permanent Japanese soldier quartered on them. They were drunks who took pot shots at their pigs and chickens and beat their children. A week later the Japanese soldiers returned.

"I am Tanaka Rikugun-Chui!" the same lieutenant had announced. "Where are the two women?" Her father had answered that he did not know that the emperor concerned himself with women. Tanaka nodded to a soldier, who hit her father over the head with his rifle. "Where are the two women?"

Saya and her mother walked out of the house and helped their father to his feet.

"The *chojin* in Bantuni Village tells me that you have not declared your two women," Tanaka barked at them. "The Emperor is not pleased. Do not hide things from the Emperor! *Wakuru? Ha!*" Tanaka had waited to make sure that they were suitably afraid, then continued. "There are certain evil men who are trying to kill the Emperor! They are on this island! Spies!"

By fits and starts Tanaka announced that he had reports of Dutch criminals who had fled Malokawi and made it to the island. This was not news to Saya or her family since by now every Eurasian small holder on the island sheltered the Dutch resistance soldiers from time to time, gave them dried pork and salted yams and told them where Tanaka and his men were. Tanaka continued.

"Because you hide prisoners from the Emperor, I assign to you a *chojin*. You are to obey the *chojin* in all things. Your first order is this: if the cowardly Dutch escaped prisoners who are hiding on this island come to this farm, you will turn them over to the *chojin*. If you hear from your fellow prisoners on any other farm or in the village that..." For the next hour they had stood in the sun while Tanaka told them their duties: they were to turn over the Dutch fighters; they were to double production of the farm; they were prohibited from communicating with anyone in the village, or on the next farm, or anyone who came to the farm, except through the *chojin*. Tanaka had then hit her father and her brothers in the stomach with his rifle butt. "And you are to submit to the *chojin*! *Wakaru? Ha!*"

Saya's mother explained to her what that meant. Saya understood.

Their *chojin*, named Moto, had been a grizzled soldier, fat, slow, and much given to *sake*. They called him Mr. Moto. Every two or three days Mr. Moto would try to slip into Saya's room at night and fumble around on her while she slept. Every time he did, Saya would grab his hands by the wrists, bind them with liana vines, and give him more *sake* until he passed out. Her brother had offered to kill him but she knew, and her father confirmed, that if anything happened to the *chojin*, Lieutenant Tanaka would burn their farm and kill them.

Saya stepped out of the rainforest into a glade, her plantation. The aroma of spices, nutmeg and cloves, came to her on the breeze. She inhaled it, inhaled the smell of home, and then glided quietly into what was left of it.

One evening, in that season two years before, soon after the nutmeg was shelled but long before the cloves had sprouted, they heard the shock of anti-aircraft fire. Far to the south, over Ambon Island, the night sky had filled with artillery bursts and tracer shells. Smoke had blotted out the moon and the constellations. Her father told them all to go into the house and do absolutely nothing. Their *chojin* hopped and sputtered and pointed his rifle at them but no one, not her father or mother or brothers or any of the Malays, did anything that he could interpret as a threat. The next day, Tanaka returned.

"I am Tanaka Rikugun-Chui!" his interpreter announced. "The harvest is ended. The Emperor has sent me to tell you that your services on his farm are no longer needed." He nodded at two burly soldiers. They lined up behind Saya and her family and pointed their rifles at their backs. "You are to go to your new home. *Wakaru? Ha!*"

The soldiers prodded them with bayonets in their backs and marched them out to the road and toward the village. The rest of the district's small holders, people Saya had known since she was born, also were on the road and being herded to the village.

At Bintuni Village the Japanese separated the men and boys from the women and girls. She last saw her father and brother, and the Boers and

Hemahas and the other young men with whom she had gone to school and trapped dingoes and raced on foot, all of them, when the Japanese led them away. She and her mother and her school teacher and the Dutch nuns and Mevrouw de Okerse the shopkeeper and her daughters and all the other girls and women were put in the back of a Japanese truck and driven to Port Haru. At Port Haru the women were herded into one of the dock sheds and held in darkness for three days.

The plantation was overgrown now. Vines snaked throughout the nutmeg trees and into the branches, brush choked out the cloves. The chemodak fruit and banana trees that had been Saya's responsibility were infested and rotted. She looked at the twisted wire and bamboo shoots that had been the cages where her grandmother had kept her songbirds and the pens where the chickens strutted before the Japanese set fire to them. There was no trace of the goat pen or the shed where they kept their tools; the only evidence of pigs was the dead soil where they had rooted and slept. The house, of course, had been burned to the ground. In only two years the island had almost completely reclaimed what her family had spent hundreds of years building and what the Japanese had destroyed in one day.

In Port Haru, a Malay opened the door to the shed and led the women and girls outside. "You, girl, this way. You, there, that way." He ordered the most indigenous-looking of them to form a line on the dock, where Japanese soldiers marched them into a boat that in happier days had transported their spices off the island. Now flying a rising sun from the mast, it sputtered away from the dock and motored toward Ambon, visible across the bay.

"And you," he continued, pointing to the Dutch and Eurasian women who remained, "you—go there!" These girls and women, mostly girls, were marched to a house about fifty yards away from the docks, a nice looking house with a porch and a veranda, a house that before the war had belonged to the Dutch port master's family. They were led up the white steps and onto the wide porch and stood in a group outside a screened door. After a few minutes a Malay woman, very pleasant, her sarong nicely wrapped, came outside and greeted them.

"Welcome," she called out, lifting her arms and wrapping them around the shoulders of the girls. "Welcome. You will like your new home.

The Emperor welcomes you," she smiled, and led them inside. They were all light-skinned girls, their hair matted from the march and the three days of confinement in the hut. "Come in. We have some clothes for you. Welcome." A smiling officer, the *chojin* of the prisoner assembly area, urged the women inside and the door closed on them.

Saya and her mother now stood alone in front of the shed.

"You," the Malay said to them. "You go back to shed." A soldier led them back inside and the door closed again.

After the sun had gone down Saya heard the lock to the shed rattle and another man, a grizzled soldier, fat, slow, their old *chojin*, opened the door. This time Mr. Moto wasn't drunk. He smiled at Saya, bowed very low, then slapped her across the face as hard as he could. Saya's mother screamed and tried to jump on him to wrestle him away, and he slapped her as well. There was no *sake* to anesthetize him, no liana vines to tie his hands. He beat them both until they could not stand up, and then raped them.

The next morning, Saya's mother was led away. The Malay who had ordered the women to the dock master's house came into the shed and told Saya to wrap her torn clothes around her.

"You embarrass the *chojin*," he told her. "The lieutenant asks the *chojin* why this girl isn't *mengandung* and the *chojin* loses face. 'You with this girl a year and she looks at you with spit,' the lieutenant says. You stupid. Very stupid. Now you go to the comfort house. The *chojin* tells me 'Now she lose face.'"

"Where is my mother going?" Saya had asked the Malay as he led her to the dock master's house. "And my father and brother?"

"The Emperor has many airplanes," the Malay told her. "He must have a new runway for his airplanes." He pointed across the bay to Ambon. War boats, gray boats flying the rising sun, patrolled the small harbor between Port Haru and Ambon. There were warehouses and cranes on the Ambon docks and, behind a stone wall and arched gateway, army barracks. Behind the Ambon docks the island rose almost straight up to a series of jagged cliffs. It would be impossible to build a flat runway there. "The prisoners build his runway. Not you. You, you go to the comfort house."

He led Saya to the steps of the nice house, then up the veranda. She waited on the porch until the Malay woman came out for her. Once inside she saw the Japanese soldiers who were visiting the comfort house, sitting on rattan chairs, smiling at Saya's friends and at girls she hardly knew, putting their hands on the girls' knees and saying clever things to them in Japanese.

*They can kill me*, she thought. *But they will never kill my spirit.*

The woman led her to a back hallway and shoved her into a bathroom.

"Clean yourself. No blood on your lip. No black eyes. You must be clean for your work," she said. She gave Saya a towel and a sarong, then closed the door and locked it. "Hurry. The men are waiting."

Saya ran the bathwater, sponging off her legs and her neck with the towel while the running bath water covered the noise she made. She stepped onto the edge of the tub, marveling at the luxury that the Dutch port master's family had enjoyed before the war, and looked out the small bath window. She took her sarong and the towel and her own ragged clothes and pushed the window open, then climbed out and disappeared into the rainforest beyond Port Haru.

After she escaped from the comfort house the Japanese burned and ransacked her family's plantation. The Dutch resistance fighters gave her news now and then of the prisoners on Ambon. Many of them died building the airstrip. Some lived, some were sent to other prison camps on other islands in the Banda Sea.

Saya had not decided whether to kill Lieutenant Tanaka or Mr. Moto, the *chojin* who had raped her. To let them live or not live was a decision she would make when the time came. It was enough that now she had the means to capture them. Olafson would be her bait.

There was still much to do to prepare Olafson for his role, to crush his desire to escape, to eat, to stare at her. She had much more training to give him about how to be tied to trees, to not scream when the snakes slithered over him or when, like the day before, she had to machete the head off a dingo that had clamped down on his arm. He had to learn to give up food. She decided that it would be better if Olafson did not see Ambon before she took him to be spotted by the Japanese.

It was time to go; it was dangerous to go home too often or to stay too long; if the Japanese could entice the Malay to become their dog boys they might also have gotten the Sawis to spy for them as well. She disappeared behind the orchards at the back of the farm, glided back into the forest, and became invisible.

SHADES OF THE DEEP BLUE SEA

She skirted around Bintuni Village, crossed the trade path several miles east of the last spice plantation, and made her way back down through the rainforest. She silently watched the hiding place where the Dutch left things: knives, binoculars, some bandages, that she had borrowed now and then. The Dutch often lost things. No one had been there for many days. She quietly picked her way around the Sawi village and the four sacred cannibal grounds, then detoured to her own hidden clearing to collect some coconut and dried fish to feed Olafson. Soon she was back at the bamboo staked water pit where she had left him.

"*Avondmaal*," she called out. "*Eten.*" She threw the rope onto the water. Olafson didn't take the rope. "*Komen*," she called out, a bit louder. He didn't answer.

Then, she realized, there was a difficulty in her plan: Olafson had disappeared.

# Chapter 15

Although Olafson was not given to solving problems by asking questions he did wonder about some things while he hid in the rock crevice of a stream bed. He wondered if the crevice was big enough, whether come morning he could see the whole island, and whether if Saya hadn't tied him up and tortured him the last two or three weeks she would have been as good sexually as Suzy had been. Those were the wrong things to wonder about. Better questions would have been why Saya had tied him up and tortured him the last two or three weeks, what there was to eat, and how he could communicate with anyone on an island populated by savages and one Tarzan woman. Unfortunately, Olafson was by nature less of a Socratist and more of a self-destructive narcissist.

Olafson had stumbled across a stream within fifteen or twenty minutes after extricating himself from the water-filled trap where Saya had left him. If Olafson was good at anything it was water. He had survived beach landings, overturned boats, and a typhoon; a water-filled bamboo stick pit was painful but not dangerous, and he was out of it within an hour after Saya left. Being good with water, Olafson understood that streams flow downhill, which was the direction of the beach, where he might find a way to float himself off this *ningen*-ridden paradise. Being bad at rainforest geography, however, Olafson did not catch on to the fact that he had been led back and forth across the island so many times that he was now on the wrong side of the ridge, and that the stream bed was flowing away from his escape plan, not toward it. When darkness began to fall he had found a crevice in the rocky banks of the stream and stopped for the day.

As for food, there were no coconuts, no cooked fish, not even a dead possum to eat, but there was a bit of red fruit and some berries. He ate some and burrowed in for the night. The rainforest was dark enough at mid-day; by late afternoon it was pitch dark underneath the canopy of hardwood trees and vines. If he had learned anything from Saya leading him around by a noose day in and day out, there were more things in the forest watching him than things that he could see. He waited until dark, ate some more red fruit, and went to sleep, thinking that he was free.

The sun was high over the eastern ridge of the island when Olafson woke up. A shaft of light penetrated the woods, beamed directly through a cleft between two large stones, and straight into Olafson's closed eyes. He blinked a few times, covered his eyes, and grinned. *I'm free*, he thought. *It wasn't a dream.*

His dreams had been good ones. He had dreamt of food, real food, ice cream, Spam on toast, navy beans, coffee, torpedo juice, and licked his lips all night. He had rolled over once, touched something wet and soft, and dreamed that Suzy was lying next to him. In his deep, unfettered sleep he remembered his nights in Honolulu with her, heaving and grunting in the bulb-lit Hotel Acme just a few blocks away from the Black Cat Club.

Cookie had come aboard *Renegade* one morning in Pearl Harbor and whispered to him, "Hey, Chief, listen up. I got this girl, Hualani." She was a Hawaiian girl who danced for Madame Rochelle at the Black Cat Club. Cookie had spent most of his shore leave, all of his shore pay, and every Black Cat Club dance card he could scrounge for the favor of spending a dozen dances and a frenzied hour with Hualani, followed by a frenzied half-hour in the Hotel Acme. Cookie's descriptions of the things that Hualani did to him were things Olafson had only imagined. "And she's got a friend."

Olafson's dream progressed to him and Cookie going to the Black Cat Club, where Hualani introduced Olafson to Suzy. Suzy introduced Olafson to a few things herself. She took Olafson's dance cards and, soon, his money, and taught him the fundamentals of the missionary position. Suzy, also Hawaiian, told Olafson, "Big boy, I love you ooh ooh," and, "You make me real woman ooh ooh," and Olafson fell hard for the first female he had ever slept with. They had paid no attention whatever to Cookie and Hualani rutting noisily on the other side of the paper thin walls of the Hotel Acme. Suzy told him after a half-hour or so, every night, that she had to go back to the club because Madame Rochelle would be mad if she was gone and she couldn't lose her job. "I support family, big family, mother and father old, brothers and sisters young, very traditional family." Olafson hugged her and promised her that he understood and would be back for more the next night. Dreaming about them was great, and the dreams were mostly true, except that Olafson edited out of his dream how he and Cookie had made a deal with Bart Sullivan to be able to afford Hualani and Suzy. He also edited out that the wet and soft thing his hand felt in his sleep might not be Suzy. It was in fact the rotting head of a rusa deer fawn that had been dragged into the eddying pool of the stream by a Moluccan python.

"GOT DUMNIT!" Olafson shrieked when he saw the reason why his hand was wet, saw the dead baby deer eyes gazing at him, its ragged neck torn away and mostly submerged in the water, nubs of antlers at the base of large dead ears that seemed to bubble as the stream flowed around and through the ragged head. "YIIIII!" he yelled, a sound interrupted only by the crashing of branches above his head. The python itself, a deer-shaped lump in its stomach, slithered out of the water and up onto the opposite bank. Olafson didn't know whether to climb back into his rock tomb or to flee. The fawn's head floated up and wedged itself against his neck; he fled.

Olafson scrambled out of his hiding place, climbed up screaming at the deer head and at the engorged python that wanted only to disappear into the brush. He gripped at the roots that overhung the cave, scrambled onto a ragged boulder, took one step to heave himself out of the rocky stream bed entirely, and snapped his ankle. He screamed, twisted, gripped his foot, and fell, hitting his head, and was crying in pain when a dozen Sawi hunters passed within a foot of him and crossed the stream.

"*Ular piton!*" "*Tombak!*" They shouted as they dived into the bush. It was clear even to Olafson that they were chasing the snake. "*Kepala,*" one shouted. "*No, tidak ada ekor.*"

For the next half-hour Olafson writhed on his rock, trying to stand up with the help of tree roots, collapsing, lifting his injured foot, dropping it, groaning, yet unable to ignore the clamor inside a thick stand of brush not fifty yards away. The Sawi were shouting and thrashing, flailing against the shrubbery.

"*Kalahkan itu! Tombak ini terlalu kecil.*" Olafson heard, or imagined he heard, a thick and painful hiss. Eventually an older tribesman arrived, a man with a thick stomach and a machete. He walked past Olafson, leapt from rock to rock, and disappeared into the bush. *"Potong! Potong!"* Eventually the hunters returned.

The Sawi carried the battered remains of a huge snake, its head bashed to a pulp. The abdomen, formerly shaped like a small deer, had been whacked so many times that it now looked more like a series of tiny snake-covered tricycles. As for the Sawi themselves, it was not difficult to see that they were all men; the purpose of the grass skirts they wore seemed unrelated to covering up their private parts. Except for those tasked with lugging the snake around, the hunters carried spears or bows with very long arrows, or both. Most of them had necklaces made of bones. The old man, however, had a bone ring in his nose and the machete. They lifted the python out of the brush, carried it up to the edge of the flowing stream, and jumped across it on the same rocks that they had used as a bridge before. They landed, one by one, within a foot or two of Olafson, who they ignored, inadvertently slapping him with the python's tail as they passed him, and disappeared back into the jungle. He moaned and stared and held his broken foot between his hands and watched them, feathered heads, dusky backs, grass skirts, bows and arrows, snake and all, glide out of view.

"I'll be got dumned!" he muttered. He took in a deep breath, grabbed once more at a tree root, took one step on his good foot, and fell back down. "I'm foked."

He had closed his eyes in pain, hoping it was still just part of the dream that had involved wet Suzy and Honolulu nights, when suddenly he was snatched up by his arm pits and lifted to his feet. Four Sawi, each a foot shorter than Olafson, held him upright under his arms and carried him off the rock. The four of them laid him out like a short, thick, sunburned, and painful python. When he passed out, Olafson was being carried through the rainforest as fast as the Sawi could run.

---

Olafson woke to find himself on a straw mat laid out on the dirt floor of a thatched hut. His ankle hurt and, again, he was hungry, but he was able to see through the opening that he was in some kind of village.

The woman who brought him a bowl of forest porridge also brought him a stout stick to help him stand on his own. She was dressed like the hunters, a grass skirt whose function was not obvious, some necklaces made with stones and sharks' teeth, and not much else. She put the bowl on the mat next to him, saw that he was awake and looking at her, and skittered back out of the hut, leaving him alone to feast with his fingers on yam and berry mush.

He put a finger in the mush, licked it, tried another, and decided that it was better than what he had been eating. When he finished he lay back on the mat, then looked around the hut. There was a small pile of new thatch a few feet away; he tucked it under his ankle, then lay back again. Before long, Olafson went back to sleep. Such was his existence for three days.

On the fourth day he was awake long before the mush girl brought his food. Morning rays of the sun filtered in through the straw walls and roof, laying patches of light on the dirt floor. Outside the hut there was the background noise of Stone Age people shuffling back and forth to begin the day. Children's voices called out, laughing, running, tumbling about while women shushed them. Roosters crowed and birds sang out in the trees. The smell of a cook fire drifted into the hut, some uncertain aroma of roasting meats and the more familiar flavor of yams and coconut with padi peppers. Now and then a naked child would dart past the door, or a chicken. A few very old women carried bits of bamboo and straw back and forth and, very occasionally, younger women, girls, would stand near the door and talk. It was all gibberish to him. The girl came in with his mush.

If she was surprised to see him sitting up she didn't show it. She never looked directly at Olafson, instead walking from the doorway to the mat while seemingly gazing at the straw wall. She was somewhere between eleven and thirty years old, he suspected, and very small. Her skin was as black as the others, not black like the Navy's stewards or the dock crews who loaded ships in Pearl Harbor, but a more cocoa colored flesh that hung on her bones like a bad drape. Her abdomen, like all Sawi's, bulged out and her chest and shoulders sagged. For the first time he noticed that her ears were pierced and studded with bones. She moved without a sound.

"Good morning, lady," he said. The girl jumped, almost spilling his porridge. "I'm Chief Olafson. You can call me Chief." The girl stood rigid, trying to be invisible. "CHIEF," he said, slowly, and grinned at her. "C H I E F." He knew if he spoke loudly and slowly that she, like all natives, would understand English. She backed out of the hut as quickly as she could.

He ate his mush patiently. He had grown to like forest porridge. Now and then he discovered a tiny bit of meat of some kind in it, and nuts softened from cooking. Berries mixed with yams and taro mash took on a flavor of their own. Better still, his ankle seemed much improved, strong enough to walk a few steps. He stood, put some weight on his foot, and picked up his bowl, then finished breakfast, wiping some of the mush out of his whiskers and wiping his fingers on his ragged pants, leaving a crimson stain on them.

*This ain't the Hotel Acme and she ain't Suzy, but it also ain't the got dumb bitin' dogs and torture pits and she ain't Tarzan Woman either,* he reflected. *Couple more days of this and I'll start figgerin' out what's next.*

For the next two days Olafson ate mush, tested his foot, and explored. Remembering the swarthy little hunters with their bows and spears, he made the decision to be on his best behavior. Their village was a cluster of thatched huts scattered around a clearing in the rainforest. There was a fire pit in the center where several women went back and forth, pulling large green leaves off the top, tossing in plantains and yams, berries, and chunks of uncertain meat. They stirred the coals with bamboo sticks, then covered the pit again, shooing the children away. Other women of indeterminate age wove straw into thatches, long stems for the roofs, shorter and more squared arrangements for walls. Groups of three and four children brought bamboo and reeds back to the village and handed their loads over to the thatch-makers and disappeared again. A half-dozen roosters strutted around in a clearing near the center of the village; small boys spent hours with switches walking in circles around the poultry and clucking them away from the jungle. Some farmed at a large plot, digging yams and taro roots and tending to a patch of padi peppers.

None of them looked at Olafson, not when he stood in the doorway of his hut, nor when he had recovered enough to try a few tentative steps out into the village, nor as he became emboldened and walked around freely, nor when he walked into the jungle, relieved himself, and walked back. He felt invisible.

On one foray he noticed that there were decorated poles at the edges of the village. Each pole was eight to ten feet high and topped by ugly leather balls. When he paid attention to the straw gatherers and food hunters, he realized that they always walked between the poles as they left the village and when they returned. Late in the afternoon of his third ambulatory day the men returned.

They arrived, gliding silently between two of the decorated poles, jogging, spears and bows and arrows in hand. Two of them slung a rusa deer between them on a bamboo pole. Others carried strings of birds, a line of small fish, and a few marginal trophies such as tree kangaroos and rats. There were no pythons, no crocodiles. They jogged to the center of the village and halted. When the women and children gathered around them they glared, unmistakably perturbed. Olafson was not clear on the precise moment, but several began to wail, holding their palms up and closing their eyes, shaking their heads from side to side. There was shouting, stomping of feet, and two of the men, the elder with the machete and another, appeared to be making declarations to one of the women and some children. Olafson suspected that not all of the men had come back from the hunt.

The remaining women and children took possession of the deer and game and fish and began to peel away the feathers and flesh. Within an hour the entire proceeds of the week's hunt had been dressed and cut up, then put into clay pots and into the large communal cook fire. Within two hours the entire village had gathered in a circle and chanted, with much raising of hands and looking at skies, all cocoa brown bodies and grass skirts, bare breasts and bead necklaces and wailing. Then they turned to Olafson.

As the faint forest sunlight began to fade two of the hunters came to where he stood in the doorway of his hut and, with a sort of Stone Age form of present arms, thumped their spear butts on the ground and spoke to him in a very clear and respectful gibberish. "*Datang. Bersama datang.*" They waited a moment, then repeated it. One of them finally reached a hand out for Olafson, took him by the forearm, and began to lead him. The other walked alongside, careful to see that he didn't stumble. They led him toward the edge of the village where the wailing family fell in behind them, soon joined by the elder with the machete and a dozen others. They stopped at the decorated poles that framed the pathway on the western side of the hamlet, then formed a circle around Olafson. The woman and children who now were, apparently, the widow and orphans, stepped forward.

"*Semgangat besar?*" the chief asked the widow, pointing at the pole on the right. "*Tau pengiri?*" He pointed at Olafson. The elder repeated himself a few times, once or twice shaking his machete at the nearest pole and, occasionally, at Olafson. The rest of the village chanted and moaned. Some threw their necklaces at the pole, others threw a few stones and beads at Olafson. He began to suspect that his status as an invisible guest was not as utopian as he had believed. Then a chant began.

"*Semgangat besar. Semgangat besar. Semgangat besar.*" One of the hunters stepped forward and punched Olafson on the shoulder. Another lowered his spear and pointed it at Olafson's bare chest. Still the widow stood silent. "*Semgangat besar!*" One of the men, a hunter who had helped carry Olafson to the village from the creek, stepped from the crowd and showed his hands, also red with berry juice. He shouted, "*Semgangat besar!*" and pointed up at the decorated pole.

Olafson looked up at the pole himself and, for the first time, perceived that the ugly leather balls were heads, human heads, small, black, fuzzy-headed heads, with huge lips and sagging lids over closed eyes, flaps of neck skin wrapped around the poles. The men grabbed him by the shoulders and marched him around the village, then to each of the paths that led in and out of the hamlet.

Each village path was marked by a pole topped by a head in various stages of rot. On the southern side of the village the heads were in no particular respect different than heads of the men of the village: small, wrinkled, and squarish in shape. The heads on the east side poles were different, however; they were marked by decaying gobs of thick white and mustard yellow war paint. Their eyes were left open, bulging, all facing east, warning the enemy tribes of that side of the island to expect the same if they went to war. The heads on the poles on the north side of the village were much like the men of the village, friendly upcountry Sawis who allowed them free passage to the north. There were only three poles on the west side and Olafson had no doubt whose heads they were. Small, skin a sallow yellow color, straight black hair, round faces, small mouths and broad noses, they clearly were Japanese soldiers.

"*Semgangat besar!*" the hunter barked again, and the men began to bend Olafson double.

"Lemme go, got dummit! I didn't..." he wailed, flailing with his arms and trying to kick at them with one leg, punching blindly in the dark. He was twice as large as the largest of them, but slow, and weak. He began to puke up his forest porridge, the hash and berries coming out in gobs that blobbed onto his chin and chest. "Turn loose of me you little savage or I'll..."

"No," a voice said, a woman's voice. "No. Pengiri. Semgangat besar, no. Pengiri." It was the widow. "No semgangat." The hunters stopped hitting Olafson, although they didn't turn loose of him. The elder went to the widow and spoke with her, nodding, shaking his head, nodding again. He turned to Olafson.

"Datang," he barked. It was not a hateful bark, or a friendly one, but a command. "Datang." He turned on his heels and walked between the poles, ignoring the heads, and marched off into the jungle.

The prisoner escort led Olafson, struggling, a half-mile, where the rainforest was so thick that it was impossible to see more than a few feet in any direction. The guards forced Olafson to his knees and bent him over. The elder lifted the machete, shouted, and brought it down with all the force he could muster as Olafson screamed. As he shrieked and waited for the fatal blow, a vision raced through his mind, a memory of another island jungle scene, of his slamming the machine gun butt into Bart Sullivan's head and leaving him dead on the beach.

The blade struck a tangle of thick vines a foot from his head. The elder raised the blade and chopped again, then cut through the vines and began to clear away the brush from around them. He chopped again, and again, and at length uncovered a stone slab at the base of a mangium tree. He scraped at the edge of the slab, digging out a hole with his machete. When the hiding place was completely uncovered the elder gave his blade to one of the men, bent over, put both hands under the slab, and dug out a wooden box.

He bowed low toward Olafson, then handed him an allied Army field radio, wood case, dials, switches, hand-cranked generator, and all.

"Dewa berada di dalam kotak ini," he said. "Bawa dia keluar," he repeated in a solemn manner. The gods live in this box. "Bawa mereka keluar."

He struck his forehead twice; his men did the same.

Olafson could have worked the radio in the dark; it was identical to the field radios the allies had used since the first landings in Guadalcanal. He wiped the dirt and tree shavings off the radio and cleaned the contact points. There were a few bugs on the dials and switches; he flicked them off and toggled the switches to see if they had been broken. He turned to the generator.

The coil appeared to be intact and the crankset attached easily. He strung the wires to the contact points on the radio, tested the crank handle, and then churned the generator. He switched the set to receive, turned the tuning dial to the open band, and began to crank the generator. For a few moments the pop and hiss of static spurted out of the box and the Sawis jumped backwards to avoid direct contact with the gods. Then a gleeful woman's voice chirped through the airwave in six solid notes. The Sawis had never heard of mopping, or a soda pop rickey, or a jukebox, but to them God sounded like Glenn Miller's orchestra, specifically the American girl singing *Jukebox Saturday Night*. The Sawis cowered against a tree; Olafson began to tap his foot, seven syncopated pats with his right toes, five with his left, all the while grinning through berry stained lips.

The Sawis listened, looked at Olafson, and listened more.

"This is the Armed Forces Radio Network," a god said through the crystal set. "And this is *GI Jive!*"

Olafson let them commune with their gods for a half hour, cranking the energy into the radio each time that the music faded. The elder was pleased. The hunters were pleased. As one song finished he turned the crystal tuner to find another. When a lull came in the music he turned the dials to lose the signal, and said in a firm voice, "We hear you, Oh God of Glenn Miller." He bowed once to the radio, disconnected it, and handed the generator to the chief to carry. The chief bowed in return, the warriors bowed, and they took the radio back to his hut in the village. That night he feasted on deer and yam mush.

Long after dark one of the Sawi females came to his hut and showed him the Sawi way. He forgot about Suzy, and Saya, and, in a small recess in his brain, he pondered his fortune.

Olafson never questioned the change in his fortunes. He only wondered, fleetingly, whether he would even bother to return to civilization after the war. As usual, Olafson was wondering about the wrong thing.

# Chapter 16

Komodo, the island, south of Molucca, had lost one of its dragons. The Dutch resistance fighters, more coast watchers than fighters, had lost their radio. Saya had lost Olafson. And, at Ambon Fortress, Lieutenant Tanaka Rikugun-Chui had lost a shovel.

Tanaka sat rigidly at his desk and looked out through the windows of the *hohei* staff quarters. Staff work was his duty, much as leading a platoon across the northern peninsula had been his duty, and capturing Dutch colonists was another of his duties. And, since the captives were now the property of the emperor, it was his duty to use them efficiently to perform the emperor's work.

Therefore, from the day he had herded all of the spice farmers and school teachers and postal clerks onto crammed barges to go to Ambon, up to the present, Tanaka began each day by instructing his *chojin* and his sergeant on the work that the emperor's property would do that day. For the greater part of those days his orders had been simple: "Today, you march the men *surēbu* slaves to Mount Salahutu. Assign one private to supervise each ten slaves." There would be minor details, such as how many buckets, shovels and picks would be issued, how many kilos of rocks each slave must dig, and how many buckets of rocks each slave must carry up the side of Mount Salahutu to build the runway they were digging out of the mountain, but even those details were simple in the extreme.

Tanaka next would march his sergeant and corporals to the prison compound, where the sergeant would assemble the spice farmers and school teachers and postal clerks into ranks and files. The corporals would assign one private to each ten male slaves and march them off. Tanaka would count them as they marched out of the compound, then return to his desk and enter on the duty roster the figures of the day, annotated by the names of his sergeant and corporals. "February 20: Sergeant Numata is assigned six shovels, twelve canvas buckets, one pick, and one hundred thirty-six *surēbu* to Mount Salahutu." His *chojin*, Mr. Moto, was Tanaka's eyes and ears on the project.

At different times of the day Tanaka would go to the work site and watch the progress, then make his report at the end of the day. "January 20: The Emperor's *surēbu* transported 134,000 kilos of building material to the runway on Mount Salahutu, compacting it in a base area of six meters by eleven meters at a point eighty-four meters from the southwest end of the runway. Six shovels, twelve canvas buckets, one pick, and one hundred thirty-four *surēbu* returned to compound. Two infirm *surēbu* stopped working and were humanely taken to the infirmary."

The two infirm *surēbu* were in fact dead *surēbu*, having collapsed in the equatorial heat while attempting to lift broken rocks and root-tangled mud out of a hole and carry them up the steep slope. The other *surēbu* shuffled all day in the broiling sun, lost weight and body fat by the hour, and wore only remnants of their underwear in vain efforts to retain any dignity. As they did, Tanaka would meet with the officers of companion platoons to agree on the following day's work schedule, inspect equipment, and attend the battalion and regimental officers' briefings. He would then inspect his platoon at the end of the duty day.

This day was different. Tanaka stared out the nearest open window of the *hohei* staff building, squinting at the harsh sunlight and also at the gash in the side of Mount Salahutu where the runway was being built with slave labor. He gritted his teeth, pursed his lips, and turned back to his desk, then looked up.

"Are you certain?"

"Yes, Lieutenant Rikugun-Chui."

"*Five* shovels?"

"Yes, Lieutenant Rikugun-Chui." Mr. Moto bowed from the neck up, his chin lowered toward his chest.

"Did you count them yourself?" Mr. Moto had counted them himself. He also had counted the workers, the sergeant, the NCOs and privates, and the canvas buckets. He had personally held the work party's only pick. "Someone has stolen a shovel!" It was more a declaration, a conclusion, than a question. Mr. Moto bowed again. "This is bad, very bad. Come with me."

Tanaka buckled his officer's belt, put his pistol in the holster, straightened his white collars, and put on his cap. He marched out of the office, Mr. Moto two steps behind, through the muggy pool of clerks and runners, then out the door.

The prisoners' compound was fenced off behind the fort; he walked along the main camp road between the prisoner barracks, a series of cement slabs with thatched roofs where the prisoners slept on straw mats. Tanaka continued on to the *surēbu* hospital, also a cement slab with a thatched roof and cots made of crude branches. He marched into the front room and demanded to see the chief.

"I am Lieutenant Tanaka Rikugun-Chui, Fourth Platoon of His Majesty's Ninth Infantry. Where are the *surēbu* who have come to the hospital today? Show them to me!" The hospital chief said that no *surēbu* had arrived today. "And the *surēbu* who did not report to work this morning?" The hospital chief said that none of the airport labor battalion had been brought to the hospital in the night, dead or alive. "Do you have a shovel?" he asked. The hospital chief was so startled that he asked Tanaka to repeat it. "A shovel." The hospital chief denied having a shovel. "And your graves detail?"

Mr. Moto was heard to say 'Ah.' It had not occurred to him that perhaps someone had taken the shovel to bury one of the *surēbu*. It didn't matter; the hospital turned the bodies over to a separate prisoner detail for burial, so had no shovels of its own. The hospital chief bowed to Tanaka and they marched out.

They walked past the cemetery, past the parade ground and women's quarters and the latrines, then out of the prison compound and onto the path that led up the mountain to the work site. Tanaka ordered Mr. Moto to one side of the road and he took the other. Between the two of them they looked at every inch of the path; they found no shovels. Twenty minutes later, they arrived at the quarry, downhill from the runway.

"Sergeant!" he commanded. "Fall the prisoners in!" All over the quarry his particular platoon of privates and corporals rounded up the prisoners. Skeletal colonial Dutch civilians, men on their knees, digging with their hands to unearth rocks, lifting rocks with their bare hands and dumping them into canvas bags, lifting canvas bags and slinging them onto yokes to be carried further up the hill to the runway, pitiful creatures, all ground to a halt, looked up, and shuffled over to the edge of the quarry and fell into ranks and files. "Bring your shovels!" The corporals shouted at the privates, who slapped some of the prisoners, who returned to the quarry for the shovels, then shuffled back to the assembly, where they were slapped again.

There were six shovels. There also was a pick and twelve canvas bags, as well as one hundred thirty-four Dutch colonial slaves in various stages of dying under the brutal sun and frequent kicks. They waited for another round of slaps and confusing orders from their guards.

"There is no missing shovel, *Chojin*-san!" Tanaka hissed at Mr. Moto. "You make a mistake." Mr. Moto bowed again, his eyes burning from the shame. "I will return to my duties. You—you will stay with the platoon all day. Dismissed!" Mr. Moto bowed to Tanaka's retreating back.

Tanaka walked back down the path to the compound to the fort, then reviewed his duty rosters and training schedules to look for an explanation of why his most trusted *chojin* had made such a bothersome mistake. He worked throughout the day and, that afternoon, inspected his platoon, the prisoners, the quarry, the path the prisoners took from the quarry to the runway, and all of their equipment. He decided that he would not mention Mr. Moto's error in judgment in his daily report, even after hearing another lieutenant gossip about the amount of *sake* that Mr. Moto was suspected of taking from the officers' mess.

Tanaka covered for Moto for the rest of the week, despite the reported disappearance of one of the canvas buckets, then another shovel, then the pick, and finally a shovel, a bucket, and a pick, all at the same time. All were accounted for. It was on the fourth day, when again Tanaka walked to the quarry, threatened to behead *surēbu* workers, and counted the tools did he realize that nothing was missing but also that each time Mr. Moto reported them to be stolen he, Mr. Moto, had just returned to the work site after relieving himself in the privacy of a *sangsana* tree.

"Show me the place of ease," Tanaka demanded. Moto led Tanaka about fifty yards away from the quarry, to a shady gully in the mountain. A tree branch grew at a perfect angle for the officers to sit and use the head, their boots on the ground, and smoke a cigarette, away from the burning sun. A cloud of flies buzzed around the filthy latrine; the aroma of digested diets dependent on rice and tropical fruit made the site unbearable. "You come here each day," he asked, "and it is when you go back to the site and look at the workers that you count the shovels and buckets and look for the pick?" Mr. Moto nodded. "I think the stink makes you dizzy," he said. Mr. Moto bowed again, deeply humiliated. "Have you been drinking *sake* when you come to the seat of ease, Moto-san?" he asked.

Moto denied drinking *sake* during his restroom breaks, but Tanaka did not believe him. Even so, there were no missing tools. The only damage had been to cause Tanaka to leave his desk again and go to the work site, that and the very brief work stoppages while he counted the shovels and buckets. He decided to give Mr. Moto one more chance.

He therefore did not mention the error in his morning report on the fifth day. He instead followed Mr. Moto at a dead run, out of the fort, through the prison compound, up the path, and to the runway itself, the entire time hearing Mr. Moto's dreaded words: "Lieutenant-san! A rifle! The prisoners have stolen a rifle!"

When he arrived at the runway Sergeant Numata had the prisoners on their knees. They kneeled in formation, hands behind their heads, staring directly in front of them. They were guarded by privates, each of them standing with his rifle lowered and aimed at them. The privates were, in turn, guarded by their corporals, also with their rifles aimed. Sergeant Numata held his rifle, bayonet attached, to the head of one of the prisoners. A Malay translator stood next to Numata. Tanaka double-timed to a halt in front of Numata.

"Is this the thief?" he demanded. He drew his sword.

"This *surēbu* is the leader, sir," Numata answered. "We observe him every day talking to other *surēbu*. He will know who stole the rifle."

Tanaka nodded at the Malay, who translated.

"Where is the rifle?"

"I don't know anything about a rifle," the prisoner answered.

"There is a stolen rifle. Who stole it?" Tanaka raised his sword above the bowed prisoner's neck.

"I don't know about a stolen rifle. I don't know who stole a rifle. I don't believe anyone here stole a rifle, sir."

"Five minutes from now I will begin to behead your fellow *surēbu*. I will stop when I learn who stole the rifle and where it is. If you tell me now, I will only behead you and the thief. Five minutes." Tanaka nodded at Mr. Moto, who took out his watch and noted the time. Tanaka then began to inspect his troops. He soon noticed an interesting fact—they all had their rifles. He lowered his sword, nodded at Numata to continue guarding the supposed leader of the prisoners, and began to walk from one corporal to the next, then to the privates. There was no missing rifle.

"*Chojin!*" he hissed. "What did you observe to say the rifle was stolen?"

It was a mildly complicated story. Mr. Moto had been supervising the platoon in its supervision of the working prisoners. At one point two of the privates disappeared at the same time into the trees to relieve themselves. Although one held both rifles as the other sat doubled over a broken tree trunk, a corporal shouted at them that they were not to leave the work party in twos. Mr. Moto walked into the bush, saw one soldier groaning over the tree latrine but without his rifle, and shouted at him. By the time he physically arrived at the latrine the in flagrante soldier had dressed and fled while the other soldier had returned to the quarry unobserved.

None of the corporals or Sergeant Numata had seen anyone missing a rifle; they had accepted without question the *chojin's* command to put the prisoners on their knees and guard them at gun and bayonet point until Mr. Moto returned with Lieutenant Rikugun-Chui.

It was a fine point. Tanaka had promised to behead at least two prisoners for stealing a rifle that, he realized, had not been stolen. He could not, however, inform the prisoners that he was wrong or that his *chojin* was wrong. He decided to march the supposed leader on his knees back to the dog kennel, where disobedient prisoners were broken in darkness, and to cut the others' rations in half while doubling their rock quotas.

"I warn you all," he said to the Malay, who shouted his translated warning to the prisoners in Malay-Dutch dialect. "You are responsible to the Emperor for his equipment. Any prisoner who makes a false report of missing equipment will be dealt with harshly. Any prisoner who takes his Emperor's equipment will be dealt with summarily. *Wakuru? Ha!*"

He then marched the leader, with one private as a guard, and Mr. Moto back to the fort.

Tanaka then punished Mr. Moto for the false report of the missing rifle. He gave Moto seven days of reduction in rank and returned him to uniform as an infantry soldier, assigned to Sergeant Numata, to personally guard the prisoners at the quarry and, as they carried rocks up to the airstrip, to march with them there as well.

Numata found no particular use for the ex-*chojin* so he had no concern when Mr. Moto spent much of the first day as usual, sitting on the rocks to ease the boiling sweat off his fat body. He was not especially concerned when on the second day Mr. Moto appeared to have undergone a change in skin color, white rather than sunburned, nor on the third when Mr. Moto returned from the seat of ease with a wild look in his eyes and spewing out the word '*ningen.*'

On the fourth day Mr. Moto vanished.

When Moto hadn't returned after a half hour, Sergeant Numata sent a corporal to fetch him from the seat of ease. The corporal returned to say that Mr. Moto was not there, but his equipment was. Numata followed him back to the latrine tree and saw, dropped into the burbling excrement, Mr. Moto's army boots, his puttees, his army cap, his pants, his shirt, and his belt. Twenty feet from the pit, Moto's canteen was tossed aside under the leaves of an *angsana* tree. His rifle was missing, as was his ammunition pouch and bayonet. Numata sent a runner for Tanaka.

Work halted. The guards ordered the prisoners back onto their knees, where they were held at gunpoint until Tanaka arrived. The corporal led Tanaka to the spot in the forest where he had last seen Sergeant Numata gazing at Moto's murky uniform.

"Sergeant-san! What happened?" Tanaka stared wide-eyed at the one man in his platoon who had never lost anything, not a tool or rifle, not a prisoner, nor even so much as a rock, the man he counted on to make the prisoners carry extra rocks and to survive on declining rations, and who whipped them when they faltered.

Sergeant Numata couldn't open his eyes. He was hoarse and his face was caked with dirt. His lips were dry. He trembled.

"*Ningen,*" he croaked. "*Ningen.*" He was crazed with terror.

Tanaka realized that, although he was personally responsible for his platoon's and Mr. Moto's failings, and for whatever Sergeant Numata had seen, his first duty was to the emperor. He therefore ordered a runner to go to the battalion, report that his sergeant had been attacked and his *chojin* had disappeared, and to request help.

The battalion commander arrived within fifteen minutes, with his entire headquarters company, the men armed with rifles, bayonets, machine guns, a 20 mm half-track gun, a Malay interpreter, and six megaphones. Tanaka stood before him in front of the kneeling *surēbu* and bowed.

"*Ningen?*" the battalion commander asked, eyebrows raised, voice doubtful? "*Ningen,*" Numata repeated. Tanaka showed him the rank latrine pit, Moto's uniform and gear. The battalion commander scoffed at the word '*ningen*' and ordered his men to begin the search. He, his company commander, their platoon leaders, and the squad leaders took the megaphones and walked into the *sangsana* forest and began to shout.

"*Chojin-san,*" they hollered, the soldiers walking abreast as best they could. "*Chojin-san,*" they yelled again, and "*Moto-san?*" and, occasionally, in case there had been a sneak attack, "To the enemy—you are surrounded. Give up." They thrashed their way up and down Mount Salahutu looking for Mr. Moto or, in the cases of the more superstitious of them, a *ningen*.

Some of them pointed out that a *ningen* would never climb up a mountain so far from the sea. "There was a Komodo *ningen* on Molucca," they said, "but that was after the typhoon, and only on the shore." Others said that *ningens* were not dragons — "That is a peasant superstition!" — but existed in the form of humans. "They have arms with claws, and sharp teeth. They can go anywhere they want. My grandfather caught one, in the ocean, fishing. It was almost like a man, except for the arms. It could climb up here if it wanted, easy." Most of the soldiers didn't believe in *ningens* at all. They instead believed that Mr. Moto was a privileged drunk and didn't care what happened to him. None of them questioned why a *ningen* would want Mr. Moto.

The search continued until four in the morning when someone from the regimental command barracks sent a runner to the search party. "Call off the search," the runner told the battalion commander. He relayed the order to Tanaka and his headquarters company officers. "Return to the fort."

At four in the morning the sentry on guard duty had marched out of Ambon Fort's ancient stone archway, stopped at the dock, turned around, marched back through the arch to the adjutant's building, made an about face, and heard the sound 'unhhhhh'. He lowered his rifle, made certain that there was a bullet in the chamber and that his bayonet was fixed, and charged. He found Mr. Moto, naked, suspended from the archway, hanging by his feet, with a gag in his mouth and a blindfold tied over his eyes. He blew his whistle. When the other sentries and the officer of the day arrived they observed that the blood had drained from Mr. Moto's face and arms, making him look white. His body was bloated and there was a deep, red gash across his back. He reeked of *sake*.

"Cut him down," the officer ordered the sentries. "Cut him down. Carry him to the infirmary." When the adjutant arrived he put Fortress Ambon on high alert.

---

Saya had been staring across the water at Ambon when she heard a sound and quietly stepped back into the dark shadows behind a tree. She stood motionless for more than five minutes, her breath so quiet that even a tree kangaroo limped across her shoulder, then scuttled down her waist and into the brush on the rainforest floor. She waited until she was satisfied that the sound was nothing more than the water lapping against the wooden hull of a rowboat, then resumed studying the shore until she was satisfied that no one had followed her. She returned her gaze across the bay toward Ambon. Suddenly, flood lights illuminated Ambon's dock. It was too far away for Saya to see human figures but she nevertheless had the strong feeling that people were scurrying around the entrance to the fort. Peering through the darkness, she saw that army trucks had turned their headlights on to put light onto the fortress walls, the docks and the gateway into Ambon. Before long, searchlights began to play across the fort, into the trees, and across the wooden huts of the old town.

She stayed to watch the growing beehive of activity on Fortress Ambon until the sun began to rise across the island. Then, despite the distance, she suddenly felt exposed, indeed felt as if someone was looking directly at her. She silently slipped back into the rainforest and disappeared.

---

Three days later a board of inquiry was assembled at regimental headquarters.

"Lieutenant Tanaka Rikugun-Chui!"

"Sir." Tanaka stood at attention. The commandant sat at his desk. The division commander, the staff officers in charge of materiel, personnel, and construction, Tanaka's battalion commander, and his company commander stood at attention on either side of the commandant.

"You are charged with the loss of one rifle. One bayonet. One ammunition pouch. Six rounds of ammunition. And *Chojin* Moto. *Wakuru? Ha!*"

"Yes, sir." Tanaka stumbled as he spoke. He was undoubtedly responsible for the disappearance of Mr. Moto, particularly for the loss of the emperor's equipment that had been issued to Mr. Moto. He might be responsible for damage to Sergeant Numata's brain and, if the commandant stretched a point, he also might be charged with the cost of the search party and the loss of time in building the runway when work halted while the headquarters company tromped around Mount Salahutu looking for his *chojin*.

"And Sergeant Numata. He is...." *Crazy*, the commandant thought. *He's nuts.* The medical officer had declared Sergeant Numata to be a case of failed *jisatsu*. "If he does not die, as he should, he will be sent to Jakarta for rehabilitation." The commandant hoped that Numata would die so no court of inquiry would look into Numata's fear of a *ningen*, or his deranged mind.

Tanaka considered his position. He had failed the emperor. He had failed the commandant. He had failed his friend, *Chojin* Moto.

"I understand, sir. I am prepared to accept personal responsibility." What he meant was that he accepted that it was his duty to go to his quarters and stick his sword in his stomach and twist it. Tanaka bowed.

"No, Lieutenant." The commandant personally believed that Mr. Moto had disgraced the service with his drinking and whoring and that Tanaka had been too inexperienced to reign the sod in. "No *seppuku* for you. You will not take any measures of a personal responsible nature. Do you understand?"

Tanaka bowed.

"You will return to duty, Lieutenant, except that each day you will search for the missing rifle, the bayonet, and the ammunition." He paused for Tanaka to acknowledge the order. "There are no *ningens*, Lieutenant. Chojin-Moto's weapon is still on this island. Dismissed."

Tanaka completed his bow, then saluted and did an about face. He would live in shame until he found the emperor's missing weapons.

---

"How long before they figure it out?" one of the prisoners whispered.

"Shhh." None of the prisoners believed that any of their fellows were spies for the Japanese, but all of them believed that sometimes men cracked, and told things. "Shut up."

They looked up from the concrete slab of their barracks, up through the thatched roof with the rain dripping through, up into the dark night, their stomachs in pain from the minuscule ball of rice and dirty water that had been their food for the day. They listened for guards eavesdropping in the night, or Malay traitors. Sound carried. It was better to shut up.

So far, all they had been whipped for was the disappearance of Mr. Moto and his rifle, his bayonet, and his ammunition. Tanaka had torn their barracks apart, cut their rations, had them dig out entire hillsides near the quarry and runway, and scoured their work path. He had even made them dig up the prisoner cemetery. Even so, they sensed that Tanaka did not really believe that the prisoners had anything to do with Mr. Moto's disappearance but also that he would be dangerous until he figured it out, as he would.

More than anything, though, all of the prisoners wondered how long it would be before Tanaka or someone figured out that there was a missing rowboat.

# Chapter 17

Saya remained hidden inside the rainforest until sunrise. Ambon's old stone fortress across the bay had been lit up all night but was too far away for her to see clearly what was happening. Her hiding place of the moment was south of Port Haru or, more correctly, where Port Haru had been before the typhoon destroyed it. It was her second visit recently.

After the typhoon blew over she had gone to a safe place to enjoy the view of its destruction. She had watched while the *chojin* and the Malays scrambled around like rats. The Japanese minions had come out from cover to survey the damage and to poke around under the wrecked planks and docks, looking for anything recognizable. Their boats and trucks had been thrown up on the sloping hill and smashed like toys. The port offices, warehouses, barracks, and buildings were flattened. Roofs, walls, windows and floors had been completely blown apart by the wind.

She had watched them, staring hard at where the comfort house had been and at the tree line to which she had escaped. The Malays had found a few people in the wreckage of the comfort house; some they led to a small boat that waited to take them across to the Ambon prison. Others they carried out wrapped in rags and laid on a board, which they took to a field several hundred yards away, tossed onto a pile, and set on fire. Saya had not recognized any of the people in the comfort house, not the Malays, not the people they bundled down to the boat, not the bodies taken away for burning. She hoped her school teacher, the girls she had known, the women from the farms had all died rather than exist as comfort women for Lieutenant Tanaka or Mr. Moto. Now, months later, Port Haru was completely abandoned.

Saya jerked up when she realized that she had allowed herself to drift off to sleep in the night. She also remembered why she had hidden inside the edge of the rainforest below Port Haru; something had been watching her the night before, and she had fled from the shingle beach.

She had experienced that feeling before, an extreme sensitivity to sounds, to changes in shadows on the trees or in the underbrush, to the snapping of roots and rustling of leaves, the certainty that she was being watched. It had happened once or twice after she had fled Port Haru, but recently more often. She had learned to be very quiet and very still, to not let any light fall on her face or her hair, and to wait until whatever had alarmed her came out in the open or disappeared. Usually it was just a tree kangaroo, or a possum. Sometimes it was a python or a cassowary, creatures big enough to make noises, stealthy enough to avoid their own predators. Now and then it was a Sawi, staring at her as if to make sure that she did not go any closer to their sacred burial grounds or the villages inside them. Sometimes she found that someone from the Dutch resistance force was looking right at her but didn't see her; they didn't resist much and didn't even know that she was present.

But last night, on the beach, she had heard nothing, seen nothing, yet was absolutely certain that someone had been looking at her. More than the rowboat on the shingled shore at the base of the promontory, more than whatever was happening in Ambon, something had told Saya to retreat into the dark jungle because she was being watched in the dark. Now, though, whatever had made her sense that she was being watched was gone. Without going out into the open, she looked back down at the shingle beach.

The boat was gone too. It had been there when she arrived at dusk the day before, but no one had climbed out of it, or into it, while she was there. She knew it was a Japanese boat, properly made, too large for Moluccans or even the Malay to use for fishing, too small to carry more than a few people. It might have had an outboard motor but she hadn't heard one as she crept toward the shingle beach the evening before, nor did she hear a motor start up or run during the night while she hid. Even so, the little boat had disappeared by morning. It was possible, she thought, that the tide had lifted the boat off the beach and floated it out into the bay. It also was possible that someone had been in the boat all along and, without her seeing them, had rowed away during the night.

The boat could not have been stolen by the Dutch resistance. She had spied on them in their redoubt near the north cliffs and overheard them say that they needed a boat now that their radio was lost. But, the Dutch never would have exposed themselves in an open boat across the bay from the Japanese. Moreover, the Dutch couldn't have hidden from her, then gotten back into the boat and rowed it away in the night without her hearing them. The Dutch resistance were not known for being silent.

The one thing she was sure of, though, was that it had not been Olafson in the boat. Olafson first would have had to get away from where she had left him tied up in a water-filled staked pit, then find his way across the island to Port Haru, swim to Ambon without the Japanese seeing him, steal one of their boats, and row it back to the same island where he had been tortured from the moment he put his first footprint in the sand. Olafson was too docile for that, too weak and flabby.

Regardless what happened to the boat, what she did know was that she had not found Olafson. She had gone to Port Haru to find him; instead, she had gone to sleep. That shook her confidence more than anything she could remember.

Saya had planned for two years how she would capture Lieutenant Tanaka and Mr. Moto and do to them exactly what they had done to her and her family. They had raped her and dragged her family off into slavery; Tanaka and Mr. Moto would be raped and dragged off into slavery, the exact forms of which she had not yet decided. But she couldn't rape or enslave them if she couldn't capture them, and to capture them she needed to trap them. Then Olafson stumbled into the mangrove swamp where she rescued him from a crocodile and a Komodo dragon. She rescued him because she needed bait for her trap.

*I've got to find him. I've got to tie him up in the open. I've got to lure Tanaka and Mr. Moto to him so that I can capture them.*

Once she was through with them, she could trade them for her family. But, first she had to capture the Japanese. As for now, though, it was time for her to go back into the rainforest. She was safer there. Olafson was there, she was sure, somewhere, and nothing good ever had come of being anywhere near Port Haru. Two hours later she crossed a stream above the Bintuni and walked north toward her home lands.

The hunting party made its way deep into the forest, working its way southward toward the Bintuni. There were fewer rusa deer than ever; even the tree kangaroos and rats were scarce. The Great Winds and Rain had destroyed not only most of the Sawis' sweet potato and taro plants but had also driven the snakes and water monitors to rage, the birds to flee, and even the philanders and possums to burrow and hide. Hunting was scarce.

Sato, the elder, remembered the last Time of Hard Eating, years before when they had been forced to steal from the *heeren* farms. This Time of Hard Eating threatened to be even worse. Everything was dead, hiding, or looking for food, just as he was. He led the hunting party in a hunting chant while the men jogged in the rainforest.

"Og immee LAN," he chanted.

"SlotsaLAN," the men chanted back in unison.

"DOAN FINS MEEINN," he chanted.

"Doan fins meeinn," they chanted, each syllable landing exactly in time to their jogging feet and hoisted spears. A cassowary hen fluttered in the underbrush.

Sato had not led them out of the village, past the totem-poled heads, and beyond the sacred grounds to hunt cassowaries. The smaller birds were too small to eat, the big ones fought back, and cassowary eggs didn't add much to the communal forest mush cook pots. He stared at the brush with some doubt and would have led the men on toward the Bintuni if the bird hadn't shrieked so loudly that all of them, from the youngest to the bravest, ducked for fear of a giant blue and gray creature leaping down on them, its huge legs and sharp claws attacking in defense of its nest.

Then the shrubs exploded, leaves trembling violently, more shrieks, and then the enormous body of the cassowary shook into view behind its gray feathers and amid the thick leaves of the forest canopy. Everyone stopped, looked, and raised a spear. The bird shrieked again, then fell back to the ground as if it had been stabbed in the heart which, in a sense, it had.

A wild forest boar had gotten into the cassowary's nest and eaten, first its eggs, then its mate, and now attacked the huge bird itself, head-on with its sharp tusks. Feathers flew in the sticky, humid air, squeals howled from the attacking pig, the daggered claw of the bird's toe sank deeply into the boar's neck, and blood spurted from them both. The Sawis were delighted. God had answered their chant.

"DOAN FINS MEEINN," they howled in gratitude for God's boun-tiful harvest. "DOAN FINS MEEINN," they sang again, and then attacked with spear and machete.

The unsuspecting forest prey had no chance to defend themselves against the hunting party, especially one so desperate to feed the tribe that the Sawis had begun to fear that God had abandoned them with his Great Winds and Rain. They unleashed a torrent of spears into the pig and the bird, jabbing at necks and underwing pits and eyes, dodging tusks and dagger toes, and killing both the boar and the cassowary in less than a minute.

They stripped vines hanging from a tree, cut and cleaned several thick saplings, and tied up their kills to carry them back to the tribal cook pot. Even if they found nothing else that day, not a rat or possum or even a snake, they had had a good day, thanks to God.

Sato, the elder, was proud to have found a direct link to God. He had given the wooden box to Why Krimma, who had known how to make the box ask God to talk to them. God, with help from Why Krimma, had told them how to chant to make the cook pot better, to love better, and to hunt. Sato told the hunters to hoist the boar and the cassowary on the carrying poles, then he took off at a jog through the rainforest.

"Og immee LAN," he chanted at a dead run.

"DOAN FINS MEEINN," they answered as they followed, passing fifteen or twenty yards away from where Saya had hidden.

Saya watched them from a safe distance. She didn't know whether they realized that she had been shadowing them from the moment they left the sacred burial ground beyond the village head poles. They probably had, she thought, but she had kept to their rules. She hadn't entered the sacred grounds. She hadn't gazed for long at the heads on the poles, just long enough to be sure that Olafson's head wasn't one of them. She had not made contact with any of the children who gathered brush and brought clean water into the hamlet. Thus, the Sawis never bothered her so long as she respected their rules, even when she followed them one or two hundred yards away, and they didn't bother her now.

Saya had decided to follow the hunting party because she had run out of ideas. Olafson had disappeared without a trace. Saya had searched the most likely places for him to have fled, the deeper forest near her hidden enclave, the rocky watercourse of the Bintuni, the more fertile and less forested lands north of the Sawi that gave way to the spice plantations.

She had turned north in hopes that Olafson might have stumbled into the Dutch. After watching them hide under rain capes for three or four days, sending out one-man patrols who walked no more than a few kilometers before holing up for the night and returning to say they had seen no Japanese, she had decided that the Dutch did not have Olafson. Indeed, the Dutch couldn't keep their own minimal affairs in order; their grumbling discussions returned over and over to the subject of a lost radio.

She then had crisscrossed the heartland of the island before turning toward the east side. She thought he might have made it back to the ridge that overlooked the beach where she had seen his footprints in the sand just after the typhoon.

As the days went by she understood that Olafson might have gotten away forever. She also understood that Olafson might simply have walked back to the mangrove swamp and been eaten by the crocodiles or, worse, the Komodo. The water monitors who lived in the ponds higher up the Bintuni were troublesome enough; as a girl she had fought them off her chickens and pigs and, later, in her own secret enclave. But the Komodo, she knew, was truly dangerous, as bad as the Japanese. If Olafson had become a victim of the mangrove carnivores there was nothing she could do about it.

That is when she had turned away empty-handed and ventured near the now-destroyed Port Haru, to see if there was any sign that Olafson had been caught by a Japanese patrol. That, too, had failed. Now she was back in the center of the island, hoping that the Sawis might find him for her and that she might rescue him before they ate him. Their hunting party jogged past her on the way home, chanting.

Something about the Sawi hunting chant bothered her. Watching them hoist their boar and cassowary carcasses, she heard the chant echoed, echoed faintly, echoed by something other than the hunting party. Saya then realized that she was having exactly the same feeling she had had the night before when she had sensed that she was being watched at Port Haru. It was the same chill of her skin in the brutal heat and near darkness, the same rising hair on her neck, the extra alertness of hearing that made her afraid she was being watched.

Without moving her feet, she slowly turned her head to the right, never allowing the dappled sunlight that made its way through the trees to fall on her hair or face. There was no one there, no sound, not even a ruffle of branches or leaves. The Sawi passed fifteen yards away and didn't see her, nor did they turn to look around as if they, too, thought someone was out there. Saya then slowly moved her head to the left. There was no one.

She waited, and waited some more, and decided that she had become skittish.

*I've looked everywhere. There's only one place he can be.*

When a cloud passed over the sun she decided that she was invisible again. She moved, heard nothing, turned around, heard nothing, took two steps in the brush, heard nothing, and set out to catch up with the Sawis. An hour later she took a deep breath, paused at the boundaries of the four sacred tribal grounds, and heard the Sawi hunting chant. Saya broke her tacit agreement with the cannibals.

She had never seen their village before. From fifty yards away, hidden behind thick mangium trees and broad leaf lou lou bushes, she held her breath and was more silent than she had ever been in her life.

The first thing she noticed was the totem. It looked like all of the totems that marked the boundaries of the sacred grounds, a solid wooden trunk with patterned markings and a wooly head stuck on top, staring with dead eyes back at her and at everyone who approached the village. Beyond the totem the village consisted of round huts woven from palmetto and vines, each large enough to make a home for a dozen cannibals. On the far side of the village, on a path that led through and beyond another headed totem, there was a small garden area that looked much like hers—struggling taro roots and a few sweet potatoes, some peppers and a few poles of winged beans growing on vines. Boys chased a frightened chicken around the yard. Women and girls made their way back and forth between the huts.

And then, there he was.

The elder who had led the hunting party walked out of a hut in the center of the village. Olafson strutted out behind him. They stood up, the elder appeared to issue a command, and then the hunters carried the boar to the village fire pit. She strained to hear them.

"OAG GIMMEE LAN," they sang out. "LAN SLOTSA LAN," they continued, rolling the wild pig onto the ground next to the fire pit. Two of the warriors fell on it with large knives, hacking at the boar's shoulders to cut the legs away. "DOAN FINS MEEINN!"

"No, whoa, whoa, whoa," Olafson called out to them.

Saya wasn't sure she had ever heard his voice before, beyond '*aten*' and '*dranken*' and whimpering. It was a crude voice.

"Let's get it right," Olafson said. "God wants it right. Listen to me: 'OH GIVE ME LAND, LOTS OF LAND,'" he sang out loudly. He paused, the cannibals waited, he resumed. "UNDER STARRY SKIES ABOVE," he continued. He put his hand on the elder's shoulder, smiled, and waved his hands around as if he was conducting music. "DON'T FENCE ME IN."

*It was the chant, the war chant. 'Don't fence me in.'* Saya wondered what it meant.

The elder bowed. The hunters bowed. A Sawi girl trudged out from the same hut and across the yard to the fire pit. The elder said something to her, she bowed and lowered her head, then stood next to Olafson, who put a meaty palm around her shoulder and publicly hugged her. The women looked away.

"Why Krimma," the elder said.

"No," Olafson said back to him. "'*White Christmas!*'" He thumped himself on the chest and said it again, slowly, as if by speaking loudly and slowly the cannibals could understand English. "I'm White Christmas." He waited while the elder bowed to him. The cannibals didn't laugh. "White Christmas!"

Saya looked on as the girl who Olafson had clamped to him with his hand looked away in shame. The direction in which she looked was directly at Saya, who was staring at Olafson from a thicket of brush and trees on the forest side of the totem pole. The girl's eyes rounded, she focused them, she saw Saya, her head jerked up, and all the cannibals followed her gaze. They saw her, too, hiding behind a tree, and jumped to their feet. Then Saya was seized from behind. A strong hand covered her mouth. She struggled, failed, and then was lifted off her feet and carried away.

# Chapter 18

Olafson named the girl Tryck, something of an homage to his Swedish roots and also to his clumsy delight in squeezing her in the dark. She named him 'Kapala,' or 'head,' not in the sense of revering him so much as in the sense of wanting to see his head on one of the village poles. Olafson tended to slap her when she called him 'Kapala' instead of 'White Christmas'. Tryck didn't slap him back; she did hope that the village hunters would catch the trespasser, link the intruder to Olafson in some way, and eat both of them.

Tryck did not share the village's view of the god box. Olafson had an elaborate ceremony for the cannibals, making them bow while he connected the wires and switches and hand-cranked the generator, then leading them in God-in-the-box singing, thus instructing them in ways to hunt, to practice love routines, and to feed him.

He had a somewhat different ceremony for Tryck, which consisted of grabbing her in the dark, squeezing her with his meaty hands, and turning the radio music low enough that only they could hear it, then flopping on top of her in a clumsy rutting ritual that she found boring and ugly. It was for this reason that she slowly but surely had begun to cook pitohui feathers into his daily forest porridge.

Olafson rolled off her and wheezed a bit, his quick rush of pleasure fading while he caught his breath and stared up into the dark, singing along with the radio. "The birds are singin', for me and my gal. The bells are ringin', for me and my gal..." He sang because, in the dark, he imagined that Tryck really was Suzy Kapuli, the Hawaiian girl who had introduced him to amore. Tryck was thicker than Suzy, that was true, and didn't moan, "Oh, oh, sailor, I love you," or grab him by the ears, not the way Suzy did, that also was true. But, Olafson could close his eyes and remember how good his life had been back in Pearl Harbor before...

He did remember the before part. Before he washed ashore. Before the typhoon. Before he jumped ship from *Renegade*. Before he had been tossed in the brig. Before the Higgins boat crew ratted on him. Before Bart Sullivan was thrown overboard. Before Lieutenant Beach came on board *Renegade* and brought with him the newspaper story that reported that Suzy was a Japanese spy. Before Olafson had tried to murder Bart Sullivan on the beach. Before Bart Sullivan had double-crossed him. Before Bart Sullivan used the stencil machine in the clerk's office to counterfeit requisition forms so that Olafson could get some detonators. Before he, Olafson, promised Suzy he would get her some explosive detonators that would make really loud firecrackers for her family's traditional Hawaiian party. He tried to remember before any of that, back to when he and Suzy did what he and Tryck now did, not in a bamboo hut but in the creaky bed of a cheap hotel a block from the Black Cat Dance Club in Honolulu, where he had met Suzy. Before giving Suzy a fortune in dance cards. Before Bart Sullivan had counterfeited hundreds of Black Cat dance cards on the stencil machine.

Before Bart Sullivan.

*And look at me now*, he moaned to himself. *Stuck here in the got dum jungle with a bunch of savages.* He moaned again, then grabbed Tryck on her bottom and squeezed. *Mebbe it ain't too bad*, he thought. *Being a got ain't the worst.*

He flipped Tryck onto her back again, experiencing the simultaneous pangs of sexual desire and, slightly higher up, in his innards, the first pangs of forest mush that Tryck had poisoned with pitohui toxins. For her part, Tryck moaned as well, rolling onto her back again to endure her tribal duty to rut with Olafson. Olafson pinned her on her back to start, at the same moment feeling a mild cramp and heave in his gut.

Neither of them noticed that the music on the god box radio had stopped, as it would do when the hand-cranked battery wound down, and as it also would do if Tryck's toe unknowingly flicked the switch from 're-ceive' to 'transmit.'

---

At the Dutch camp on a different part of the island, Captain Van Muis looked out over the northern cliff and confirmed that Private Boer had indeed seen a signal lamp out at sea. A series of dots and dashes quickly beamed across the midnight ocean and stopped.

"What do you think, Boer?" he asked. They huddled behind a growth of bikkia shrubs.

"I'm pretty sure it's English. Not so sure what it says. One word is 'island': dot dot, dot dot dot." He spelled it out. "Then 'SOS'. What do you want me to do?"

"Do? Nothing. It could be a Japanese trick; if you answer, they know where we are." Van Muis didn't like the idea of telling anyone that his resistance fighters were hiding on the north side of the island.

"Sir? Don't you think he knows where we are? Why would he be sending us Morse codes by signal lamp if he didn't think we're here?"

Not for the first time Van Muis regretted the loss of the field radio. There was, to be sure, a backup system to communicate with Section 22; if the resistance failed to send a coded radio signal to the control group for more than a week, Van Muis was to send Boer by boat all the way to Nampali to hand deliver a message to the coast watchers who would, in turn, memorize it, eat it, and verbally pass it up the chain until it reached Manokwari. If the resistance went for a month without sending or replying to a signal and Manokwari didn't receive anything from the coast watchers, Section 22 was to send someone out to the island to find out what had gone wrong with its local resistance team. It had now been almost six weeks.

"Maybe it's Control, from Section 22, come to check on us," Boer said, hopefully. Boer wanted to be checked on; he and Corporal Kluit, once trapped between a Japanese patrol and a cannibal hunting party, had hidden the radio in case they were captured. The dangers disappeared, but so did the radio.

Van Muis had ordered the team to scour the island all the way to the nutmeg plantations and west to Port Haru with the forlorn hope of finding it. After a week, he decided to send Boer to Nampali to confess to Section 22 that they had lost it. Boer's little boat crashed on a hidden reef a hundred yards offshore, below the cliff, and he barely made it back to land. Then, a few nights ago, Morse code messages began to appear at night from a lamp out in the ocean.

"If Section 22 sent someone to find us and we don't answer it they won't know we're here. Sir." *Here, hiding like rats, running out of food and supplies, stuck on this god-forsaken island, waiting for the Nips to catch us if the cannibals don't,* Boer thought. The lamp signaled again.

"Dot. Dash. Dot. Dot." Pause. "Dot. Dash. Dash. Dot. 'L. A.'" Boer repeated it to Van Muis until he had spelled out the word. "Landing, sir. Oh, shit!"

"What's the matter, Boer? What do you mean 'oh shit?' What is landing?"

"Landing, sir. It's English for *landen,* sir. Landing. They're landing!"

"Who's landing, Boer?" Van Muis picked up his binoculars and peered out to sea. There was no landing fleet. The north side of the island would have been the worst possible place for anyone to land, the very reason why Section 22 had chosen it as a redoubt. The signal started back up.

"Dot dot dot. Dash. Dot dash dot. It's another SOS, sir. Has to be English, but he spelled it wrong."

They waited for the signal lamp to repeat the SOS. The signal was not repeated.

"What was the first signal, Boer?"

"Island. SOS."

"Did he spell it right? The SOS?" Boer thought about it a moment, then agreed that SOS had been spelled correctly. "Aren't they supposed to repeat it?"

They quietly acknowledged that something didn't add up: SOS spelled correctly, then a warning of an island landing on an island that couldn't be landed on, at least not where they were hiding, then SOS spelled incorrectly.

"My mistake, sir. It's not SOS. It's 'strip'."

"What does that mean, strip?" Boer didn't know. Another word lit up across the water.

"Dot dot dot." Pause. "Dot dash dot dot. 'S. L. A. V.' I think it's slave, sir. Or slaves." Boer waited for Von Muis to acknowledge. "Dot dot dash dot." Pause. "Dash dot dot." Boer read them off. "In dancers, sir."

"In dancers? I N D A N C I..."

"Oops. G, sir, not c. Sorry."

"In danger, Boer. It's English."

They put the messages together: Island. SOS. Landing. Strip. Slaves. In. Danger.

"One more, sir."

"Dot dot dot dot." Pause. "Dot." Pause. "Dot dash dot dot." Boer spelled it out. "Help, sir."

"Help?"

"Dash dash. Dot. Me, sir. 'Help me'."

"Help who, Boer?"

Van Muis waited at the edge of the cliff, debating with himself. The messages were not clear. None of them comported with Section 22 protocol, particularly since they weren't coded. But, put together, it was possible, just possible, that someone was doing what his team was supposed to be doing, spying on the Japanese on Ambon. He considered his choices and their likely consequences: a reply by lamp would announce his position to an unknown someone out at sea. If the signals were Japanese tricks, a reply in code would give them clues. But a reply in the clear would violate Section 22 orders. And, regardless, any reply by lamp could let a Japanese patrol locate them.

"Boer, stand by." Van Muis pondered, then ordered. "One word reply, Boer." Boer raised his head and opened his mouth to protest, but Van Muis held up his hand to stop him from arguing. "In code." If it was Section 22, code was the only way to communicate. If it was not Section 22, heaven help them. "This is the word."

Boer coded it, then showed it to Van Muis, who agreed that it was correct. Boer uncased his signal lamp and flashed a single word:

"Identity?"

Then they sat down to gaze out at the ink-black ocean where the Morse code had come from, and to wait for the reply. No reply came. When sunrise came Van Muis was still staring out to sea. There was no boat. They studied the bottom of the cliff, where the tide was running out. The beach was undisturbed by boat, footprint, or any other evidence of human activity. It was as if there had been no signal in the night.

———

Lieutentant Tanaka Rikugun-Chui compared the evening report of the day before to the physical evidence in front of him: more *surēbu* had reported for duty this morning than had been fit for duty at the end of yesterday. Sergeant Batsu, his new sergeant, stood at attention, waiting for Tanaka to

order the prisoners back to the runway to resume making the surface sufficiently hard and compact for the emperor's airplanes to take off and land.
Tanaka looked again at the report.

"April 13, 1945: The Emperor's *surēbu* loaded 8,000 kilos of building material into pavement rollers and compacted an area of the runway
on Mount Salahutu..." it started. "...Konsutorakuta Oshira discovered that
the new surface was not level and instructed Sergeant Batsu to punish the
*surēbu* for sabotage..." Then, "Five infirm *surēbu* stopped working and were
humanely taken to the infirmary. One hundred twenty *surēbu* returned to
compound."

He questioned Batsu: "And one hundred twenty-*four surēbu* reported
for work this morning, Sergeant?"

"Yes, Lieutenant. Four *surēbu* recovered from their illnesses in the
night and are fit for duty, sir. And one died."

Tanaka ordered Batsu to form the skeletal prisoners into ranks and
files, then took the unprecedented step of inspecting them, row by row. He
looked at their faces, their eyes, their pitiful arms and hollow cheeks, walking past every man. He then made an about face and inspected the wretched
nutmeg farmers and colonial merchants again, this time from behind. He
saw nothing to explain how four of them had survived the beatings.

"March them to work, Sergeant."

"*Hai*, Lieutenant Rikugun-Chui!" Batsu commanded four privates to
prod the prisoners to pick up the tools and roll the wheelbarrows, and to
march out of the compound toward Mount Salahutu.

Tanaka returned to the junior officers' quarters to compose his morning report but, for the first time, was uncertain how to do so. Never since
the Army had captured the Dutch colonists on the island had he begun a
morning report in which more prisoners showed up for work in the morning than had returned from work the evening before. Something was wrong.
He began to write the prescribed words:

"April 14, 1945: The Emperor's *surēbu* have volunteered to increase
the productivity to compensate for the act of sabotage that violent *surēbu*
criminals attempted yesterday and will today load 16,000 kilos of building
material into pavement rollers...."

He lifted his pen. Oshira had ordered Sergeant Batsu to correct the
*surēbu* for their sabotage. Five *surēbu* survived the correction. *Yet four of the*

*five criminal surēbu resumed work this morning*, Tanaka thought. *How is that possible?*

He had missed something. Something had happened, something with the *surēbu*. He would be expected to explain to the commandant why seven of his *surēbu* had attempted to sabotage the runway, why he, Lieutenant Rikugun-Chui, had not been present at the work site when it happened, and how four of the criminal *surēbu* not only had survived the engineer's punishment but had actually returned to work this morning. Such an explanation would be difficult.

Ever since that bitter day when he had stood before the board of inquiry and the commandant had ordered that, "each day you will search for the missing rifle, the bayonet, and the ammunition," that Mr. Moto had lost when the *ningen* took him, Tanaka had worked twice as hard, three times as hard, to push his *surēbu* to build more of the runway than the others. While they worked he personally climbed around ridge lines, through rain-washed gullies and thick jungle, looking for a single rifle and one bayonet. *And ammunition*, he bitterly reflected. *As I was doing yesterday when the surēbu sabotaged the flat runway.*

There could be only one greater shame than for his *surēbu* to have rebelled while he was absent, and that greater shame was that *surēbu* had survived a correction. Tanaka expected to be called to the commandant to confess his shame, then stripped of his lieutenancy. He had sacrificed everything to the Emperor, yet one weak *chojin*, a cowardly sergeant, some criminal *surēbu*, and a harsh commandant would make his sacrifices meaningless.

*How had four surēbu survived?*

Tanaka left the unfinished morning report on the desk and walked to the infirmary.

"I am Lieutenant Tanaka Rikugun-Chui." The hospital chief bowed. "Five *surēbu* were brought here last night. Tell me their treatment."

The hospital chief told him that the five suffered from the disease of bleeding from cuts on their backs and shoulders. One of them bled from the disease of a cut on his head. The treatment had consisted of wiping off the blood. None had been given medicine, food, or water, as the emperor's physicians had observed that these did not cure patients of the disease of bleeding from beatings.

"The Emperor's physicians were correct, Lieutenant; this was the proper treatment. Four of the diseased *surēbu* left the hospital this morning, on foot, and returned to their teams of fellow workers."

Tanaka considered this information. He, too, had learned that providing food, water, or medicine directly to *surēbu* was a waste of the emperor's food, water, and medicine.

"And the one *surēbu* who did not report to work this morning?"

"His disease was too great, Lieutenant. His illness bled until he died." The hospital chief bowed again.

"Where were the diseased *surēbu* treated last night, before they returned to their work?" Tanaka asked. The hospital chief showed him the single pallet where they all had been laid out. It was a flat platform made of poles, elevated a meter or so above the concrete slab. There was a stain on the floor beneath it.

"Where the one *surēbu* died, Lieutenant." The hospital chief bowed. Tanaka gazed at the spot; it was disgusting. A rat scampered across the floor, snagged a single grain of rice, and scampered away.

Tanaka left. He returned to his desk and resumed the chore of writing his report. He did not mention that he had inspected the slaves; they were beneath the dignity of being inspected. To explain why he had done so would not be soldierly and would likely make the commandant even more disdainful of the young lieutenant. He reviewed the numbers again, signed the report, folded it into the proper form and left it for the courier to collect.

Tanaka gazed through the window toward the prisoner compound and, beyond, to Mount Salahutu. He felt neither pride in the runway nor hope for what it would do for the emperor. Months had passed since the last fleet of battleships and cruisers had steamed past the islands. The official reports were that the Imperial Navy had won a great victory over many American ships; the unofficial report was that many American ships had been destroyed in the typhoon. Tanaka decided to ask his battalion commander to recommend him for transfer to a combat battalion in the Philippines; Tanaka also knew that there would be no such recommendation until he had removed the stain that Mr. Moto had left on his record. He put on his field jacket, buckled his officer's strap belt and holster, and left the depressing office to walk to the equally depressing runway.

*They did not look different*, he thought. *They looked this morning the way they looked yesterday, and the day before: skinny, hollow, angry, but not dying, not enough to keep them from work. In fact,* he reflected, *they looked exactly like they looked since the last wave of surēbu died a month ago.*

Then it hit him: they did look exactly the same. They did not look worse, as they should have. He began to jog toward the runway. He was stopped by the courier.

"Lieutenant, sir, you must come to the castle."

"The castle?" The castle was to be avoided. The castle was where Mr. Moto was found strung up at the main gate, where the post command offices were installed, where his board of inquiry had left him in shame. "I am going to the runway to supervise the..."

"Excuse me, Lieutenant, sir. The company commander has told me that you must hear something. In the communications office." He paused. "An allied radio, sir."

Tanaka reluctantly changed course to walk to the castle. He crossed the parade ground, walked through the stone archway at the rear of the castle, then across the courtyard to the command offices.

*The surēbu should be worse now than a month ago,* he reflected. He entered the communications office. *Not the same. Not better. Worse.*

A crowd of officers were laughing at an allied broadcast on the direction finding radio. *I have no time for laughing at enemy broadcasts. I must look at the prisoners.* A particularly loud burst of laughter erupted. His company commander elbowed Tanaka in the ribs.

"Listen," he said. "They're *kuso!*" He leered and made an obscene gesture with his fingers and pointed at the radio. "Listen."

"Sszzszs pop buzz Oh Suzy Suzy bzzz..."

The men laughed. The signal faded. The technician rotated the direction finding antenna.

"Oh oh Kapala sszz pop buzz... OOH." A female voice, less enthusiastic than the male voice, then a slap of hand on skin. "Luv oo Why Krimma. SSZZ Buzzz Ooh ooh."

Everyone laughed.

"Listen, Tanaka. The technician says the radio is on the island!"

*How could the surēbu sustain their body weight on rice gruel and slave labor?* he thought. An uneasy suspicion had begun to form in Tanaka's brain: *the surēbu are eating something.* He thought of the shrubs that lined the runway, the quarry, the road that led from the prisoner compound to the mountain. *Berries? Cane? Sandal fruit? It isn't the season for sandal fruit.*

"Lieutenant Rikugun-Chui!"

*Cuscus possums?* He thought. *It would take a lot of possums to feed prisoners for a month.*

"Lieutenant!" Tanaka looked up; the post commandant was speaking to him. "Lieutenant. You were responsible for the occupation of the plantations and villages in the center of the island, yes?" Tanaka replied that he was. "You know the island well, Lieutenant? The highlands? North of the Bintuni?" Tanaka said that he believed that he did. "There is an allied radio transmitting from there, Lieutenant. The language is gutter, but it can only be the criminal Dutch resistance." Tanaka acknowledged that it must be so. "Your captain requests that I permit you to lead a patrol to find the radio, Lieutenant."

*They must be getting more food,* Tanaka thought. *Real food, like rice. Where would the surēbu get rice?*

"Captain Samura will detail men to you. You will form a patrol and land it on the island near the mouth of the Bintuni, then lead it into the jungle. You will locate the radio and capture the criminal resistance on the island, and..."

"Sir! I have it!" Tanaka blurted out. "I know what it is." Tanaka gathered himself up to his full height and smiled. "It's rice, sir!"

"Rice?" the commandant answered? He wondered if it was a mistake to give the lieutenant a chance to redeem himself. "What are you talking about, Lieutenant?" He crossed his arms and glared.

"Sir, I know why the *surēbu* aren't dying." Tanaka had a crazed look in his eyes. "Someone is smuggling extra food to the prisoners!"

The commandant turned to Captain Samura to order that he remove Lieutenant Rikugun-Chui from the room. Before he could do so, Tanaka finished his statement.

"In the infirmary, sir," Tanaka answered. "The *surēbu* infirmary. I saw it. This morning." He waited. The commandant stared at him, incredulous. The other officers were stunned. *Lieutenant Rikugun-Chui had lost his mind,* they believed. He continued. "With my own eyes, sir. I saw it—a rat ran across the floor. It snatched a grain of rice!"

Tanaka smiled, as if he had just completed an intricate crossword puzzle or broken a vexing enemy code. The commandant turned red. Captain Samura turned pale. Then the speakers popped and buzzed again. The officers stopped to listen. A voice came through the airwaves.

"Got dumb savage!" the radio blurted out. Another slap. "I'm *White Christmas*. And it's 'Big boy, I love you ooh ooh!' Say it!" Slap. "Owww!" came a woman's pained cry.

And then a different sound, a sound like *hakike*. A sound like someone who was vomiting up his jungle porridge.

# Chapter 19

A wet paw clamped over Saya's mouth, another pinned her arms from behind, and she watched helplessly as she was carried through the jungle. The *ningen* dodged left and right, jumping over tree roots and snakes, but struggle as she did, Saya could not break away from him. They fled as the cannibals' war song curdled the air behind them.

"IGOT SPURZAT!" the elder shouted, running close behind.

A dozen enraged Sawi warriors followed him, spears high, bellowing, "ZINGL ANGL ZINGLE!"

"IGOT SPURZAT!"

"ZINGL ANGL ZINGLE!"

The cannibals were almost close enough to throw their spears. Saya's mind raced with thoughts of what came next: a spear in the back, a shout, her body hitting the ground, a machete in the air, her head stuck on a pole, her skin flayed for the village cook pot. The *ningen* ran, carrying her past the water pit trap where she had left Olafson so long ago, past the sacred grounds, running for higher ground and the cold stream that flowed into the Bintuni, her familiar landmarks passing by. She sensed that the *ningen* was tiring.

"IGOT SPURZAT ZINGL ANGL ZINGLE!"

The first spear thudded into a tree next to her head. The *ningen* dodged left. Another spear zipped past on the right. A third spear flew by and the *ningen* leapt into the shallow stream. Then they began to fall.

"AZ IGO RIDY MURLY LONG!"

Spears pierced the water, missed, then more spears. The *ningen* pulled her through the stream, bouncing them against rocks and branches until the rushing water dragged them over a steep waterfall and dumped them far below in the deep pond. Then they sank, sank, sank, and finally touched bottom.

The *ningen* held her tightly and kicked to the edge of the pond, surfaced, took its paw off her mouth, flailed a moment, then pulled her underwater again. She choked, coughed out water, and struggled until the *ningen* stuck a reed in her mouth, a hollow reed. Gasping, she sucked in the air, breathed through the straw.

A thought flickered through her dying mind: *I can breathe through the reed.* A second thought. *It knows there are reeds. It knows about the waterfall.* Another thought. *It knows this is my bathing pond. It knows....* Then the cannibals arrived, their spears jabbing, poking, probing the water. Saya stopped struggling.

*Whatever will happen, will happen,* she thought, and closed her eyes. *It's out of my control.* She relaxed and let the *ningen* hold her, hidden from the cannibals until her mind drifted away, into a jumble of vague memories. Her search for Olafson. The typhoon. The Japanese at Port Haru. The hated *chojin*. Her family's nutmeg trees and clove bushes. There were her pigs, the picket fence, the chickens, the root garden. Saya let herself go completely and was rewarded by the comfort of her own bed, where she listened to her mother and her brother in the next room, talking, planning her father's birthday, planning a day in the village, planning to walk Saya to school. They were right there, all of them, she could touch them. Everything was all right.

Everything except the *ningen*. *I've seen it before,* her mind whispered. *At the plantation. A shadow, a shape, something in the trees at the edge of the farm.* Her last thought was to realize one thing: *That's when I began to sense I was being watched.* Then it all began to fade, her family, her farm, the *ningen*, all of them, their edges and shapes dissolving, their colors fading, then—nothing.

Saya awoke to find herself in her cave behind the waterfall, a place known only to her, her place of safety where she bathed, hid, dried her few clothes, a cave that she had used since fleeing Port Haru two years before. Her hair was still wet, and her clothes. But, apart from a bit of soreness where the *ningen* had gripped her arms, she found nothing to suggest that she had been touched in any way, at least not any physical way. Then Saya began to take stock of her life.

*I've lost my family, their plantation, and my hostage. And, now,* she realized, *I'm not even invisible anymore.* The cannibals had seen her. The *ningen* had seen her. Her ability to simply disappear in plain sight was gone. She sat through the night, thinking.

She waited in her cave all the next day, never once looking out through the waterfall to see if the cannibals were there. In the end, it came down to one false step. *I shouldn't have gone past the totem poles, trespassing into the Sawi village, to get a closer look at my fat sailor.*

The implications took shape. If she couldn't make herself invisible, she couldn't safely hunt for food, or dig her garden or, most especially, kidnap her sailor back from the cannibals. If she couldn't hunt or dig her garden, she would starve. If she couldn't re-capture Olafson, she had no bait for the Japanese. If she had no bait for the Japanese, she had no plan to seize Tanaka and Mr. Moto or to bring her family home.

The solution was obvious.

---

"Signal, sir," Boer reported. Van Muis perked up.

"Coded?" he asked.

"Dash. Dot dot dot dot. Space. Dot. Hmmm." Boer jotted down the dots and dashes and announced his translation. "Six, sir." Then, "Dash dot dash dot. Dot dash. Cans, sir. Six cans."

Van Muis flipped through the months-old decode book; 'six cans' was not in it.

"'G', Sir," Boer continued. Dash dash dot dot. "'A roo,' sir. Six kangaroos." Boer beamed at his work. "He got the 'c' wrong, though.' It should have been a 'k'. Kangaroo, with a 'k'."

'Six kangaroos' also was not in the codebook. Van Muis doubted that the code was current. Maybe the message wasn't in code. Maybe, just maybe, Boer had made a mistake.

"I don't think it's Section 22, Boer. Maybe it's our little friend. Maybe it's in English."

Boer went back to work.

"Dot dot dot dot. Dot dash." Boer jotted away and announced the first word. "'Have', sir. I think it's Dutch. Now, dash dot dash dash." He worked on the next word. "'Your,' sir. Is that English?"

Van Muis thought that maybe 'your' was English, and re-thought the message. *'Have' wasn't a mistake; that's Dutch for garden. Or maybe it was 'haven'?* No. *Garden,* he thought. Secret codes never referred to havens. He worked it out. *Six kangaroos have your garden.* "Oh, shit!"

Van Muis raced down the path to the resistance fighters' camp. His sentry challenged him, he barked at the sentry and told him to get Sergeant Kaas on the double.

"Signal, Kaas. Urgent. I think there's a Japanese patrol on the island. Six men, in the jungle. Or maybe it's six patrols, the message wasn't clear. Pick two volunteers; send one to Port Haru, one to the fishing village down by the mangrove swamp. You, personally, head for Bintuni Village. If there's a Japanese patrol, you three have got to find it. Now. Go!"

He watched the men rush away in the dark, worried that he should have sent two-man teams in case one of the patrols needed to send a runner back. *No time for second guessing,* he thought. *I've got to send a reply.*

He climbed back up the cliff and went into his dugout, then began to work out a coded reply. 'Patrols sent to all points. Will report enemy sighting.' *If it's Section 22 Morsing us, they'll recognize the old code.* He pondered whether to ask Section 22 for re-supply, coded that message as well, then decided it was too much. *Out she goes.* He handed the coded words to Boer and told him to send the reply.

"Yes, sir. Wait. Look, sir."

Another signal from the sea.

"Dot dash dot. Dot dash. Dash dot dot. Dot dot. Dash dash dash."

"Radio, sir."

"Radio?" Van Muis thought the world had gone crazy. "No one would ever use the word radio in a code." *No one who was sending in code,* he realized. He read the notes again. "Six kangaroos garden radio? It's gibberish. It's a trap." He ordered Boer to stand by, then lifted his binoculars and peered out to sea in the ink-dark night. There, at the far end of his sight, was a boat, a tiny open boat. *It has to be a trap. Six kangaroos.* "Boer, read it to me again."

"S. I. X." Boer paused. "Hmmm. Maybe he meant dash first, then dot dot dot, sir. 'T' and 'h'. "'The', Boer said." Not 'six'. 'The'. My mistake."

Van Muis thought back. '*The* kangaroos' wasn't much of an improvement over '*six* kangaroos'; Japanese patrols were Japanese patrols, however many and wherever they were. "Was there maybe a mistake on 'k' also, Boer?

You said 'c' should have been 'k'?"

There was. 'C' was 'c'.

They worked it out. It was not coded. It was English.

"The cannibals have your radio."

Van Muis was stunned. His first thought was to recall Kaas, then or-ganize a fire team to go after the cannibals and re-capture their radio. *If we can find the right cannibals,* he thought.

His second thought was, *Who's out there who could possibly know we lost our radio?* Then, *And who would know that the cannibals have it?*

He peered out to sea again. The boat was gone.

---

Saya climbed up the vine wall behind the waterfall, then waited to see whether the parrots or the kookaburras scattered; when the birds returned to the branches she concluded that no human was near and began to make her way through the rainforest. Her own familiar paths were easy enough to follow but, until two days ago, there hadn't been any signs that anyone but she had used them. Now, moving quietly and only in the shadows, she picked her way through the rainforest and looked for what she was sure was there. After less than fifty yards she found it: a small branch, waist high, was bent. The branch had been disturbed by something taller than she, not by much, but enough so that if in a moment of carelessness she had bent it, it would have been knee-high or thigh-high on her. And, it was bent going away from the waterfall, not toward it, and so recently that she knew it was neither her nor the Sawis.

A hundred yards further on she found a vine that had been wedged underneath another vine, shoved there by a foot, not by a hoof or a paw or the antics of a tree kangaroo. Beyond that, and continuing to the north and west, she found more minute proofs that the *ningen* had used her secret trail not only to follow her, but also to leave her. A rock pressed into the leaves, a dab of mud on a dry fern. A button.

She was more angry than surprised when the trail led to her redoubt. It was true that her treehouse was inside the vague territory between the village lands of the central island Sawis and the northerly cannibal tribal lands. She had chosen the location because neither tribe felt impelled to hunt there out of concern of starting up a war with the other. At the same time, the northern tribes wouldn't care what happened to her so wouldn't care if the Sawis destroyed her secret clearing. She left the hidden path and entered her forest home.

The Sawis had already been there. She checked her traps; all had been destroyed. Her meager garden was wrecked, her remaining chickens and the last piglet taken. Tell-tale signs of water stakes and tree snares blocked every conceivable route to the treehouse. The cannibals had destroyed everything that was hers. But, unlike the *ningen* using her secret trail, the cannibals had made no effort to conceal their work. She said goodbye to her scattered treehouse and pilfered garden and resumed the search for the *ningen*.

The trail led to Port Haru. One bent twig and footprint at a time, Saya followed it until the clues veered, beyond Bintuni Village, then westward toward the island's coast.

The further the trail led, the less she understood who had snatched her away from the cannibals and had done so without making the slightest sound. That ruled out Van Muis and the Dutch if for no other reason than their inability to walk anywhere on the island without sending flocks of birds out of the trees and dozens of snakes and possums fleeing. It also ruled out the other tribes; if they had wanted Saya as a hostage to barter with her Sawis, they would have kept her. The same was true of the Japanese and their Malay dogboys; if they had rescued her, they would have her now, probably tied to a bed somewhere on Ambon. The clues ended when the old commercial road turned from the upland path to lead down the escarpment to the ruins of Port Haru, facing Ambon Island across the strait.

Saya searched for hours, creeping through the trees that flanked the dirt road, studying the debris that the typhoon had left of Port Haru, retreating into erosion gullies on the hillside above the beach where she had looked for Olafson and seen the fevered activity across the water at Ambon fortress.

*The boat! There was a boat on the beach. Then the boat was gone*, she thought. *I watched from over there*, looking about a mile away, *and felt it!* 'It' was the feeling of being watched. She looked again at the shingle beach where the little fishing boat had rested on the shore in the night, then began to study the location. *The only way someone could have gotten to that boat was from the sea.* No one had motored up to the boat and the tide had been strong enough to make swimming up to it from the sea very hard.

*That, or by walking across the strand, from that direction.* She studied the landscape between the beach and Port Haru, then beyond to the cliffs where the island faced the open sea. She slipped back into the cover of the trees, made her way back to the road, and returned to the last bent twig she had found. She looked around once more, then turned into the tall tree ferns and dogbane shrubs and struck out for the cliffs. The clues led her to a hidden cove near the northwest corner of the island.

The *ningen* had made a nice home for itself on an islet fifty yards off shore. Covered by thick mystica trees that grew out of the coral and limestone, the islet looked like hundreds of others that dotted the reefs alongside the island, except that it had a slender opening in a cleft of the rock that would be underwater at high tide. Saya watched for an hour, then swam out to the islet, quietly pulled herself onto a hidden rock shelf and studied the cave's opening. The small boat she had seen was drawn up inside the cave. Its opening was covered enough that someone could pass within a few feet and not see it. Inside the boat there was a faded life ring like the one that Olafson had abandoned on the beach when he first set foot on the sand. Saya listened, heard nothing, and waded into the *ningen*'s lair.

Its cave was clean, neat, and dry. The den was not large, room enough for a straw pallet and three jute sacks imprinted with Japanese markings and filled with rice. There was a crude hearth and an iron cook pot. She knew better than to open the sacks but the cook pot would leave no trace of her lifting the lid. The cook pot was filled by more than a hundred thick, round cooked rice balls. *What,* she wondered, *did it do with so much food?* She wanted to eat one so badly that she shook, but if the *ningen* could track her to her most secret place behind the waterfall and into the Sawi hunting grounds, then the *ningen* could count rice balls.

By stepping between the rice sacks she found a sliver of light in the rocks through which someone could see all the way across the straight to Ambon. Behind one bag there was a Japanese rifle, an ammunition pouch, and a bayonet. Behind another there was a long handled shovel. A flashlight, mirror, and batteries were hidden underneath the third bag. Shadows began to creep across the hidden doorway; it was time to go.

Saya waded out to the rock cleft and saw that the tide was coming in. She studied the *ningen*'s islet, the shore fifty yards away, the water approaches on either side, and dived in to swim back across the coral lagoon.

Without a sound she waded out of the water and onto a rock shelf that would leave no trace of her wet feet. A slight wind blew over the strand and made her shiver as she hurried back to the fern where she had hidden her ragged sandals.

The ferns weren't disturbed but her sandals were. A small scrap of paper was stuck in the thongs.

She stared at the folded page fluttering in the late afternoon breeze. Slowly, quietly, she turned to look in every direction. The *ningen* wasn't there. Then she unfolded the note.

"We're alive. I hope you're safe. This man helps us."

The handwriting was cramped, the penciled letters dim, but there was no doubt that the note had been written by her father. She had not had any word of her family from the day the Japanese took them to Ambon. Saya began to tremble. The note had been written recently; the paper was neither yellow with age, nor damp, or faded. She read it again. Her family was alive.

Saya hid the note in a tree, then went back to the lagoon just as the last bit of evening sun sank into the ocean. There, disappearing in the gathering dark, was the boat, the *ningen* rowing it quietly around the northwest corner of the island, out to the open sea.

# Chapter 20

"Mama's little baby loves shortnin', shortnin'."

Tryck hummed along, happily believing with all her heart that The Andrews Sisters were the best of the god box's messengers. "Mama's little baby loves shortnin' bread." She did her best imitation of them with clear, crisp unintelligible tones while she fed Olafson poisoned porridge, one ladle at a time.

His flat gaze peered up as Tryck stuck more pitohui mush into his drooping mouth. He opened up, obedient, and waited while she ladled more of the thickened gruel through his fading lips. Tryck closed his mouth to make him swallow, and smiled, the bones in her ear lobes bobbing up and down as she nodded approvingly at his big bite.

"Trcyk, be a goot girl," Olafson moaned. He trembled with fever and had trouble seeing clearly. He vaguely wished he hadn't shown Tryck how to crank the radio and turn the dials, a poor decision he had made when, after she began to show some skill at imitating The Andrews Sisters, she withheld sex and mush until he gave in.

"Bring me some water." She smiled and offered another ladle. "No, not food. Water." He tried to lift his hand to mime taking a drink. "Tirsty."

"Tirsty," she answered. She stuck the ladle back into the mush and smiled. The pitohui feather toxins had acted faster on Olafson than she had expected. She had experimented with other pitohui bits, some skin and bone from one bird she had trapped, a heart from another, but had to stop when her mother caught her skinning one near the cook pot. "*Lahedo kikini! Ua alaia emui tau!*" her mother had snapped at her, to which Tryck thought, yes, indeed, she did want to kill her man.

"Tirsty," she said again, and stuck another ladle of mush into Olafson's mouth. He rolled over and tried to vomit. *Just a few more days,* she thought. She shoved him back onto the pallet, ladled the last few spoons of pitohui mush into Olafson's mouth, then picked up the radio and sneaked out of the hut.

The dark of night didn't slow her down, but the radio did. As strong as she was, and as familiar as she was with every root and bush in the jungle, Tryck nevertheless struggled to carry both the radio and its hand-crank generator. She sneaked out of the village, past the northern totem pole, touched her forehead in honor of the dead grandfather who looked down from it, and lugged the radio into the woods. Hiding it, she connected the wires, cranked the handle, turned on the power switch, and watched as the needles jumped on the meters and the tuning dial illuminated, exactly as Olafson had shown her. Gripped with excitement, she turned the knob in search of The Andrews Sisters. She got nothing.

*Oh,* she thought. *The shiny switch. Push the shiny switch.* Olafson had yelled at her once when he discovered that the shiny switch had been pushed the wrong way. *I must have done it again,* she thought. She pushed it the other way, turned the signal dial again, and God began to speak directly to her.

"...Troops have conquered all of Okinawa except for some holdouts in the..." God had a deep voice that night, which Tryck didn't much care for. She liked it better when God sang, so she dialed again. "...and have raised an American flag over Nuremberg..."

Tryck dialed again, and again, but neither God nor The Andrews Sisters were singing just then. She wondered if there was a secret to the god box that Olafson had hidden from her and considered how she could learn it before she finished him off. She tried one more time, hoping that God's booming voice hadn't carried into the village. She heard a twig snap.

Sato was there, watching her. She stepped in front of the god box.

"What are you doing, Daughter?" he asked. He slapped his machete against his thigh. "Where is Why Krimma? We need him to talk to God. We need to hunt."

"He is *gorore*, Elder," Tryck answered. "A bit *gorore*." Then, with a bit of inspiration, she added, "I think his white men made him *terluka*. He was *terluka* when you found him."

"That is true, Daughter," Sato replied. He remembered that when they had plucked White Christmas out of the stream he had a broken ankle and was covered with bites and scratches. "Why Krimma did stay inside his hut while we fattened him up for *kapala* and *ania.*" A good sacrifice and a good feast. "You must take very good care of Why Krimma, Daughter," he said. "He is God's messenger."

"Yes, Elder," Tryck answered.

"Does your mother help you?" Sato asked. "We can send more mothers to help you, Daughter," he continued. "Or more *kekinis?*"

Tryck thought over the offer of Sato sending more virgins to help make White Christmas healthy. There was some merit to the idea; she suspected that the village women had nominated her to be White Christmas's love girl out of jealousy, because she was pretty, with a nice big belly and sagging breasts, the sort of girl who drew looks from their men and envy from the other *kekinis. Maybe I should stop poisoning him and make a few other girls rut with the slob,* she thought.

"No, Elder," she answered. "He is satisfied with me." She rubbed her belly to assure Sato that White Christmas was well-served. "And I am satisfied with him," she continued. *And when he's dead,* she thought, *only I will know how to crank the god box. I will be the one to dial God's voices.*

She bowed to Sato and hoped that he was persuaded; this was not how she intended for him to learn of her radio skills. She had planned for days how, after Olafson snuffed out, she would show everyone that she could take his place in communicating with God. And, she was sure that White Christmas would make good *kapala*, good *ania*. The idea of Olafson's head on a pole pleased her very much.

Then the god box spoke to them.

"And in the Pacific, a kamikaze dive bomber has struck the American troopship...."

Sato stepped forward, gripped Tryck by the shoulder, and shoved her out of the way. The god- box was perched behind her on a tangle of vines, its needles and dials glowing in the dark.

"...casualties have not been fully determined..." God continued.

"Oh, Daughter!" Sato barked at her. "What have you done?"

———————

Farther north on the island, near the cliffs, Van Muis finished inspecting his troops. It was time to go. The ragged soldiers picked up their rations and rifles, rain capes and spare socks, and waited for the order.

"Move out, men. Quietly."

That the cannibals had their radio had not been enough by itself to make Van Muis start the mission right away. That was delayed until two of Van Muis' scouts returned from looking for either six kangaroos or for six Japanese patrolling the island, finding neither. Sergeant Kaal had gone through the abandoned spice plantations, all the way to Bintuni Village, and back: "No sign of a Japanese patrol anywhere in the north, sir." As for Corporal Witt, he had patrolled to the rocky harbors on the west coast of the island: "No Japanese at Port Haru, sir, or anywhere else on the coast," he reported. "Not likely to be anytime soon, either. There's a merchant ship docked up across the harbor at Ambon." Witt tapped his binoculars to imply that he had been especially successful at spying on a ship anchored over a mile away. "It'll take them days to unload it."

Armed with their reports, Van Muis concluded not only that Boer's translation of six kangaroos in the garden was wrong but also that it was time to take their radio back. That did leave Pee Pants unaccounted for.

"What about Pants Broek?" The last scout, whose name was Van Meer but who everyone called Pee Pants, had not returned. No one wanted to leave Pee Pants behind.

"He's looking for Japs all the way down south to the native fishing village," Van Muis answered. "By the mangrove swamps. We're going in that direction so we'll meet up with Pants Broek when he comes our way or when we get all the way down to him. Sergeant, lead them out."

"Which cannibals are we looking for, sir?" Boer asked. Boer wasn't in a hurry to feud with the cannibals. "There's natives all over the island."

"The ones that have our radio," Van Muis answered. "We know they're not the northern tribe or Sergeant Kaal would have seen them. They aren't on the west coast or Corporal Witt would have seen them." Neither Witt nor Kaal had seen any natives, it was true, but neither Witt nor Kaal had been told to go look for natives and, if they had been told to do so, it was no sure bet that they would have been able to see them. "So, we march to the center, down the river until we find them. Enough! Forward, march!"

The Dutch resistance group thrashed its way single file, down from the cliff, into the upland scrub of thickets and rocky outcrops. After several hours they made it to the remnants of the trade road. By evening they reached the Bintuni River, where Van Muis ordered them to turn south. They chopped and stumbled through the jungle for another half hour and, by good luck rather than design, stopped just before stumbling through the sacred grounds.

"Enough for today, men," Van Muis decreed. "Too dark to go any farther. Kaal? Set up the guard rotations and an outpost. I'm turning in."

The men scattered, some taking up guard positions, others reluctantly creeping into the jungle as outposts, the rest uneasily nesting in the ground roots of the giant candle wood trees, none aware that the northern cannibals had shadowed them from the moment the troops left the road and approached their territory. The cannibals walked unseen past the outposts and between Van Muis's guards, looked at the remainder of the force asleep on the ground, then withdrew to their own stone markers at the entrance to their lands, and waited.

---

Lieutenant Tanaka Rikugun-Chui also contemplated how he would get the Dutch radio. After dark, hidden by the *Jigoku Maru*, Tanaka's launch slipped away from Ambon to motor quietly across the bay, then along the south side of the island.

The commandant had approved his plan. Tanaka had spent the day standing conspicuously on the wharf at Ambon harbor, watching the merchant ship *Jigoku Maru* lumber slowly up to the dock to unload its cargo, certain that by his being so obvious he, too, was being watched.

All that day the soldiers had prodded the *surēbu* into and out of the ship's holds, making them carry hundreds of bags of rice to the warehouses where Tanaka had hidden guards to catch the thief who had been stealing rice for the prisoners. Other *surēbu* unloaded bales of uniforms, shoes, dried fruit, and supplies. More prisoners hoisted oil drums out of the cargo ship and, whipped by their guards to assure that none of the drums rolled into the harbor, carted the oil to a storage yard alongside the main path to Mount Salahu. Ship cranes reached into the *Jigoku Maru* and, slowly but surely, unloaded anti-aircraft guns. The next cargo was a dozen bomb trolleys, followed by hand trucks to tow airplanes onto the flight line. One by one, everything

166

necessary to supply the garrison and fly airplanes on the emperor's new air-strip was taken out of the ship and transported to the staging area on the road to Mount Salahu. Tanaka had watched it all, and by late afternoon, the *Jigoku Maru* had been emptied.

Tanaka was pleased. He had been given the chance to recover from his shame, not only by setting a trap to catch the food thief but also by being given leadership of the patrol to capture the Dutch and their radio. He also smiled because Mr. Moto, out of the infirmary, had been given a last chance and would be on the patrol. And, finally, Tanaka was pleased that the war was going so well, a conclusion he drew from how little food was unloaded and, he thought, less oil delivered than he had assumed would be needed to supply the airplanes that would arrive any day. *If the Emperor sent so little*, he thought, *victory must be in sight!*

Just before twilight another squad of soldiers had arrived from beyond the rice warehouses, leading a gaggle of prisoners onto the quay. Tanaka's squad had marched them to the gangplank of the *Jigoku Maru*, then halted. The frightened prisoners shuffled to a halt, clutching their ragged dresses, pitiful scarves, and each other. Tanaka drew out his sword and pointed up the ramp. The escort saluted, then prodded the women prisoners onto the ship. One by one, they stumbled, trudged, fell, and moved until all of them disappeared into the boat. Tanaka felt alien eyes peering at him from a hiding place and, certain that the hidden thief was watching, smiled.

Then, under cover of the late afternoon shadow and hidden by the large ship, Tanaka had addressed his squad:

"Men," Tanaka announced. "You have been particularly chosen for the next great mission. We will board a launch and motor across to the island. We will go with all stealth to the bay of Bintuni and land in the night. Specialist Kiku will use his equipment to locate the criminal Dutch soldiers hiding on the island. We will find their camp, capture their radio, and destroy them. That is our mission. We will not fail. *Wakuru? Ha!*"

"*Ha!*"

Now, as they neared the fishing village, he ordered the crew to cut the engine and drift up to the primitive dock across from the mangrove swamp. The launch glided silently the last few yards, touched the dock, and held close by as Tanaka's crew disembarked. Once on shore, his path illuminated only by the moon, Tanaka led them away from the bay, through the fishing village, to the river, then uphill toward the jungle. Once inside the cover of the trees, he held up one hand. The men stopped and gathered round him.

"We wait here until first light. You," he pointed to a private, "and you—outposts. Fifty yards upriver, you on the left bank, you on the right. *Wakuru? Ha!*"

"*Ha!*"

"Moto, I post you as rear guard. You must not let anyone leave the fishing village. If anyone has seen us, they must not be allowed to get word up the island that we are here. Do you understand?"

"*Ha!*" Moto accepted his assignment, one both shameful and important, and retreated toward the village.

"The rest of you do not move, or even breathe aloud."

"*Ha!*" The men settled in.

"And Kiku, listen to the radio to see if the criminals are broadcasting."

Kiku put on his ear phones and switched on his direction finding equipment, then began to search for a signal.

---

When Pants Broek heard the launch motor into the bay, he gaped in the dark, then took off as fast as he could to warn Van Muis that the Japanese were coming. He had only gone ten yards before something hit him with enough force to knock him into the mangrove swamp. There, lunging at him, was a monster! Pee Pants leapt, grabbed a low-hanging branch, and pulled himself just clear of the dragon. There he stayed while the Japanese disembarked, marched upriver, and disappeared. Now, his feet dangling dangerously close to the fetid water, Pee Pants leaked from every opening in his body and prayed that the monster would go away. He was still praying when Mr. Moto walked out of the darkness, marched through the village, approached the edge of the swamp, lit a cigarette, turned around and began his patrol.

---

On the north side of the island, far below the cliffs and out in the darkened bay, a single lamp flashed a message: "Dot dot dot. Dash dash dash. Dot dot dot." SOS. "Dot dash dot. Dot dot dash dash dot."

For almost fifteen minutes the lamp signaled that a supply ship had arrived at Ambon and unloaded fuel and antiaircraft guns for the new runway, which was almost completed. When the last word was complete, the signal paused, then resumed.

"Dot dot. Dash dot. Dot dot dash dot...." It was the most complex message the lamp had sent so far. At length the last letter was sent.

"SOS. Japanese removing all women prisoners by same ship. Do not torpedo. SOS."

The lamp waited a half hour, then repeated the signal.

There was no reply.

---

"Where is Why Krimma?" Sato demanded. "Only Why Krimma may touch the god box!" Sato slapped his machete against his thigh and glared at Tryck with all the fury he could muster. "Did he bring the god box here?"

White Christmas did not bring the god box because White Christmas was on death's doorstep back in his hut. Tryck made her decision.

"This life is leaving Why Krimma, Elder," she answered. "But he taught me how to communicate with God and told me to bring the god box to the sacred tree to speak with God." She held her breath; Sato did not cut off her head. "I was reaching for God when you came, Elder."

Sato was skeptical. Then the god box announced, "Marines have captured Shuri Castle near the center of..."

"That is not God, Daughter," Sato said. "God sings. I do not believe that...."

"No, Elder. God has many voices. I will show you." Tryck frantically dialed up God's voices, all of whom sounded like English-speaking news broadcasters, none of whom sang. In the end, she flicked the shiny switch once more. The god box went silent as soon as she changed it from 'receive' to 'transmit.'

"Where is God singing, Daughter?" Sato shouted at her. "Where is Why Krimma? Where is God?"

---

"Sir, I have a signal," Kiku whispered. "Listen." Through the radio came the sound of a whimpering voice. "It is the same woman, Lieutenant. The radio is still there, exactly where we thought it was."

Tanaka smiled.

169

Olafson rolled his face to one side, trying to wipe his numb mouth against the straw of his filthy pallet. He wanted to wake up, but could not, and wanted to stop the nightmare, but could not.

He dreamed that Tryck had forced more of the tart forest porridge into his mouth, then hummed that got dumned song about shortnin'. He had tried to tell her to stop but could only manage to groan the word 'thirsty,' which Tryck had ignored while she carried the radio out of her straw hut. Now the hut seemed even darker, like a shadow, as if someone had come inside it. He hoped that this time it was Suzy and that she had come to help him. Suzy would make the nightmare better. He forced his eyes open to look at her. It wasn't her.

"Not Suzy," Olafson groaned. The darkness, like a shadow, hovered just above him.

"Shh, Chief," the shadow whispered back to him. "Shh. Be quiet."

"Not Tryck," Olafson groaned. Then he did open his eyes, and the nightmare got even worse. *What was he doing in the hut?* "Go away," he muttered. "You're dead."

"Shh," the nightmare shadow whispered back. It put a finger on Olafson's lips, as if it was shushing a child.

"Tryck," he moaned at the finger's touch. "Zat you?" *Not Tryck. Fat black girl. Good screwing.* "Not Suzy." The shadow shushed him again. "Tryck?" he asked. The shadow put one hand under Olafson's head and tried to lift him up. Olafson began to remember where he was and how he got there.

*Oh, yeah,* he dreamed. *The got dumned savages. They fixed my leg. Then they...* Olafson's nightmare reminded him of the cannibals leading him to the cooking pit and arguing about him. He remembered the totem poles, and the heads stuck on top of them. *That old bastard took me in the woods and was going to cut off my...* And Olafson screamed in his sleep.

The shadow clamped a hand on his mouth.

Olafson opened his eyes wide, looked at the shadow, and his dream got even worse.

"Got dumb you," Olafson moaned. "Go away. You're dead. Again."

"Please, Chief," the shadow whispered. "Be quiet. I've got to get you out of here. Before she comes back."

Then the shadow lifted Olafson from his nightmare and carried him away.

# Chapter 21

"Listen, sir." Kiku gave the headphones to Lieutenant Rikugun-Chui, who listened and smiled. "They're still broadcasting, sir. And they haven't moved."

Just before dawn, Tanaka marched his patrol up the Bintuni River to the center of the island. After several hours he didn't need to ask Kiku if the radio was still broadcasting; he could hear it for himself, echoing down the river's rocky banks, music blaring about rum and coca cola.

Tanaka raised his right hand. The patrol stopped. Without a word, he signaled to load rifles and fix bayonets and to follow him. In almost complete silence, the patrol hiked out of the river bed and into the jungle, walking directly toward the sound of the Armed Forces Radio broadcast.

A quarter mile upriver, Van Muis raised his right hand. The bedraggled Dutch troops shuffled to a halt.

"Listen," he said. "Radio! Our radio!" The men perked up when, for the first time in months, they heard the sweet sound of the Billboard Honor Roll of Hits. "Lock and load, men. Fix bayonets. We're going to get our radio back." Van Muis grinned the smile of the overconfident, then thrashed his way into the brush toward his date with The Andrews Sisters.

A quarter mile to the east, at the right side of the rather oblique Japanese-Dutch-Sawi triangle, Sato waited patiently for God to finish speaking to Tryck. He had put his machete down on the ground to make clear to the village's hunters, who had come out at dawn to listen to God, that he was not angry with her.

"Where is Why Krimma?" the hunters asked, seeing only his *kekini* turning the knobs of the god box. "Why Krimma isn't in his hut."

"Why Krimma was *gorore*," Sato told them. "So he taught Daughter to communicate with God." Sato nodded approvingly at Tryck, who had spent the last hours dialing nervously in hope of avoiding a cannibal's fate, occasionally flicking the switch from 'receive' to 'transmit' to demonstrate to Sato that she really could connect to God any time she chose. "Why Krimma is with God."

The hunters accepted Why Krimma's fate without question. What they wanted was to hear God himself.

"Igot spurzat, Daughter," the hunters begged her. They loved I've got Spurs. "Ask God for zingle angle zingle." Hunting songs, such as 'Og imme lan,' also were favorites, but the hunters were still frustrated over the loss of the white woman trespasser and wanted to hear the war chase song.

"Shortnin' shortnin'," Tryck answered them. "That's what God was singing when Why Krimma left to join Him." In truth, Tryck was uneasy about where Olafson actually had gone; if he was no longer in the hut, maybe, she thought, maybe White Christmas really was with God. Maybe she really was anointed to succeed him as the priestess of god box communing. She turned the radio dial in search of spurs that jingled and jangled, and raised the volume, unaware that White Christmas was no more than a few hundred yards away.

———————

A flock of Moluccan hanging parrots burst out of the forest above Saya's head. *Something's walking through the jungle*, she thought. She edged into the shadow of a mangium tree and waited while a medium bush python slithered into the brush and a pair of mating tree kangaroos broke apart and scampered up to the highest limbs. Then she heard the snap of a twig, the soft whish of khaki on leaf, and gasped.

*Where did they come from?* Tanaka's patrol passed within twenty feet of where she hid. There was more: just in front of her, Olafson lay hidden by a thicket of ferns. *Where did he come from?* she asked herself a second time. Saya stared at all of them, holding her breath and ignoring the spiders on her neck while her most hated enemy led his Japanese soldiers toward the radio.

Saya then focused on her long-lost bait, and was surprised again. Olafson lay crumpled on the forest floor and there, cradling his head, was the *ningen*. It looked up at her, smiled, and held a finger to his lips to suggest that even Saya should be quiet. She liked its smile and smiled back in reply. It was clear that the *ningen* was comforting Olafson, why she could not imagine. Olafson looked a lot worse to her than the last time she had seen him, but then the sounds of another snapped twig, another khaki-brushed leaf, and Tanaka's patrol passed them by. The radio started up again.

"In San Francisco, delegates to the United Nations have approved the right of the major powers to veto...."

"*Stil,*" Saya whispered to the *ningen*. "*Heel stil.*" The *ningen*, even more silent than she, smiled at her. Olafson moaned. "*Ssst! Stil!*" The *ningen* put a hand over Olafson's mouth.

"I wondered if you would find me," the *ningen* whispered to her. Saya shook her head to remind him to be quiet. "Find me," the *ningen* whispered very slowly.

"*Vind me,*" she whispered back. "*Je vinden!*" She shrugged to show how easy it had been to find him. The *ningen* smiled again, but kept his fingers on Olafson's lips to prevent him making an inconvenient outburst. "And him," she went on. Neither of them quite knew how, but it seemed they could understand one another. "What do you want with him?"

---

Tanaka heard the Dutch before he saw them. His first view of the enemy was of a small squad of bedraggled colonial soldiers, their rifles pointed toward a dozen nearly-naked natives who were gathered round a radio that a somewhat chubby native girl was dialing frantically in hope that God would tell them how to rid the village of the white men who wanted to steal their god box. Tanaka nearly laughed, but checked himself and signaled his troops to spread out to encircle the Dutch soldiers. The Japanese quietly moved through the dark rainforest and positioned themselves behind the enemy, all of whom were entranced by watching Tryck fondle their radio. Then, with a flair for the dramatic, Tanaka walked alone into the clearing and aimed his pistol at Van Muis's head.

Van Muis spoke the first and, almost, the last words of his short-lived victory: "Where did you come from?" his startled voice gawped out to Tanaka. "There are no Japanese on the..." And then it occurred to Van Muis that waiting for Pee Pants to return from his patrol might not have been a bad idea. He swiveled his rifle toward Tanaka. "You are my prisoner!"

Tanaka laughed. *"KŌGEKI!"* he shouted.

Van Muis looked up to see Japanese riflemen rushing out of the jungle behind his own pitifully small and unfortunately inattentive group of outmanned scouts. A dozen Japanese rifles poked themselves into the backs of a half-dozen soldiers, and the battle was over without a shot.

Sato alone understood what had happed. He faced Tryck and in clear, plain Sawi, asked her: "Daughter, see what have you done?" Tryck would not look Sato in the face or answer him because, she knew, something had gone slightly wrong with her plan. "You have made God angry with us. Where is Why Krimma?" he demanded.

Tanaka ignored the cannibal gibberish and spoke to Van Muis.

"I am Lieutenant Tanaka Rikugun-Chui. You are prisoners of the Sun. *Wakuru? Ha!*" He exhibited his most stern samurai expression. "Order your men to put their weapons down. Ha!" Van Muis nodded the signal to capitulate. "Order them to stand in a line for the march. Ha!" One by one, the bewildered Dutch soldiers shuffled into place under the menacing glares of their Japanese captors. "Kiku! Take the radio from the fat one!"

Kiku gave his own radio signal-finding set to one of the Japanese soldiers, then walked up to Tryck and slapped her. Every Sawi in the circle bristled and gripped a spear. Tanaka raised his pistol, fired one shot, and the Japanese soldiers aimed at both the Dutch and the Sawi. Kiku seized the transmitter, the crank-handled generator, and the wiring of the god box, and hoisted them onto his shoulders.

Sato, Tryck, and the hunters stood by as the god box left them.

"Daughter," Sato said to Tryck in a very harsh voice, "Daughter, you have brought this down on us. God is angry. I do not know if you will make good *kapala* or good *ania*," he continued, "but you will never again make bad crimes." He picked up his machete, his hunters retrieved their spears, and two cannibals gripped Tryck by her arms just as the last of the white men filed out between the grisly totem poles and onto the battered path to the river.

"No, Elder," she answered. "God was only testing us. Look!"

---

Pitohui toxin metabolizes readily when treated with a lot of fresh drinking water and cooked rice balls. Trembling, fearful, and weak, Olafson knew only that he had been carried out of the hut by his worst nightmare, who had rinsed him out and deposited him on the floor of the jungle. Olafson sweated out the worst of the poison, took another sip of water, chewed the remnants of a rice ball, and looked up to see not only the *ningen* but also Saya, and screamed.

"Shhh!" the *ningen* ordered him to be quiet, and clamped a hand over Olafson's mouth.

"MMMPHHH!!!!" Olafson surged against the hand that kept him quiet. "MMMPHHH!!!"

Olafson's life might have turned out very differently if he had done no more than groan in captivity. Instead, he found the energy to kick out with his feet and legs, thus clearing away the ferns that hid him and tripping the leg of Tanaka's point man. As for the soldier, he felt a sharp blow hit his thigh, stumbled, and swiveled his rifle to prevent falling. His bayonet pushed aside the ferns and there, quivering, was the mostly naked leg of a white man, a leg with a bare foot attached. Just above the bare leg was the emaciated body of an American sailor, clad in the remnants of shredded blue denim sailor pants, a tee shirt that was more hole than shirt, and a garland of feathers and bones that failed to conceal the dog tags around his neck.

"Lieutenantsan! There," the point man pointed. "There!" He pointed his bayonet at the quivering and emaciated Olafson, who no longer knew whether he was dead or alive, awake or asleep, having a nightmare or living in one. "Shall I kill him?" the soldier asked, raising his rifle and chambering a round with the bolt. He aimed at Olafson's head.

"Stand up!" Tanaka ordered. Olafson quivered. "Stand up!"

Saya and the *ningen* retreated into the shadows. She took the *ningen*'s hand and, for the first time in weeks, felt invisible. She looked at it, the *ningen* himself almost invisible in the dark, dappled light of the dense rainforest, and pursed her lips to make clear that, hard to see or not, they should be quiet. They watched, helpless to stop what the Japanese were doing.

Tanaka held a pistol to Olafson's head while another Japanese soldier jerked Olafson to his bare feet. Two Dutch prisoners were pressed into service; they draped Olafson's arms around their shoulders and waited.

"Who are you?" Tanaka demanded. Olafson hung his head. His body sagged. Tanaka prodded the Dutch to hold him upright. "Who? Are? You?" Olafson could only mutter the word 'sick.' "Who is he?" Tanaka demanded of Van Muis, who answered truthfully that he had never seen Olafson before. Tanaka then turned to his men and announced:

"Then this man is a spy! Shoot him!" He ordered the Dutch prisoners to hold Olafson upright to make shooting him a bit easier. He picked out three of his riflemen, ordered them to aim at Olafson, and raised his sword to give the command.

Olafson, at last, finally saw his past life race through his mind. His childhood thefts, the fights, the hooky from school, the judge, reform school and the Navy, shore leaves and captain's masts, the landing on Guadalcanal and the Black Cat Dance Club, nights with Suzy and the theft of detonators and the clubbing to death of Bart Sullivan on the beach, all of these visited Olafson in his last moments. He waited for the end that had not come to him at the hands of hostile beach landings, or in a life ring flinging about the Pacific in a typhoon, or to a crocodile or Komodo dragon, or in a bungee noose or a water-filled stake pit, or even from poisoning. Kiku, struggling under the awkward weight of the god box, looked downward and saw the rice ball at Olafson's feet.

"Sir!" Kiku said. "Sir!" He pointed to the ball of rice, partly eaten, partly intact, entirely like the balls of rice that the benevolent emperor provided for the *surēbu*. "Look!"

Lieutenant Rikugun-Chui saw what he wanted to see. In a bedraggled and half-dead American sailor he saw a spy! In a rice ball he saw not only a spy but a thief.

"Halt!" he ordered the firing squad. "Halt!" He picked up the rice ball and shook it in Olafson's face. "You!" he shouted. "You have stolen the Emperor's food. It was you who helped the criminal *surēbu*!" Tanaka couldn't contain his glee; he had captured not only the criminal Dutch and their radio, but he also had captured the man he had set about to trap the day before in the Ambon rice warehouse. "You have stolen the Emperor's weapons and subverted his *surēbu* with stolen food to prevent them from finishing their work. You have tortured my *chojin* and you drove my sergeant crazy. And now, I have caught you!"

Even as he shook the crumbling rice ball in Olafson's face Tanaka could not keep from smiling, thus adding to Olafson's confusion. "My plan worked," he continued, even though his plan had been to have the thief caught inside the warehouse on the docks. *And*, Tanaka thought to himself, *you are my prisoner. I will parade you to the Commandant!* Visions of promotions, command of a combat unit, glory for the emperor, all flitted through Tanaka's imagination. He lowered his sword.

The *ningen* watched as Tanaka ordered the Dutch prisoners to carry Olafson's sagging body and resume the forced march back to the bay. He held Saya's hand and, for the first time, he and Saya saw each other clearly. Tanaka saw nothing. "March!"

---

Saya watched the Japanese lead their prisoners away, then turned to look at her *ningen.*

"*Ben jij een man?*" she asked.

"Am I a human?" the *ningen* answered. He nodded, but not firmly. "Watch this." He released her hand; Saya became more visible than she had been only a second ago. The *ningen* took her hand again and she felt as if she was diffusing into the shapes and shadows of the jungle around her, just as she had been able to do before she had trespassed the Sawi village. She was not invisible, not exactly, but then she could not be seen either, not exactly.

"*Ben je leven? Of dood?*" She had lived between life and death for two years, but on her own terms, and without sharing it with anyone. She wondered if he was like her, or she like him.

"Am I alive or dead?" the *ningen* answered. "I'm not sure. I was dead once, but it didn't last. Then I was thrown off my ship, and drowned, but didn't, not exactly. I think I'm somewhere in between alive and dead," he went on. He doubted that she understood it but, then, he didn't understand it very well himself. "The Japanese think Olafson is me," he continued. "I have to go." He released her hand again, and stood up.

"*Een moment,*" she replied. "*Mijn familie?*"

"Your family? Alive," he answered. Her father and brother were alive, he was sure of that. He was less sure of her mother; she had been herded onto the *Jigoku Maru* with the other women. "*Leven.*"

He stood to look at the path the Japanese had taken but, before he could start, Saya took his hand again. When he turned to look at her she took his face in her hands and kissed him. It was the first time she had kissed anyone, even counting child's play at the school in Bintuni Village. For him, it was the first time a girl had kissed him without him trying to get

177

her drunk or trapped inside his father's old Ford. But, they were touching, and no one saw them.

This time, when he turned to follow Olafson and the Japanese, she came with him.

---

Despite the stumbling resistance of the dispirited Dutch and their burden of dragging Olafson along, the patrol and their prisoners arrived at the dock relatively soon, in the heat of the afternoon. The humidity from the fetid swamp and the shimmer of thick air from the bay hung over the delta as Tanaka led his triumphant patrol. Pants Broek watched in horror from his tree limb above the swamp when he saw Van Muis and his fellow resistance troops arrived under armed guard.

"MOTO!" shouted Tanaka. Mr. Moto trotted out from behind a village hut, pulling up his pants. "Fall in!"

The *ningen* watched it all as the longest-running victim of his bedeviling the Japanese marched to Tanaka, snapped to attention, presented arms with his rifle, and stood ready for orders, at which point the tree limb on which Pants Broek was perched gave way with a loud snap. Everyone looked up to see the last Dutch soldier on the island splash into the swamp.

"Moto! Take that man prisoner!" Tanaka shouted.

"*Ha!*" Moto lowered his rifle and stalked manfully from the dock to the edge of the swamp. Pants Broek floundered in the foul water, looked up, saw Moto's bayonet pointed at his face, and raised his hands. He waded out of the ooze and into captivity. Moto stood over him, pointed his rifle at Pants Broek's chest, and saw the flicker of green lights fluttering through the darkness of the mangrove trees, twinkling across the swamp. Moto shrieked.

"NINGEN," he shouted as he recognized the *ningen* he had first seen from his seat of ease at the *surēbu* work quarry and had last seen when it had stripped him naked and left him hanging upside down over the gate to Ambon castle. "*NINGEN!* Capture him! HELP!" Tanaka stared at Moto, unable to see what the shouting was about. "*NINGEN!* Help me!"

Moto aimed at the flickering swamp lights, fired, missed, aimed again, and missed a second time. A second cluster of flickering green lights hovered near a towering hardwood tree. Moto shrieked again, lurched backward, and was jerked off the ground by the same tightly strung vine snare that had caught Olafson on the first day he set foot on the island. The astonished Japanese watched Tanaka's *chojin* pop upward and dangle in the air. Moto himself bobbed up and down, feet in the noose, his head dangling above the swamp.

No one came to help him.

The Komodo dragon came to help itself. The last thing Moto saw on this earth was a dinosaur. It erupted from the water, jaws open, tongue out, eyes flashing red, and clamped onto Moto's dangling head. As he screamed, Tanaka stood, transfixed on the dock, wondering what he had just seen, then realizing that, whatever it was, he would be returning to Ambon without his most trusted *chojin*.

"Into the boat," he ordered. "Now. Prepare to cast off!"

The soldiers, Japanese and Dutch alike, scrambled over one another to get into the launch. Kiku, bumped and shoved with everyone else, tumbled to the dock, dropped the god box, and was pulled into the boat.

The *ningen* stood by Saya, watching the Komodo eat the man who had tormented the *surēbu* on Mount Salahutu, the man who had raped Saya at Port Haru. Mr. Moto's time had come. Saya spoke.

"I wanted to capture Mr. Moto so that I could trade him for my family," she said. Watching the last of Mr. Mojo had made her less happy than she had expected. "Now I have nothing to bargain with. I have no plan."

The *ningen* understood.

"I have to go," he said. "To Ambon. To try to help." He looked toward the boat, its engine revving up, the bow-man tossing the docking line into the cockpit. "Will you come with me?" He took her hand. She took his.

"I will."

---

Olafson, feeble in body and mind, was pinned down between two Dutch soldiers on the deck planking of the Japanese boat. No one, not him, not the Japanese, not their Dutch prisoners, could shut out the sight of Moto's half-eaten body dangling from a rope while a giant reptile made repeated passes at his head. No one suggested that Tanaka try to rescue his hapless *chojin*, in part because it was clear that saving only Moto's remaining half would involve more risk than they wanted and in part because of the horde of cannibals that came running down the river bank and on to the dock. Led by a short chubby black woman, all of them shouting "IGOT SPURZAT! ZINGL ANGL ZINGLE."

It was through this fog that Olafson heard a splash in the water, followed by a heavy, wet weight that settled down on him. He lifted his weary head to see that Bart Sullivan had come to rest on his chest, along with the island woman who had tried so long ago to kill him with snakes and spiders and water pits. He looked at Bart through dull eyes.

"I thought you were dead," Olafson muttered.

"Not exactly," Sullivan whispered back to him.

No one in the boat paid any attention to Olafson, focusing instead on the scene unfolding back at the dock. The cannibals mobbed the dock, shouting and waving whatever spears they still had. Their chubby native girl leader bent over, straightened up, and held up the god box. The launch's motor was too loud to hear the music but soon the cannibals began to sway and nod in rhythm. The spear-throwing stopped.

"Listen, Sullivan. I was like a king. They named me White Christmas. And they gave me a girl." Olafson still wanted to be important, even if only to the shipmate he had tried so hard to kill. "How'd you get here anyway? You were tossed overboard. Lost at sea."

"It wasn't my time," the *ningen* answered.

Van Muis shuffled down onto the deck to lift Olafson's head a little higher, to shield it from the sun. "Anyone know who he is?" Van Muis asked. No one did. "Look at him. Wonder how long he's been wandering around in the jungle, poor bastard."

"He's crazy," Private Boer said. "Listen to him. He's raving."

Van Muis agreed, but he shaded Olafson's eyes anyway, and soothed his forehead as they looked toward Ambon Island across the open sea. Then Van Muis and the others forgot all about Olafson when they heard the sound of airplane engines. Everyone on the boat looked westward, toward Mount Salahutu rising in the distance, as the first allied bombers streaked across the red sunset toward the emperor's new runway.

# Part III

Red Sky at Morning, Sailor Take Warning

# Chapter 22

Madame Rochelle looked at the prison visitor registry, raised her eyebrows, and laughed, then handed the pen back to the duty clerk. The waiting room was filled with anxious visitors, some who hoped to arrange for bail for an unfortunate family member, others who had arrived for a weekly visit with someone already doing time.

"You can fill this out for me, I'm sure." Madame Rochelle had never made a practice of writing on government records, much less signing them. "I'm sure you know what to put where," she said, winking.

"Got to fill in the form, ma'am. No form, no visit," the clerk said. "Fill it out or leave, all the same to me. Next!" he barked at the line of mostly-Nisei hopefuls.

"Oh, my, soldier," she went on. "How times do change a man." Madame Rochelle cocked her head slightly to one side, the better to show off her high cheek bones and full lips. "Come, come. Surely your memory can't be that bad." She turned again, lowered her eyes to gaze directly at the befuddled young man behind the barred windows, and gave him a pouty smile. "Black Cat Club? 'Show me your dance cards, sailor, and I'll show you a girl.' Does that help your memory?" The clerk's head jerked up, his eyes opened wide, he stuttered a few syllables, and she continued. "You like the young ones, if I remember. You always ask for Shirley Temple. Nice little blondie, looked more like Betty Hutton, only pretty," she said. "If I remember."

The clerk swallowed, hard.

"Shhh, ma'am. Don't let my chief hear you...."

"A little *oke*, a little pineapple, no straw, and..." she interrupted him. "Baily, isn't it? Private Baily? I may forget to pay the rent, but I never forget a client." The MP band on Baily's sleeve seemed to shrivel as his mind swirled. "You always get your glass of *oke* and steer little Shirley off into the corner behind the palms, in case some other MPs drop in and you need to scram." She waited for Baily to stop looking around to see if his duty sergeant had overheard her. "As I said, Baily, I'm here to see a girl. Why don't you fill out the form for me? So it's done right?"

"Yes, ma'am," Baily said, looking at the form on his window shelf instead of looking at the madame whose memory could sink Baily's boat if anyone found out that he was a regular at the Black Cat Dance Club. "Who is it you want to see, Miss..."

"Call me Veronica Lake," she said. "That's the ticket. Veronica Lake."

Fifteen minutes later, a block guard opened a steel door and ushered Madame Rochelle into a gloomy room furnished with a table and two chairs. Madame Rochelle dazzled the guard with a smile, then took a seat. The guard left and locked the steel door behind him. She studied her nails. A few moments later, on the opposite wall, a second steel door creaked and jolted, then swung inward. Another guard stepped into the room, followed by a haggard young Nisei woman who was dressed in a clunky striped prison dress, hands cuffed, hair matted, eyes dulled.

"Ten minutes. Do not reach across the divider in the middle of the table. Do not touch the prisoner. Do not pass anything to the prisoner."

"Sure, honey," Madame Rochelle smiled again, then looked at the prisoner. "Hello, Suzy. How're you doing, kid?"

Suzy Mazuka looked up for the first time and saw that, instead of her lawyer, she was meeting with her former employer.

"How am I doing? They going to hang me. Me and Hualani. That's how I'm doing." Suzy showed a little life for the first time. "They say I'm a spy! Hah, some spy! War over. Japan over. Emperor over. I don't do anything. They going to hang me."

Madame Rochelle watched her former employee gather up her anger at the injustice of being hanged for merely stealing the Navy's sailing orders and some feeble little explosives.

"And you!" Suzy went on. "It was you who turned us in."

"Just for stealing, Suzy, I just turned you in for stealing, not for spying. But," Madame Rochelle put on a remorse face, "I will say that a girl who steals from her friend should be a bit more careful when she steals from the

Navy, especially if she's going to keep stolen sailing orders and explosives in her apartment."

"You were not my friend," Suzy snapped. "You hire girls to dance with the sailors, get sailors drunk, take sailors money. Girls make a little on the side, you want take that too! Some friend!"

"Sorry about the hanging, Suzy. Tell me again why the judge sentenced you to hang?"

"I spy, he said."

"Well, yes, you were a spy, but if I remember from the newspapers, at first the judge hadn't decided he was going to hang you. You must have done something more."

"What do you mean? I don't do nothing more."

"Oh, yes," Madame Rochelle feigned to remember, putting her chin in her right hand, gazing up at the naked light bulb hanging from the ceiling. "That's what it was. Instead of doing something more, you did nothing more. That's why the judge decided to hang you. And hang Hualani too, of course."

Suzy glared at Madame Rochelle across the table divider. The heat from her burrowing eyes was so intense that the guard stepped closer to the table and put his hands on his billy club. As for Madame Rochelle, she reached down to her purse, opened it, and pulled out a yellowed page from an old newspaper.

"'Sentencing has been delayed while the authorities search for the identities of the two sailors,'" she read out loud. She put the newspaper away and continued. "Of course, I wasn't in court when the judge convicted you, so maybe the papers got it wrong." She looked over the top of the newspaper and smiled innocently at her former employee, who would have strangled Madame Rochelle but for the presence of the guard. "But that's what was in the newspaper so I just assumed that the judge wasn't going to hang you automatically. If he was, he would have said right then that he was going to hang you, no need to wait to see if the sailors turned up." She blinked at Suzy with yet another dazzling, innocent smile. Suzy's angry eyes opened a little. "So I suspected that if you helped them find the sailors who gave you the sailing orders and the explosives the judge would go easy on you. Is that how you figured it, Suzy? That if you helped them find the two sailors who got you and Hualani into trouble, the judge might not hang you?"

Suzy nodded. It seemed to Suzy that even though Madame Rochelle was not in court when the judge convicted her of spying she had certainly figured out what the judge planned. As for Madame Rochelle, she had figured it out because the judge told her.

"But Navy no find the two sailors," Suzy moaned. "No find nobody. Navy say not two sailors, we lie. I say how we get money and sailing orders if not from sailor, huh? How I get Navy explosive if not from sailor? Navy say I just lying."

"Were you lying, Suzy?" Madame Rochelle looked the prostitute spy in her eyes and asked again. "Were you lying?"

"No. How you think we get thousand dollars? We get from dance cards we turn in. Where we get dance cards? Two sailors with lot of dance cards. Lot of dance cards! Not lying. No."

"And the explosives? Same two sailors?"

"No. Just one sailor. Same as the money we get from the two sailors, but just one of of those two sailors get firecrackers." Suzy was not a very good spy. "One night I take Bingo card from him. Navy say is not Bingo cards, is secret sailing orders. Next day he bring me little firecrackers. Navy say they explosives. Not much explosive I tell you that. He doesn't say anything about secret sailing orders, so I forget, they still in apartment when Navy arrest me. I don't give the papers anybody. I don't know what is sailing order. They going to hang me."

For the second time Madame Rochelle reached into her purse and took out a newspaper.

"Did you tell the Navy who gave you the explosives Suzy? When the judge said he would wait to sentence you while the Navy searched for the two sailors?"

"No. I don't know his name. Fat guy. Talk funny. He never come back. Not after he give me fireworks, he never come back. Navy say you know how many fat guys talk funny in Pearl Harbor? I say no."

"How about this fat guy?" Madame Rochelle held up the front page of the *Honolulu Star Bulletin*. The headline read "Prisoners of War Return to Australia." The photograph depicted a dozen emaciated men, Australian soldiers who had been liberated from Ambon, being escorted into a hangar at Cairns, Australia. In the middle of them, one man stood out, taller, heavier, rounder than the Australians. Suzy's eyes bulged as she focused on the picture.

"That him!" Suzy shouted. "That him." The guard had to restrain her from reaching across the table to take the newspaper away. "That the sailor!"

"When Australian authorities liberated the Tan Tui prisoner of war camp on Ambon Island," the news story reported, "they found one American sailor among the starved and tortured soldiers who had been captured by the Japanese."

"That him!"

"Well, Suzy, I thought it might be. Remember what we said at the Black Cat? I may forget to pay the rent, but I never forget a client." She put the newspaper clippings back in her purse and stood up. "Sorry, my ten minutes are up. I have to go." Madame Rochelle gathered her coat and purse, then flashed an insincere smile at the woman she considered to have cheated her out of her share of the proceeds from Olafson's counterfeit dance cards.

"No! You can't go. They going to hang me!"

"Stay in touch," Madame Rochelle called back over her shoulder as she headed for the visitors' door. "Eat your vegetables." She waved cheerily without turning around, then swept out the door and disappeared.

The guard stood Suzy up and turned her around. The steel door opened and the spy was led back to her cell.

"They going to hang me!"

––––––––––––––––

The *Honolulu Star Bulletin* was not the only paper interested in war heroes who turned up in Japanese prisoner of war camps. A Navy liaison officer in Australia saw the same photograph in the *Cairns Post* newspaper, got Bart's name from the Australian prisoner of war repatriation dog tag list, and notified the Third Fleet that one of its sailors had survived in the Ambon POW camp.

The fleet public relations office telegraphed back that American prisoners were being collected at Clark Field in the Philippines "but if you can get him on a plane right now we might be able to reunite him with his ship, which is en route to Pearl Harbor." The liaison officer telegraphed in reply that he could get him on a plane to Hollandia right away.

Thus it was that a few days later a Catalina seaplane descended over the Cyclops Mountains, banked, waggled its wings, and circled Humboldt

Bay, then glided in to land on the far west side of the Hollandia harbor. The seaplane taxied up to the Base G dock and cut its engines. A very small motor launch was waiting when the door opened from inside. One by one, men tumbled out, some stretching, others stumbling, all cramped from having flown almost a thousand miles.

The boat's crew hauled them to the VIP jetty where a small but determined Navy band struck up *Stars and Stripes*. The band made it through most of a stanza while a public relations officer looked at each new arrival, then wobbled to a halt when the public relations officer shook his head 'no'. Finally, after the fourth boat load arrived, the men stumbled out of the launch, onto the dock, the band struck up again, the public relations officer gave a thumbs up to the cameramen from the *Stars and Stripes*, and flash bulbs went off like firecrackers.

The startled passengers, all of them Navy ensigns and lieutenants, Army majors and captains, and a few Marine officers of indistinct rank, looked around to see who the celebrity was who had flown with them all the way from Australia without any of them knowing. All were surprised when the public relations man turned his attention to the one enlisted man in the group, an ordinary seaman dressed in new-issue dress blues, and saluted.

"Sullivan," he called out. More flash bulbs went off. "Sullivan, welcome to Hollandia. How's it feel to be back in civilization?" he asked. Another flash bulb popped. A pimply-faced nineteen-year-old apprentice poised his pencil to record the momentous answer of the hero of the day.

"Uh, uh," was all they got from the hero. "Uh."

"To be alive?" the officer asked, smiling. "How's it feel to be alive? The whole Navy thought you were dead."

"I thought I was dead myself," he said. It would later be remembered that he looked around at the dock, saw the battered destroyers and warships out in the harbor, the flash bulb cameras and the news reporter, and seemed nervous. "This ain't Pearl, is it?"

"Pearl? Pearl Harbor? Oh, no, this is Hollandia, sailor. Tell us, what's the first thing you want to do on free soil? Get a beer? See a USO show? Phone call home? Nothing's too good for a rescued hero."

"Why're we in—where are we?" He was told. "Why're we in Landia? I thought they was flyin' me to Pearl."

"All in good time, sailor. But first, a few days of R&R, a medical checkup, and like I said, how about a beer? A show? And guess what? The Navy's putting you up at the general's headquarters. How about that?"

"The general?"

"General MacArthur. Until you get cleared for home, Sullivan, that'll be your barracks. Welcome home." He waved at the band, the conductor lifted his baton, and the band struck up again. More cameras flashed. The public relations officer smiled and shook his hand, then saw a jeep careening along the wharf.

"And we've got another surprise for you too, Sullivan. Look who's here to greet you!"

A Navy jeep lurched free of a crowd of sailors, dollies, cranes, and trucks and spun to a halt at the dock. Two officers hopped out of the first jeep and trotted up to the little throng gathered around the Navy band, then stopped short. The public relations officer waved them forward.

"Sullivan, this is Captain Burger. He's the base judge advocate, the man who cut all the red tape to get you here." Burger saluted. "And now, Sullivan, the biggest surprise of all. We couldn't get *Renegade* back here but we did get your captain, Captain Hull."

It was a pretty big surprise.

"*Renegade's* on the way to Pearl Harbor to take soldiers home. But Captain Burger commandeered a Catalina and picked up Captain Hull in the middle of the ocean, just for a hero's reunion." The public relations officer had the uneasy feeling that hero Sullivan wasn't sufficiently gleeful, given how many planes and ships had been diverted to have a photographic reunion of heroes.

"Sir," Hull answered, "this isn't Bart Sullivan. This is the man who killed Bart Sullivan." The band stopped. The other passengers stopped. Even the squawking gulls stopped when Hull grabbed the celebrity hero by the arm. "Chief Petty Officer Olafson, I charge you with killing Bart Sullivan by throwing him overboard from my ship. You're under arrest."

Olafson, now wanting to be in Pearl Harbor more than ever, decided to try to swim there. He wrenched free to be able to jump off the dock, but only made it as far as the edge of the dock, where he was tackled by the tuba player.

---

Hull and Burger turned Olafson over to the shore patrol, then found Admiral Petty.

"Admiral?" Burger explained. "This is Captain Hull. We just arrested one of his sailors for murder."

"Who'd he murder?" the admiral wanted to know.

"Bart Sullivan, my best Higgins boat crewman," Hull explained. "I'm off *Renegade.*"

"Okay," the admiral said. "Hang him." Then he thought a moment. "What's he doing here?"

"Remember the big typhoon, sir?"

"Halsey's typhoon. December of '44. Should have hanged Halsey too. So what?"

"Olafson jumped ship during the typhoon, floated up to a Japanese POW camp a couple of hundred miles away. We just got him back today."

"Okay. Hang him. Dismissed. Oh, what are you doing here, Captain. Where's your ship?"

"My ship's on the way to Pearl Harbor. Someone thought the killer was actually the victim and flew him here for a reunion. Fleet thought it was good for public relations for me to be here. "

"Okay," the admiral said. The admiral wrote out an order charging Olafson with the murder of Bart Sullivan, Seaman Second class.

"Got it," Burger said after he read the order. "We can have the court martial next week." Then he began the task of rounding up a dozen battle-tested gunnery officers, submarine commanders, and combat pilots as jurors who would be willing to hang someone.

# Chapter 23

*B*iggest *Court Martial of the War*, blared the headline of *Stars and Stripes*. "Escaped sailor found in Jap POW camp wearing victim's dog tags."

The story reported how Olafson had been tackled on the dock after being identified by his commanding officer and accused of escaping from his brig on *Renegade*. Otherwise the story was short of details. Lieutenant Mason, Olafson's new lawyer, read the story to him in the stockade and shook his head.

"I hope there's more to the story than that," Mason asked.

"More?" Olafson answered. "I done a lot of stuff in my time but I didn't toss Bart Sullivan off the ship. It ain't true!" Olafson decided that now was not the time to mention that he had first tried to kill Sullivan with his machine gun and again by dropping a huge bag of salt on his head from one of the *Renegade*'s Higgins boat hoists. "I didn't do it," he added. "And when I tell my story, there's not a man in the Navy'll convict me. I'm the hero here."

Olafson did hold back a bit from Mason but, for that matter, Mason held back telling Olafson that he had only been a Navy lawyer for a few weeks. Mason did have one suggestion.

"Not too late to ask the judge to move the trial to Pearl Harbor. That's where the witnesses are. What're their names?"

"Barker, Hantsel, who they call Gretel for some reason, and Smith. But I don't think that's such a good idea."

"And your squadron commander, this Lieutenant Beach. You said you taught him everything he knew. He's there too."

"I think maybe we're better off here."

"Or a delay."

"I think the sooner the better," Olafson answered. He had the idea that a delay might backfire.

Thus exactly nine days after he landed on one dock Olafson stood and faced a Navy jury in another.

"Chief Petty Officer Olafson," the judge faced him. "You're charged with the murder of Seaman Second Class Bart Sullivan by throwing him overboard from the troopship *Renegade* on November 14, 1944. And then escaping from custody during a typhoon in December, 1944. How do you plead?"

"I didn't kill him," Olafson answered.

"*Habeas corpus*, Your Honor," Lieutenant Mason chimed in. "*Ex Post Facto!*" He let the words sink in. "*Erratum.*"

"What are you talking about, counsel?" the judge snarled. "Speak English," he continued, without adding 'you idiot.'

"He pleads not guilty, Your Honor. Mistake! Error! Alibi! Therefore, *habeas corpus*." Mason's preparation for his first criminal trial involved a mixture of reading an English law dictionary and drawing on selected phrases from the Navy procurement contracts that had taken up his first two weeks as a Navy lawyer. "It's criminal pleading, sir. And, there is no party of the second part," Lieutenant Mason said hopefully.

"Okay, prosecution, call your first witness."

Captain Hull took the stand, identified Olafson, and told the jury all they needed to know.

"So, in my experience, Seaman Sullivan was the best Higgins boat man in the Navy. Olafson was his chief petty officer. But Sullivan, he basically saved his crew at Peleliu, maneuvering their Higgins boat around and around, under heavy fire. Then he ran ashore himself and rescued a whole boatload of wounded Marines on the hottest beach on the island." He waited; the jury listened. "Then, a week later Sullivan was on watch and sounded a periscope alarm, which got my ship turned just in time to escape a torpedo. The torpedo hit a whale."

Every single man on the jury wished they had had such a man in their boats.

"Now, this is the hard part. We made port here in Hollandia a few days later to load troops for the Philippines and there was a set of orders waiting here for Sullivan; he got a transfer back to the states to work for some congressman in Washington. But, listen to this; he turned it down and stayed with the ship!"

That was all the jury needed to hear. Some of them began to doodle on their scratch pads, little drawings of nooses and axes.

"So, we were back out at sea on November 14. It was a black night in the middle of the ocean. Sullivan had the middle watch. He made his last round and then disappeared. And here is this entry from Lieutenant Beach's duty log: 'Sullivan's Higgins boat crew reported that Chief Petty Officer Olafson was right there on the deck.' Gentlemen? Olafson had no duties on deck." The jurors murmured their disapproval of a chief petty officer lolling on the deck after hours. "And there's one other fact. Sullivan had almost a thousand dollars in his sea bag; Chief Petty Officer Olafson knew it."

Even the doodlers and hangers jerked up at this part of the story. The judge would have banged his gavel for order but he was just as agitated as the jurors. Budding lawyer Mason tried to act inconspicuous, facing Captain Hull while whispering under his breath.

"You didn't tell me about the money, Olafson."

"It'll be okay. Wait'll they hear my story," he whispered back.

"So," the prosecutor summed up. "Sullivan was on deck conducting his watch. Olafson knew that there was a lot of money in Sullivan's sea bag. And Olafson was on deck, in the dark, where he had no duties. Sullivan disappears from the deck, in the night, in the middle of the ocean. Is that when you arrested him?"

"No," Hull answered. "We spent all our time at sea searching for Sullivan, but we had to give him up. After several hours we notified the convoy that he had disappeared at sea. It wasn't until weeks later, after we made some troop landings in the Philippines, that we learned the rest of what had happened. During the landings, Olafson sent Sullivan's old Higgins boat crew to land on hostile Japanese beaches instead of on our landing beaches, which was plainly going to get the crew killed. The crew figured that Olafson was trying to get them killed in the Philippines to get rid of the witnesses to his killing Sullivan. They'd already been afraid of Olafson but once they figured he was going to kill them one way or another they had nothing to lose by telling what they knew. They came up to me and reported that before we docked at Hollandia Olafson already had tried to kill Sullivan once. It had been the same setup; Sullivan was on watch, middle of the night. That time Olafson went up on deck and tried to kill Sullivan by dropping a fifty-pound bag of salt on his head from one of the landing boat hoists. I heard them out, then put Olafson in the brig."

"You tried to kill him with a bag of salt?" Mason whispered.

"I didn't kill 'em. The bag landed on the crew ladder," Olafson whispered back. "Quit worrying."

"How did he get free, Captain?"

"Well," Hull answered, "when the task force went out to sea for refueling, we got caught in the typhoon. *Renegade*'s hull was torqued around in the storm and the brig doors twisted open. Olafson disappeared."

"Anything else, Captain?" The prosecutor was almost done with Hull.

"Well, this," Hull answered. "The other things in Sullivan's sea bag were some Bingo cards, some dance club cards, and Sullivan's diary. I had it copied. Sullivan wrote on one page, quote, 'I'd be safer in combat than I am on board the ship.'" He handed the page to Captain Burger, who showed it to Lieutenant Mason, who had never grasped the concept of hearsay. "That was after we left Hawaii. Oh, and one more thing." He paused. "When Olafson showed up here in Hollandia, he was wearing Sullivan's dog tags."

The officers on the jury had heard enough. If there was any mortal sin in the Navy it was to take another man's dog tags. They began privately thinking of the different ways they could recommend how to do away with Olafson: firing squad, hanging, cutting his head off, or something a little slower. Some of them were visibly annoyed when the judge told them that Lieutenant Mason was allowed to ask questions of his own.

"Captain Hull? Did you ever see Sullivan's dead body?" Hull conceded that he did not. "Did Chief Petty Officer Olafson ever admit to you that he killed Bart Sullivan?" Hull agreed that not only had Olafson not admitted killing Bart, he had actually denied it. "Was there anybody else on board who might have a motive for Sullivan to disappear at sea?" Hull said that he didn't know of anyone.

"Well, how about the three crewmen? If they reported that they saw Olafson on deck right before Sullivan disappeared, doesn't that mean they were on deck right before Sullivan disappeared too?" Hull agreed it might be the case. "And aren't they the ones who discovered the money in Sullivan's sea bag, back at Eniwetok." Hull agreed that they were.

"So, who's got the money now? And where are they?" Hull agreed that Sullivan's mates not only had the money in his sea bag, but had gone on to Pearl Harbor with *Renegade* and were being processed for discharge 'right now.'

Olafson beamed. The jurors frowned.

"And where's the rest of this diary, Captain?" Hull agreed that he had left it in Sullivan's sea bag. Mason sat down.

"Next witness, sir," the judge told the prosecutor. He called to the stand the sailor who had started to toss Bart's body overboard, but didn't.

"Lieutenant Commander Calvin Hobbes, sir," he said. "I was the executive officer on the convoy's flag ship when *Renegade* sailed from Hawaii in September. Our first day out was over to the big island for a beach landing exercise. One of our corpsmen on shore came across Sullivan's dead body lying on the sand under a coconut tree about twenty yards from where his landing boat had pulled up to put its troops on the beach. There was a big bash in Sullivan's helmet. They brought his body out to the ship and laid it in the sick bay and the convoy got underway to Eniwetok. I was about to order them to bury him at sea when his body made a couple of sounds and, I'm serious, Sullivan came back to life, I swear to God."

The jurors thought this was one of the best sailor yarns they had ever heard. One or two tried to write down what Hobbes had said to write into their own war memoirs.

"By then," Hobbes continued, "we were underway. So we took care of Sullivan on the flagship. He slowly but surely returned to the land of the living, if you know what I mean. He stayed with us until we refueled at Eniwetok. And like Captain Hull said, Sullivan turned out to be a good man. Spent a lot of time with our chaplain, as you can imagine, and the padre liked him so much that he offered to keep Sullivan on as his chaplain's assistant. Sullivan turned it down to get back his own ship."

Images of Saint Bart danced in all their heads. Hobbes didn't know about the krait.

"What does that have to do with this case, Commander?" Prosecutor Burger was warming up.

"Well, when Sullivan was dead, I had to set up a board of inquiry. Olafson was called over to the flagship to testify but by the time he got there, Sullivan was alive again, sort of. A pharmacist's mate had stuck a sharp probe into his foot and Sullivan jerked, and then croaked. Then he had a heartbeat. So, we didn't have a dead body to inquire about. The convoy was headed to war and I let it drop. But then Olafson came back to my attention in the Philippines. He kept sending this one Higgins boat to shore under heavy Jap fire on beaches where we weren't landing any troops. That's when I got the rest of the facts about what happened to Sullivan on the training incident back in Hawaii."

"What facts did you get?"

"Sullivan was the sternman on his Higgins boat so he would have had the machine gun when the crew went on shore, which was part of the exercise. The bash in Sullivan's helmet there on the beach was exactly what you get when someone takes a machine gun by the barrel and swings it at your head. When the corpsman found Sullivan on the beach, his body was all alone, dead under a palm tree, but—no machine gun. After the Philippines I thought there was more to what happened, so I got the ship's armory logs from Captain Hull. As I suspected, it was Olafson who carried the machine gun back to the *Renegade* and checked it in after the exercise. It looked to me like Olafson picked up the machine gun, bashed Sullivan in the head, and left Sullivan on the beach. You can add two and two for yourself."

"Objection," the defense declared. "Irrelevant, incompetent, and immaterial."

"Overruled," the judge replied. "You sound like a movie lawyer, Lieutenant. Do you even know how to object?"

"Let me try this, sir," Mason answered. "Objection. Damaging to my client's case."

By then one of the jurors was busy drawing a noose on his notepad. Another played a game of hangman with a third, a good speller who had completed drawing three fourths of the gibbet.

"You didn't tell me about that, either," Mason hissed in another aside to Olafson.

"It's alright. Wait'll I tell 'em what really happened."

Despite the pangs of doubt growing in Mason's stomach he stuck to his questions. Commander Hobbes agreed that, despite all appearances, when he saw Bart Sullivan for the first time he wasn't really dead. When he saw him for the last time Bart Sullivan was still alive. Hobbes admitted that he had a chance to question Olafson about what happened on the beach and, for that matter, to question Sullivan's crew mates, but never asked a word about who left Sullivan knocked out under a palm tree or who carried away his machine gun.

"And, sir, regardless, you have no knowledge of what happened on *Renegade* when Bart Sullivan disappeared, do you?" Hobbes agreed; he did not. "So, in a nutshell, a coconut shell, all you can say is there was no dead body. Just a live sailor."

———————

The trial didn't move to Pearl Harbor but the news did. The wire services reported the parts that the jurors really liked. "Commanders testify that chief petty officer tried twice to kill hero," blared the next headline in *Stars and Stripes*. "Sullivan left sea bag full of money to his crew mates."

The case was discussed in all the officers' clubs, the demobilization processing centers, and in every bar and waterfront dive in Honolulu. *Renegade* became a tourist attraction; bored sailors waiting for demobilization orders hiked over to the wharf to take snap shots of the murder boat. That was enough for Barker, Smith, and Hantsel to beg shore leave and take a taxi into Honolulu. When the cab driver asked 'where to?' they named the only place they had ever heard of. By the time the sun had set they were drinking warm beer in the Black Cat Dance Club.

"That goddamned Olafson's trying to blame us," Barker hissed. Barker took it personally; this was beyond the mere business cheating of swamp traders. "You see what they're sayin'? Goddamned Sullivan's crew mates found his money and then wound up with his money. Olafson's going to tell them to blame us for killin' Sullivan."

"Well," Gretel said, "we did try to kill him. With ectoplasm, remember? And we do have the money."

"Yeah," Smith chimed in. "But we didn't kill him. We didn't even toss him off the boat."

"Pipe down, idiots. Someone'll hear you." Barker drank some beer and fumed, then added. "Tell ya' what. Anyone comes around askin', we don't know nothin.'"

"Hey," Gretel looked up from reading the news story. "Did you know that Lieutenant Beach put it in the search log that we saw Olafson on deck that night Sullivan disappeared?" Neither Smith nor Barker knew it. "We didn't have to tell him that we saw Olafson tryin' to drop a bag of salt on Sullivan's head, either." They nodded in agreement. "All that did was just put us on the deck. We're screwed."

"I just want to get out of the Navy and go home." Smith didn't like being screwed.

"Listen, stupid," Barker commented. "If Lieutenant Beach says he saw us on deck, that's a lot worse for us than if it was just that goddamned Olafson claiming we were on deck. So like I said, our story is we don't know nothin.'"

But a pair of ears behind the palm trees in the Black Cat Club were pretty sure that the three sailors did know something, so the next day Madame Rochelle began to call old friends in the Navy. One of them answered.

"Hello, dear. Listen. An old friend needs a favor."

# Chapter 24

*J*udge says circumstantial evidence 'pretty strong,' read the morning headlines. *Olafson to take the stand. Courtroom packed.*

"Lieutenant Mason, are you ready?"

"Yes, sir," he answered.

"Call your first witness. And no monkey business, you hear?"

"Yes, sir. I call Chief Olafson." Olafson made a show of marching to
the witness stand, stiffened to attention, then took his seat. "Tell the court,
Chief Petty Officer. Did you kill Bart Sullivan?"

"No, sir. I didn't kill 'em," Olafson answered. He paused, and then:
"And he ain't dead. Bart Sullivan's alive and livin' it up with a native girl on
some island out there. Not only didn't I not kill him, I saved his life over and
over." The jurors sat up in their chairs. "Here's what happened. First, I didn't
escape from my ship. We was in this typhoon and the *Renegade* is getting'
herself tossed about this way and that and suddenly the doors sprung open.
So, I went up on deck to my duty station to help out with the ballast. A big
wave knocked the boat almost over and I was washed overboard. So, for the
next however long, I was tossed about on the cruel seas. I thought I was dead
a thousand times over, starving, tirsty, clingin' to life." He paused to be sure
the jury was paying attention. "And then I washed up on this island. Well, I
was cruel hungry and found some kind of fruit growin' on a bush and this girl
come along. Native girl, good lookin', sort of like me Tarzan her Jane. Well, I
thought she was gonna help me out but instead she has a bunch of natives tie
me up and they carries me off to her treehouse in the jungle."

The jurors had never heard such a good story, not even in a comic
book. They listened carefully.

"Well, this girl, I found out later her name was Sigh Yuh, she has me roped up in that treehouse and she starts starvin' me until I'm nearly dead. Then she starts torturin' me, puttin' me in water traps, curlin' snakes all over me, puttin' monster spiders on me that drank my blood. So one day she ties me up in a water pit filled with sharp sticks and she takes off. I work at the ropes and I get free so I take off too and hide in this river." Olafson had rehearsed; every man on the jury had been trained about the dangers of being marooned on a Pacific island. He could tell the officers on the jury liked his story.

"Well, I was hidin' from her but I wasn't hidin' from the cannibals. They were out huntin' this giant snake," and he spread his arms as far as he could and shook his head because the snake was even longer. "They got the snake and then they got me, and carried me up to their village. When I saw their heads on poles there at the cannibal village I thought my goose was cooked, but here's what happened." He paused again. "Listen to this. The cannibals had found this field radio, one of them crank sets, and didn't unnerstand it, not a bit. They musta figured I was a white man and all so they showed it to me and I cranked it up an' dialed around and found the armed services broadcast. You shoulda seen their faces, all them cannibals, all painted an' grass skirts an' bones in their ears, shocked when they heard the radio play GI music."

This was by far the best story anyone in court had ever heard. The jurors grinned; the reporters jotted furiously on notepads. Olafson kept talking.

"So, they would sit at my feet and I'd crank up the radio and dial up some songs and they'd pick up their spears and go off huntin'. They liked 'em all: *Don' Fence Me In, I Got Spurs*, all them songs. But they liked *White Christmas* better'n anything else. They called me White Christmas and give me my own hut and a girl—they was makin' me a king they was so grateful. But I was tryin' to find my way back to the war so I went scoutin' on the island. One day I discovered all the way over to one side there was a bay and across the water there was another island, with a bunch of Jap boats and like a castle. I thought *Jesus, didn't know they was over there.* But it was just right across the water and you could see from across the way the Japs was makin' poor white people do slave labor. So I figured I've got to help 'em. I found me a rowboat and I begin sneakin' across the bay at night and takin' food to the slaves and savin' their lives. Those prisoners was buildin' a runway so then I started sneakin' food to 'em and all that. Well, I kept 'em alive. I saved 'em."

"How did you come to be in the Japanese prisoner of war camp?"

"It's a bad story, that. See, I didn't know it but there was a bunch of Dutch soldiers hidin' on my island. One day they come along and picked a fight with my tribe and tried to take away the radio. Well, I looked up and guess what! Right behind the Dutch there was the girl. And right beside her was Bart Sullivan! I had to blink my eyes. I figured he was dead but there he was, right on my island. I think he had washed up there. Well, the Dutch was fixing to kill my tribe to get that radio but they was sorry soldiers and not very many of 'em. They was so bent on gettin' that radio back that they didn't post no guards and a Jap patrol walked right in and captured everybody—the Dutch soldiers and Sullivan and the girl. Well, I'll be honest, I didn't care much if the Japs got her or not but I wasn't gonna let'm take my old shipmate, so I followed the Japs, lookin' for an opportunity, you know?" He paused to see if the jury knew. "Well, the Japs marched all of 'em—the girl, Bart, and the Dutch soldiers—down the river to the fishin' village. They was puttin' them on a boat to take 'em over to their POW camp. But, there's one more thing. There's a Jap guard posted there at the dock by a swamp. They're puttin' everbody on the boat and we hear this scream and look up and this Jap guard gets tangled up in a bunch of vines and then..." Olafson paused and cleared his throat, wiping away a tear. "And then this dragon jumps up out of the swamp and bites this guard in two! I mean a real dragon—a green one, with red eyes, long teeth, a roar what'd make a man lose his bowels. And I stopped in my tracks and watched it like everyone else. And that's when they see me. I just put my guard down and they got me. Well, everyone piles in the Jap boat and they take us all over to their island and put us in the POW camp. That's how I come to be in Ambon when the Aussies come to liberate the camp after the war is over."

"And Bart Sullivan? Did they take him, too?"

"That's right. And the girl, too. So, from then on for the rest of the war, there I was. But I didn't quit. The Japs was starvin' all of us, so I figured out their guards and where they kept stuff. I'd hide from the guards and sneak out every night and steal food to give the prisoners. I'm what kept 'em alive."

"How were you treated?" Mason asked. "In the POW camp?"

"Cruel bad, sir. Cruel bad. The Japs were run by this officer Tanaka who would show up every day and say somethin' to us and then pick out men and march 'em off. Sometimes we never seen 'em again. So I figured out what they was doin' and I stood up to 'em for the prisoners and it stopped. They still tried starvin' us but I kept feedin' 'em. The prisoners loved me."

"And when was the camp liberated?" Mason questioned him.

"Well, we don't even know the war's over and one day this Aussie boat shows up and we think there's gonna be a battle but instead all the Japs put their rifles down and sit down on the ground. The Aussies come marchin' in and lead us to this boat and take us to Australia."

"And Sullivan?"

"He comes up to me in the line and says he ain't goin', that he and this girl is stayin.' It's her island we was on with my tribe and they're goin' back there to live. That's the last I seen of him."

"He was alive, then," Mason postured, "when you were rescued."

"Yessir, he was alive as you and me. As far as I know, he's still there, livin' it up with this girl."

The officers on the jury loved the story. One of them said it reminded him of a movie he saw with Bob Hope and Bing Crosby on the road to somewhere. Another wanted more details about the girl. They all liked the story about the dragon eating the Japanese guard. The prosecutor had a few questions of his own.

"Tell the court, Chief Petty Officer, how you wound up wearing Seaman Sullivan's dog tags."

"Don't know, sir. They was took from us at the POW camp. I expect the Japs mixed 'em up. Never read 'em myself, sir, not my best skill."

"Is it your best skill to try to kill Bart Sullivan with a machine gun in a training exercise?"

"Sir, I didn't kill 'em. I didn't even try to kill 'em, although I will say he was a sorry sailor. He was a coward. When we landed on that beach he said he wasn't goin' into combat because, get this, he had orders. That was a crock. So, I think all of us wanted to kill 'em, but we didn't. We left him on the beach and went off into the jungle with the Army like we was supposed to. I took the machine gun because it ain't no exercise without the machine gun. But I didn't do nothin' to him."

"Who did?"

"Don't know as anybody did, sir. Coulda been a coconut. It sure wasn't me."

"And trying to, what was it, drop a fifty-pound bag of salt on his head?"

"I was just tryin' to help my friend the ship's cook. We was heavin' this bag of salt out of the ship's stores and it come loose. I wasn't tryin' to kill Sullivan. Whoever heard of someone tryin' to kill someone with a bag of salt?"

Even the worst of the jurors had to admit that Olafson had a point.

"And the girl, please? What was her name?"

"Sigh Uh, somethin' like that. Sullivan told me it was her island. Her family was farmers there until the Japs took 'em all prisoner. She got away and hid out in the jungle until Sullivan come along."

"And these Dutch soldiers on your little island? What were their names, if you please?"

"Don't rightly know them all, sir. One of them was called Pee Pants. Another one's name was somethin' like a mouse. They was kind of like the leaders."

"Just one last question for you." Burger bided his time. "All of these stories are interesting, but they have one thing in common. Do you know what that is?" Olafson sat, a bit uncomfortably. "There's no one to vouch for you."

"What do you mean, vouch?"

"Well, Olafson, you say you didn't assault Sullivan on the beach, but someone did. Where are the Higgins boat men who were with you on the beach to tell the court that it wasn't you?"

"Objection, Your Honor. He's trying to infect the proceedings." Mason sputtered. The judge sighed and told Olafson to answer.

"Well, I don't know exactly. Last time I saw 'em was on the ship before I washed overboard."

"They're still with the ship at Pearl Harbor, waiting to be discharged," the prosecutor said. "So, they're not here to tell us what happened on the beach, are they? They're not here." True enough, Olafson agreed. "And there's no one else here who can say what happened on deck the night Sullivan disappeared?" Not as how Olafson knew. "And when the court said it could move the case to Hawaii, your lawyer said having the trial here, 5,000 miles from Hawaii, was just fine. There's not a single person here on Hollandia who can contradict your tale of heroes and dragons."

"I wouldn't know, sir."

"And as for the POW camp, well, there's no one around from Ambon either, is there?" There wasn't. "Or Sullivan himself. If he's alive, he's on some island, you say. What's the name of this island?"

"We just called it the island of cannibals and dragons, sir."

"Cannibals and dragons?" Olafson nodded vigorously. "I think you've told your story, Chief. No more questions."

---

Five thousand miles away the three men who were with Olafson on the beach were marched under guard, single file, into the Third Fleet Welfare and Morale office. At the command, they dropped their sea bags on the floor and looked around.

"Stand at attention, men," the shore patrol officer told them. "Do not look around, do not move, do not fall out, do not head for the door or the head or the window."

The outer room of Welfare and Morale consisted of a couple of time-worn couches, a bulletin board covered with anti-venereal disease posters, the results of a Waikiki volleyball tournament, and some steel desks. Startled clerks made their way back and forth putting out piles of mimeographed announcements about upcoming demobilization lectures, the cancellation of USO shows, and 'Life as A Civilian: What you Need to Know.' The three witnesses tried to act nonchalant, but being rousted out of their cramped berths and ordered to report to Renegade's accommodation ladder with all personal gear at 0700 was out of the ordinary. Being led away by military police was even more out of the ordinary. When they were marched past the stockade and into Welfare and Morale even Barker was dumfounded. The only thing they could see that hinted what was to come was the morning newspaper sitting on a rickety coffee table three feet in front of them. Its headline blared: "Murder Suspect Tells of Island of Cannibals and Dragons."

Eventually the door behind the steel desks opened. Lieutenant Beach walked out.

"Come with me, boys," he said. "Bring your bags."

The trio was even more dumfounded when they entered and the door closed behind them. In front of them there was a somewhat flaccid officer sitting behind a desk on which a nameplate spelled out 'Commander – Third Fleet Service Group.' Next to the desk was one-half of a ping pong table, without the net. Next to the ping pong table there stood a rather over-dressed and over-made up woman with thick red lipstick, arched eyebrows, and a hat with a demure veil. Next to her stood Lieutenant Beach.

"At ease, men," the commander said in a voice that didn't sound very easy. "Are you men ready to move out?" he asked. He didn't wait for them to answer. "You're shipping out today." He studied their faces; they knew something was up. "Whether it's to San Francisco or back to Hollandia is up to you." He turned to face the woman and Lieutenant Beach. "You see, we think you have something that belongs to Lieutenant Beach, which means it belongs to me. If you agree, you go home. If you disagree, you go to Hollandia. Do you agree?"

Even Barker could see that, though it was just business, the trading had come to an end.

"We agree."

The commander nodded. Barker didn't even wait for Smith or Gretel; he simply took his sea bag and upended the contents onto the ping pong table. His bag contained the ragged remnants of his deck denims and underclothes, the battered topside blues that he wore for inspections, his deck shoes and dock shoes, a Dixie cup hat, and a smattering of illegible letters and orders. "You too, fellas," he said to the others.

Their debris was roughly the same, differing mainly in degrees of grime and salt and one particular; the last thing out of Smith's bag was a stack of Bingo cards. Gretel's bag had a few extra dance cards with black cats imprinted on them. Madame Rochelle raised an eyebrow. Lieutenant Beach raised two. The commander didn't raise either. He crossed his arms and made a comment.

"Looks to me like you boys don't agree. Something's missing. So, Hollandia it is."

"Sorry, sir," Barker answered. "This musta got stuck." He shook the bag. A false bottom came out. A stack of cash came out on top of that. "Is this what you're missin', sir?"

It was.

"Where'd you get this, boys?" the commander asked.

"It was left to us by Bart Sullivan, sir. He handed it over the day he disappeared."

"I didn't hear that last part, son. Did I hear you say Bart Sullivan gave you his sea bag? I think that's what you said. You said he gave it to you, right?" Gretel agreed on behalf of them that he had said exactly that. "And sometime long after he disappeared at sea, you got bored one day and opened it up and this stack of money fell out? Is that what happened?" Gretel agreed again that the commander had it right.

"Well, boys," the commander continued, "this money seems to be connected to those dance cards, and those dance cards are connected to Lieutenant Beach. So that money is his. You do agree, don't you boys?"

"Yes, sir." Even Barker had no difficulty pronouncing the words clearly and loudly.

"And if you boys will hand it over to Lieutenant Beach, you're dismissed. The good ship *Sumpter* is headed for San Francisco at 1700; here are your orders. Don't miss the boat."

"Yes, sir. Thank you, sir."

"And get that crap off my ping pong table. Dismissed. Out." He glared at the stinking skivvies and tee shirts and salt-crusted denims. The Higgins boat swamp ghost killers gathered their rags and papers, stiffened to attention, did an about face, and left. "Not you, Beach."

"No, sir," Beach answered with a quaking voice.

"Let's inventory the property, shall we, Beach?"

Beach nodded and, when the commander nodded back, he began to count the money. He put twenties in one stack, tens in another, fives in another, and made two stacks of all the one dollar bills. He also put the dance cards in a separate stack and, for good measure, put Bart Sullivan's orders and the surviving pages of his diary in yet another stack.

"Guess that Captain Hull was right, eh, Beach? Here's some orders sayin' he's to report by first available transport to Congressman Wirtle. Pretty good orders, eh?" Beach agreed that most men would have liked to have those orders. "And some orders to stay out of combat. Now, you don't see that every day, do you, Beach?" Beach did not. "And maybe it's just me, but do you notice anything about those orders? They sure look like they was made up on the same machine that printed out those dance cards. What do you think, Beach?"

"Couldn't say, sir."

"Even the same typewriter, eh?"

"Hard to know, sir."

"And the money, Beach. Looks to me like it's about $1,000.00. Want to count it again?"

"No, sir."

"Well, well, Lieutenant. Remember when you were here at Welfare and Morale and you lost about $1200.00 on Black Cat dance cards we were giving the troops? That was..."

"Last September, sir. A year ago."

"So, it seems to me, Beach, that we found the missing money. But it looks like some is still missing. What do you want to do, Beach?"

It took Lieutenant Beach a lot of guesses but eventually he guessed right.

"I'll sign a chit for pay and finance, sir. They can take it out of my pay."

"Well, thank you, Lieutenant. Thank you. Sign here."

"Interest, Commodore?" Madame Rochelle chimed in. "Dollars are like a lot people. When you treat them right, they make you a little more."

"Well, yes, I guess they do, ma'am. How much interest?"

Beach signed a chit directing the Third Fleet Pay and Finance office to withhold another $754.00 from his pay and allowances.

"And one more thing, Beach?" He paused. "Do you read the papers?"

"The papers, sir?"

"Yes, the goddamned newspapers. The ones full of sailors being thrown off boats and cannibals and dragons, those newspapers, do you read them?"

"No, sir," Beach lied.

"Well I'm going to ask you something about the news, Beach, and you better listen carefully to what I'm going to ask you. Understand?" He did. "If you were to testify in a court martial in Hollandia and someone asked you 'Lieutenant Beach, did you see Chief Petty Officer Olafson throw Seaman Second Class Bart Sullivan overboard?' what would your answer be?"

Beach was not the brightest one in his class; he began to say 'I didn't see...' but he was cut short.

"That's right, Beach. You didn't see. Whatever it was you didn't see I don't care. Olafson's a bum. Those three idiots who just left here are bums too, but they're not smart enough to be murdering bums. As for you? I don't know." He let Beach think about how easy it was for the commander and, probably, everyone who read the newspapers, to figure out what the commander had figured out. "We don't like scandal here in Welfare and Morale, Beach. We don't like rumors or gossip. You're through. Sign this." Beach read what the commander passed to him, then looked up. "Unless you want me to fly you to Hollandia so you can start answering some questions." Beach signed. "Now, get your ass over to payroll and finance, give them your allotment chit, then go straight to fleet personnel, give 'em this." He added his own signature. "Dismissed. Go. Get out of my sight. Never show up here again."

He waited until the door was closed, and the outer door, and he could see Lieutenant Beach, soon to be ex-Lieutenant Beach, stumbling along the rock-lined path outside the building. He turned to Madame Rochelle.

"Here's your money."

"Thanks, sweetie. Come by and have another drink sometime." She smiled her cat-got-the-cream smile and gave him a kiss, not enough to mess up her lipstick but enough to leave the odor of cheap perfume on his shirt, just in case. "Got to run. Have to see an old friend."

---

The next day, the judge told Mason to call his next witness.

"There aren't anymore defense witnesses, Your Honor."

# Chapter 25

On the following Monday morning the judge told the jury to wait, then told Burger and Mason that he wanted to know how much longer the court martial would take. Olafson sat at the table, smiling.

"Well, Captain Burger, are your witnesses coming?"

"No, sir." Burger unfolded a teletyped message and handed it to the judge. "Please read this."

CincPacPersCom
Third Fleet, USN
Pearl Harbor, Territory of Hawaii
Serial 1044544 of 20 September 1945

To: Staff Judge Advocate
USN Base Hollandia, WPAC

Subj: Witnesses US v. Olafson

Action:

1. Seamen Barker, Hantsel, and Smith ex APA 3-38-14 *Renegade* no longer at this station, en route San Francisco.
2. Lieutenant Sonny Beach, ex APA 3-38-14 *Renegade* resigned commission and is no longer in Navy. No forwarding locator.

Signed: Everett Landrum, Lt. Cmdr, for CincPacPersComThirdFleet

"So, Captain, you're in the Navy. You know what happens when you run out of ammunition; the battle's over." He handed the message to Lieutenant Mason. "Unless you've got somebody else ready it looks like the last gun's been fired. We can sum up for the jury right now."

Captain Burger couldn't contain himself and exploded:

"He did this, Your Honor," Burger snapped, pointing at Mason. "He set this whole thing up as a trick. He knew there wasn't anybody here on Hollandia who could tell the truth about this cock and bull dragons and cannibals story." He paused, caught his breath, and pointed at Olafson. "As for him, he's not just a murderer, he's a cheat. I want to get the truth to come out."

The judge agreed that there wasn't anyone on Hollandia to challenge Olafson's tale, but he did not agree that Lieutenant Mason was smart enough to plan how to keep the Navy from finding its own sailors to testify. What the judge didn't anticipate was that Mason had been reading more English law dictionaries.

"*Corpus delicti*, Your Honor," he declared.

"What did you say, Lieutenant? *Corpus delicti*? Body of the crime? What are you talking about?"

"There isn't one, sir. There's no body. No body, no crime," Mason replied.

"Oh, you mean *non corpus delicti*, counselor. No corpse, no crime." In one instant the judge realized that Mason had made a real objection, just like a real lawyer. "Never mind me. Shouldn't be stating your objections for you. Disregard what I said. We're off the record."

Burger wasn't the smartest lawyer in the fleet either, but he at least had read some of the law himself.

"It doesn't matter, Your Honor. "*Corpus delicti* isn't a defense. The jury can convict, even without a corpse, if there's enough circumstantial evidence. Otherwise murderers could just dispose of their corpses and get away with it."

"I think that's right, Captain Mason," the judge said.

Mason was ready again; Black's Law Dictionary was full of *corpus delicti* nuggets.

"The bloody shirt case, Your Honor. They hanged a man in England after his master disappeared because the servant had blood on his shirt. A few years later the master turned up alive; he had skipped the country to not pay a debt. They hanged an innocent man. After that, the law was you had to produce a corpse."

The judge thought about it a while and made a decision.

"Here's what we're going to do." He then worked out the terms of a letter.

Staff Judge Advocate
Third Fleet, USN
Hollandia, WPAC
Serial 69 of 23 September 1945

To: Allied Liaison,
8th Division, Second Australian Imperial Army
Cairns, Australia

Subj: Witnesses / US v. Olafson

Action:

1. Request you locate Dutch soldiers who were prisoners of war in the Japanese camp at Ambon Island, particularly two Dutch officers named approximately 'Mouse' and 'Pee Pants.'
2. Need named Dutch prisoners to testify in military court USN Hollandia about facts of American Navy chief petty officer Gustav Olafson, accused of murdering American Navy seaman Bart Sullivan.
3. Court martial in recess one week pending your reply.

Signed: Robert F. Burger, Captain, Staff Judge Advocate

Burger sighed with relief. Mason objected. The jury full of submarine commanders, combat pilots, and gunnery officers left for the bar and took a week off. Olafson smiled and told Mason not to worry; Mouse and Pee Pants weren't in Australia.

Exactly one week later to the day the fleet intelligence officer in Hollandia received a coded message from a group named Section 22.

"Hey," he called out to his chief clerk. "What is Section 22?"

"Dutch guys, Colonel. Coastwatchers, radar watchers, spied on the Japs out in the islands."

"We got a message from Section 22. Can you decode it?" the colonel wanted to know. The code was sufficiently complex that he wasn't even sure which side of the paper was up. "It says something like antenna, rowboat, crab, umbrella, headphones. And a bunch of letters that don't make words."

"Got it, sir. Stand by." The sergeant took the message, looked at pictograms of an antenna, a rowboat, a crab, an umbrella, and headphones. "It's allied code August 5: listening only, SW Pacific, do not share or leak, message to follow." He looked up the code pages in the book, rearranged the letters, and revealed Van Muis's reply.

"DF 22-Haruku was captured by Japanese patrol due to Olafson using the unit radio to broadcast in the clear and listen to music. DF 22-Haruku and Olafson imprisoned Ambon until Japanese surrender. One of the DF soldiers was called Pants Broek, 'pee pants,' real name was Piet van Meer. Signed, Michiel Van Muis, Colonel, Moluccas Garrison, Royal Dutch East Indies Army."

"Who's Olafson, Chief?" the intelligence officer wanted to know. "Does this make any sense to you?"

It did. The code clerk personally walked the decoded message to the courtroom where the most famous case of the war was on hold. An hour later he returned with a message to be sent back to Van Muis.

"Request you come to Hollandia to testify."

The following day, one day after the deadline, Burger begged the judge to wait a bit longer. Mason objected. Van Muis' reply arrived in the middle of the debate.

"Unable to come to Hollandia. Interrogating Japanese officers. Piet van Meer discharged, on way back to Netherlands."

---

"NAVY JUDGE DISMISSES CHARGES," the headlines read. "Olafson freed." The *Stars and Stripes* journalists wasted no time in getting a special edition onto the newswires as soon as the judge ruled. Bookmakers all across the Pacific collected winnings and paid off the very few bets they had lost.

Like most jurors in such cases, the submarine commanders, gunnery officers, and combat pilots who had agreed to hang Olafson were dismayed to discover that they had spent a week sitting in a court martial, followed by a week sitting in a bar waiting for a witness who didn't come. To a man they felt cheated of getting to see Olafson squirm when they announced their verdict.

"Oh, he murdered that sailor," they reported to the judge after he told them his decision. "No doubt about it. Great story though." There had been some disagreement over which of them liked which parts best, the gunnery officers having especially enjoyed the story of the cannibals hunting Saya while singing Billboard hit songs and the submarine officers preferring the Morse code messages that were sent to the Dutch. The combat pilots liked the shocking urgency of the Komodo dragon erupting to eat Mr. Moto in the swamp. "There aren't any cannibals in those islands," they added. "Or Komodo dragons. They're a thousand miles south of Ambon. Why can't we hang him?"

"There's a chance that Sullivan's alive," the judge told them. "Not much of a chance, but Olafson survived going overboard and made it to Ambon, so maybe Sullivan did too. And there's no one to say different. So, the law leaves me no choice." Fifteen minutes later, Olafson was free.

Twenty-four hours later, Olafson was packed into the troop deck of another ship headed to Pearl Harbor.

———————

The atmosphere on deck was electric as the troopship neared the islands. Sea birds, then clouds, then the low peaks of Kauai appeared off the port rail hours before the island itself was in plain sight. A bright red morning sky glowed down on a thousand soldiers who began to yell and cheer as the ship passed a few miles to starboard of Waimea and began a slight turn to the south southeast.

"Boy, this sure is purty," a war-weary soldier said to a fat, thick, square-faced sailor dressed in blues.

"Red sky in morning," Olafson said back. "Hope we make port right away. Could be a blow comin'. 'Red sky in morning, sailor take warning.'"

But the blow didn't come, not right away. A few hours later the men yelled again as the ship made a hard turn back to port. Diamond Head rose off the starboard rail, and the ship made directly for the channel into Pearl Harbor. Every soldier on board crowded toward the troop ladder and the ship soon wallowed to a halt and threw out its docking lines.

Olafson stood behind them, his own new sea bag ready to go ashore. He gazed at the docks, the wharf, the sheds with numbers painted on the roof where troops would be received and send on to their next ship and home. The ship snugged against the dock. The gangways rolled out. The boys were back in America. They let out a roar and threw their caps in the air.

"Where's home, sailor?" one of the soldiers asked him, noticing that he was dressed differently than the crew and had his own sea bag on the deck.

"Here," Olafson said. "Just waitin' orders for my next ship."

Olafson had to wait his turn. He didn't care; he had lived on ships most of his life and would be living on a ship again as soon as he found the Third Fleet assembly point and reported for duty. He looked up and down the wharf. Two more troopships were docked ahead of his; another brought up the rear of the convoy in the channel. Even so, for the most part, the wharf was orderly and mostly free of civilians. Army liaisons held up cardboard plaques with unit numbers painted on them to guide the disembarking soldiers. A few ambulances stood at the ready to take on the men who had been too wounded to go sooner but too fragile to stay in Hollandia. A few dark blue sedans were parked in the concrete yard beyond the wharfs and the troop sheds. And a few women in dresses stood near them, watching for their men to come home at last. Then he saw her.

"Suzy!" he shouted. The nearby soldiers heard him, turned, saw the big sailor with the thick stomach and blockish head yell for joy. "Suzy! By got, she come to meet me." He waved and jumped up and down on the deck, but Suzy was too far away. For the first time in his life, Olafson was in a hurry to get off his ship.

It took more than an hour to disembark the wounded, then the soldiers, and then the few sailors in transit. Olafson stood as close as he could to the midship gangway, hoping his work dress blues would stand out against all the Army green so that Suzy could see him, too. He watched her leave the parking lot, make her way toward the sheds, and reappear on the wharf. He waved and yelled again.

*I think she saw me,* he grinned and thought to himself. *Good old Suzy.* He scratched himself in anticipation.

The last of the soldiers filed down the gangway. Olafson pushed his way to the rail, saluted the officer of the deck, and lugged his sea bag down to the dock. There she was.

"Suzy!" he yelled. "Suzy! It's me. Over here." He jumped up and down, waved his arms from side to side, and shouted again. Suzy turned to face him, smiled, and nodded. "Suzy, I'm here! I'm coming for you!" At last he got past the milling battalions and companies and soldiers and dock hands and pushed his way to Suzy, and stopped.

Suzy wasn't alone. She stood next to a woman who seemed familiar, a woman in a nice black dress, lipstick, hair slightly covered by a fancy little hat with a veil, and a man in an overcoat. Suzy pointed at Olafson.

"That him," Suzy said to the overcoat. "That the man who give me sailing orders. He give me Navy explosives. He the one."

The man walked toward the bewildered Olafson and opened his lapel to display his badge. Another man appeared from behind and gripped Olafson's arms. Madame Rochelle smiled, turned, and walked away.

Olafson's time had come.

# Part IV

Afterlives

# Chapter 26

Two Maoli, surfing the Makapu'u Lighthouse breakers, were caught in a shorebreak barrel that dumped them at the base of a cliff, where they saw a 1947 Ford convertible that had landed wheels-up on the rocks. Two legs dangled out of the driver's side door. One of them looked after their surfboards while the other climbed up to the highway to flag down a passing car. Its driver turned around and drove back to the first hotel he could find, where he called the Honolulu police. The police traced the license plates back to the Honolulu Ford dealer, who said that he already had sent someone to the police station to report that both the used car and one of his used car salesmen had been missing for two days.

"I was worried, to be truthful," he told the police. "Sonny had been acting upset for a couple of weeks now," he added.

"Sonny?" the police asked.

"Sonny Beach. He was one of our salesmen. He checked the car out Thursday to go home and never came back."

"Upset, how?" the police followed up.

"Hard to say, you know? He was always quiet, a little jumpy when one of the cars backfired, that sort of thing. You see a lot of that in guys who were in the war. But for the last couple of weeks it was like he wasn't really here. He'd be sitting at his desk or walking the showroom and had this look in his eyes, you know? And shaking."

"Anything else?"

"To be honest, there was. I drove him home after work a couple of weeks ago. He asked me 'did you see that? Did you see it?' And I said no, but he insisted I look. He lived off Farrington Road, you know? And he kept pointing at the swamp over there."

"Pouhala swamp?"

"Yeah, you can see it from the house he was renting. And he kept saying 'Do you see it?' and I kept saying 'No, what?' and he kept saying there were lights there in the swamp, little green lights. But I didn't see anything. And the next day when I picked him up to go back to work, he was just shaking all over. I told him to go see the doctor."

"Any family?" the police asked.

"None I know of."

It took the police two more days to winch the car off the rocks and up to the coast road. The wrecker driver was used to seeing cars that had gone over the cliff but not used to seeing crushed bodies still under the steering wheel when he showed up on the scene. He helped the police turn the car over onto its wheels, then walked away.

"Yeah," the Ford dealer said, "that's him. Say, who's gonna pay for the car?"

Not until the police got the body out of the car did they find anything of a lead. There was a month-old newspaper in the car with a heavy pencil mark under a headline: "Navy carries out sentence on traitor, former chief petty officer." The story summarized how last-minute appeals had failed.

"Say," one of the officers mentioned. "That story came out about the time you said he was seeing things? Little green lights in the swamp?"

The Ford dealer said that it might be.

It was the coroner who found the note in Beach's shirt pocket: "I confess; I helped push him."

The police detectives checked all the crime reports for the island; none seemed to involve either an assault by a mid-thirties white male of Beach's description or anything involving a late model Ford convertible. Beach did have a bank account with a very small balance, but no record of recent deposits or withdrawals. There was no hidden money, or photographs, or letters, or anything of interest inside his house. The police did send a man and a dog to wade through the swamp; they found nothing to see or sniff. In the end, the case was closed as an accident. The Ford dealer made an insurance claim for the value of the car, and was paid.

It was as if Sonny Beach had never lived at all.

"UH DOF," Tryck sang out.

"UH DO," everyone in the village chimed in.

"DREDNOZ," she continued.

"DREDNOZ." The cheery notes bounced off the lower leaves of the mangium trees, reverberated against the totem poles, and perhaps even reached some very trill notes by whistling through the gaping eye sockets of Sato's skull, facing down from above the village path. It was a very joyous day in the village, a banner day. The hunters had brought home a rusa deer and two cassowaries; the gatherers had cooked up a crude pot of taro roots and beans. The celebration was lively.

"RINDR."

"RINDR." Spears were lifted, fermented berry water drunk, bottoms pinched, war paint shared.

Tryck cranked the radio again, twiddled the dial. The airwaves warped and crackled. Children swayed to the crisp swing of the *Chattanooga Choo Choo*. Life was good, and it was long after the darkest hour when the last of the Sawi staggered to their respective huts and fell asleep. Tryck flipped the switches, disconnected the wires, and carried the radio back to her hut, one piece at a time. It was dark inside.

"Hello, Tryck," a calm voice said from the shadows. She stopped in her tracks, dropping the hand crank generator. "Did you miss me?"

Tryck's mind raced back and forth, trying to place the voice. It was too crude to be one of the men from the village, too fresh to be Sato or any of the other men they had eaten in the last few years. Then, it struck her.

"Why Krimma! Why are you here?" She had last seen White Christmas in the soldier boat, going with the Japanese to their island across the bay. "Go away."

"Soon, Tryck. Soon. I brought you something." He held out a gob of Crisco, dripping from his fingers. "It's shortening. Mama's little baby loves shortening, remember?" He walked across the darkened hut until he was only a few inches from her. She then was able to make out his form in the dark, even though his features were obscured, as if they were fading. "Here." He smeared the white fat across Tryck's face and, to his amusement, she began to lick at it.

"Go away. I call the hunters," she said.

"Call them," Olafson said, or Olafson's shade said. "What are they going to do to me?"

And Tryck knew, the way that people say they know when someone steps on a grave, or a raven caws, or when the lights at prisons flicker, that someone is about to die.

"I've come for you, Tryck. Just like you came for me. Just like you came for Sato." He waited for her to argue, but she knew as clearly as Sato had known when it was his time, as Mr. Moto had known when it was his. There was no argument to be had. But, she tried.

"Where you come from, Why Krimma?" It was then that she realized that White Christmas's body was twisted a little, like his head wasn't on straight. "What you want with me? I don't kill you."

It was true; Tryck had tried to kill him, and had gotten very close, as close as Olafson had gotten to killing Bart and as close as Moto had gotten to killing Saya. And eventually White Christmas did see a light in the afterworld, too, but it was more like a boatman's lantern on a river of the dead than the white light that Bart and Saya had seen. And, instead of the window to the future that the bright light had opened for Bart and Saya, what Olafson had looked through was more like a trap door.

"You were greedy, Tryck. The radio, then me, then Sato." She didn't know how he knew she had managed to turn the village against Sato, but he knew. "And now it's your time, Tryck. Mama's little baby. Shortnin'. Have some." He forced Crisco down her mouth until she gagged. "And it's Rudolph, Tryck, not UH DOF. Rudolph the Red-Nosed Reindeer. You never did learn to sing."

Tryck's body was found in her hut the next morning, her mouth packed with thick white paste that the village women tried to lick. However, it and she were so rotten that the hunters declared she was not fit for *kapala* or for *ania*. Her remains were taken beyond the totem poles and left for the animals.

As for Tryck's shade, neither hers nor Olafson's were ever seen again.

––––––––––––––

Not everything that Olafson had told the jury in Hollandia had been a lie. Bart and Saya were still in the islands, although living it up might not have been the correct description of their existence.

They swam across the gentle lagoon, splashing each other and laughing. She was much faster than he, she having lived on the island all her life and he having grown up afraid of the water. For most of the early morning they raced from the rocks that sheltered their cave, across the shallow water to the sandy beach, and back again. Now and then they would run up into the trees, dry off, and let the sun warm them. With the Japanese gone and the colonists making their way back to the island, there wasn't much for them to do.

Saya lay back on her elbows, her wet hair falling almost to the sand, and closed her eyes. Bart watched her, still fascinated by the fact of her, her slender body and tawny skin and sad eyes, fascinated that she hadn't told him to go away.

It had been hard on them at Ambon. Saya had been frantic when she first saw her father and brother in the line of *surēbu* being marched out to clear the debris from the runway that the allied planes had bombed. They looked like skeletons, wearing pitiful ragged cloths for underwear. She had wanted to run to them, to hold them, to take food to them, to attack the guards. Bart asked her not to try.

"They won't be able to see you," he had warned her. "A glimpse, maybe, or just your shadow. But, if they even see that much it could go bad for them. If your father calls out to you, or runs to where you're standing, they will kill him. If the guards find them with food, or a shovel, anything, they will kill them." It had been painful to see her cry for want of touching them. "If the Japanese see them do anything unusual," Bart had told her, "they will kill them. On the spot."

It was no different with Saya's mother. They had taken the rowboat across to Ambon again when the *Jigoku Maru* came into port under guard and disembarked all the women who had been taken away. It was the first time that Saya had seen her mother since the day Mr. Moto had trapped them in the customs shed at Port Haru, before the typhoon. But, like her father and her brother in the *surēbu* camp, Saya's mother had been able to see no more than what she believed she could see. She had been told that Saya was dead, and could not see her.

So, Bart and Saya continued to do what Bart always had done, sneaking across the bay, making rice balls, giving pitifully small morsels to the *surēbu* and to the Dutch and Australian military prisoners who barely survived until the camp was liberated.

223

"I don't understand," she said. "I thought they could see me, like the cannibals saw me. Or Olafson."

"I don't understand it all either," Bart told her, "not very well, but most people don't believe in us at all. They think we're dead and gone. Since they don't believe they could ever again see us, they can't. But the cannibals can see us. I think they've always had something, I don't know, some connection between living people and shades, like us. Maybe they..." He had almost said 'maybe they get that from eating people.' Instead he said, "Maybe they know the difference between who's really alive and who's really dead. And who's like us, somewhere in between." Bart was happy; being in between with Saya was better than anything he had before, when he was alive. "So the cannibals aren't surprised by us. If they know to look, they see us."

"Is that how we can understand each other? And the cannibals? Because we're in between?"

"Maybe. I'm not sure."

"Are there others like us?" she wondered.

Everyone sees someone who they thought was dead, turning a corner, walking in a crowd, showing up in a picture in the newspaper. The same haircut, or jaw, or shoulders, the same way of walking, just a glimpse. And, yet, when they follow who they've seen, the person isn't there.

"I think so. I don't know. Maybe."

Bart didn't know everything. He didn't know why her father could understand Bart when he had whispered to him in the night to write a note to Saya. He didn't know how Olafson survived the typhoon or why Olafson could see them. It might have had to do with the cannibals or it might have had to do with something else, but Olafson—who should have died in the typhoon, or in one of Saya's water pits—had definitely been alive, yet could see both of them, who by then were just shades.

The sun warmed them. They looked at the fat white clouds overhead, and the horseshoe crabs skittering across the sand. She began to talk about her family.

After the Japanese surrendered, Bart and Saya had tried to visit her plantation. Her father and her brother had been clearing weeds from the nutmeg trees and rebuilding fences for the pigs that the Dutch relief mission had brought out to them. Her mother had been tending a crude cook pit that would keep them alive while they worked to recover their wrecked farm.

All of them saw glimpses of Saya. Her mother ran to tell her father, "She was there, walking behind the banana tree. It was her. The way she walked, just so, the way she swung her arms..." She had called out to Saya, couldn't find her, and was trembling. "She was there. It was her."

Her father had seen a glimpse, too. "She was over there, just inside the tree line, turning her head the way Saya always did, her hair swishing just so. I know it was her." It had been Saya, but when they went to find her behind the banana tree and at the edge of the jungle, she wasn't there, not that they could see.

"They believe I died in the comfort house," Saya said. Tears flowed down her face. "Or in the typhoon."

"I know," Bart answered. "They know what happened to you. They know you couldn't have survived. They were told you were dead, so they can't see you. But because they want to believe you might have survived, they want it with all their hearts, sometimes they can get a glimpse of you."

Saya's family had never known Bart, so never saw any of him, not even a glimpse or a shadow. He was just a voice in their hut at night, or in the hospital, a voice who left rice balls and told them to write a note. Mr. Moto had seen Bart's body when Bart had washed up on Ambon, but thought that he was a dead American sailor so left him for the *surēbu* to bury. Afterward, when the natives told Mr. Moto that there was a *ningen* on the island, he was terrified when Bart appeared at Mount Salahu. None of the other Japanese believed in *ningens* so couldn't see him.

Bart had told Saya about Olafson killing him on the beach, and of Beach and Olafson throwing him overboard. He told her how he had been tossed about in the sea and how he washed up on Ambon with no sign of life.

"Moto was the first person I saw," he told her. "Then the prison."

Saya had told Bart what had happened to her in the comfort house, dying but not dying, and seeing the white light as she fled, then being caught by the typhoon.

"They killed us, Saya, but they didn't kill our spirits. We both saw the white light and then we both came back. It just wasn't our time." Bart stopped and tried to find the right words for what he had figured out. "So,

225

we're stuck here, in the middle. Not alive, but not quite, you know, dead."

She told him that she had decided to sacrifice Olafson to trap Mr. Moto and Lieutenant Tanaka.

"They didn't deserve to live, not after what they did to my family. Not after what they did to us in the comfort house." She let her speech catch up with her thoughts. "Why did you rescue Olafson from the cannibals?" she asked. "He didn't deserve to live either. He stole from the other prisoners and ratted on them when they hid food from the guards. And he killed you, twice. If anyone should have died, it was Olafson."

Bart took his time to answer. He had been tempted to let the cannibals have Olafson, and to let the Japanese starve him to death. In the end, he had made sure that Olafson survived.

"It was not his time. Olafson had some unfinished business to take care of," Bart answered. "He owed a debt and had to go back and face it."

There was a lovely sky in the west. Thin clouds rose low above the horizon as the sun set, casting a brilliant red glow to the evening sky.

"Red sky at night, sailor's delight," he said. "Sailors have a lot of those sayings."

She sat up and looked across the little lagoon to their cave. They had changed it a little to make it easier for the two of them. They had made a wider cot and opened up the window to allow for more light. They dried driftwood so that they could cook more than rice and fish. Eating was one of the habits of life that they still enjoyed.

They swam back across the lagoon, dried themselves on the rock at the cave's entrance, and went inside to be alone. They still were not clear when someone, another shade, maybe, or a hant, might be able to catch a glimpse of them. Even in their state there were some things that gave more comfort when done in private.

Later, that night, Bart told her what it was like to travel, the places he had seen by train and by ship. Saya said she would like to see what it was like, to see other places, to go where Bart had gone.

"We will," Bart said, and smiled. "I promise."

It was an easy promise for him to make. After all, Bart Sullivan had seen the future.

# About the Author

Jack Woodville London is the author of four novels, including the acclaimed novel, *French Letters: Children of a Good War*, winner of the 2018 Gold Medal for Book of the Year in war and military fiction. He also wrote *A Novel Approach*, a non-fiction book on the craft of writing, is co-author of *Texas Pattern Jury Charges*, and author of more than thirty articles on history, literature, travel, law and art.

Jack studied the craft of fiction at the Academy of Fiction, St. Céré, France and at Oxford University. His writing career began with his appointment as managing editor during law school of the University of Texas International Law Journal.

In addition to writing, Jack teaches the craft to others. He is Director of Writing Education for Military Writers Society of America and regularly conducts writing programs for beginning writers, especially veterans.

Jack lives in Austin, Texas.
*Visit with him at*
jwlbooks.com
jack@jackwlondon.com

# Also by Jack Woodville London

*French Letters Virginia's War*
*French Letters Engaged in War*
*French Letters Children of a Good War*
*A Novel Approach*